Carving a Future by Carla Olson Gade
Ship figurehead carver Nathaniel Ingersoll has apprenticed for many years under his Uncle Phineas and hopes to become a master ship carver in his own right. Indentured servant Constance Starling arrives on the Connecticut coast too ill for anyone to accept her indenture. Will Nathaniel jeopardize the future he has worked hard to achieve for the welfare of a weakly servant?

Trading Hearts by Amber Stockton
Jonathan Ingersoll is a successful merchant trader along the Connecticut River. When flooding forces him to take sanctuary in an unfamiliar inn along his route, he meets the innkeeper's daughter, Clara. Immediately attracted to her shy yet caring spirit and quiet faith, Jonathan makes a point to return. But animosity from Clara's brother gives him pause. Will learning the source of his resentment spur Jonathan to try that much harder to prove his worth?

Over a Barrel by Laurie Alice Eakes
After being wounded while fighting on the frontier, Micajah Ingersoll figures his future lies in making the town bakehouse a success. He doesn't expect to find a woman willing to marry a partially lame man. He especially doesn't expect to meet her in his storeroom after hiding her daughter in an emptied barrel. Sarah Chapman can't be up to any good. But being near Sarah may mean losing his heart regardless of her past.

Impressed by Love by Lisa Karon Richardson
Phoebe Carlisle is traveling with her uncle, captain of the HMS *Aries*, until an attack forces them to seek refuge along the Connecticut River. Doctor Alden Ingersoll prefers to be in control of any situation, but his fate is ripped from his grasp when he's pressed into the Royal Navy to tend an injured captain. But in Phoebe's company, Alden finds his desire to escape fading. . .even if pursuing her means abandoning his medical practice.

COLONIAL COURTSHIPS

COLONIAL COURTSHIPS

FOUR-IN-ONE COLLECTION

Laurie Alice Eakes
Carla Olson Gade
Lisa Karon Richardson
Amber Stockton

BARBOUR
PUBLISHING

Carving a Future © 2012 by Carla Olson Gade
Trading Hearts © 2012 by Amber Stockton
Over a Barrel © 2012 by Laurie Alice Eakes
Impressed by Love © 2012 by Lisa Karon Richardson

Print ISBN 978-1-61626-694-3

eBook Editions:
Adobe Digital Edition (.epub) 978-1-62029-026-2
Kindle and MobiPocket Edition (.prc) 978-1-62029-027-9

All scripture quotations are taken from the King James Version of the Bible.

Cover design: Kirk DouPonce, DogEared Design

Published by Barbour Publishing, Inc., P.O. Box 719, Uhrichsville, Ohio 44683, www.barbourbooks.com

Our mission is to publish and distribute inspirational products offering exceptional value and biblical encouragement to the masses.

 Member of the
Evangelical Christian
Publishers Association

Printed in the United States of America.

CARVING A FUTURE

by Carla Olson Gade

Dedication

To Joyce Buckley—my "first editor", research companion, and amazing mother! Thank you for our big birthday road trip and all our excursions for the research of this book including Colonial Williamsburg, Glastonbury, CT, & Mystic Seaport.

With special thanks to the Glastonbury, Connecticut Historical Society for their assistance; and for so faithfully preserving the history of this charming New England town on the Great River. To the curators of the ship carving shop at Mystic Seaport; and for the spectacular display of historic figureheads. And to world renowned figurehead carver and historian, Martin Jeffery, whose expertise was essential to my writing about this legendary craft. Fair winds to all!

And whatsoever ye do, do it heartily, as to the Lord,
and not unto men. . .for ye serve the Lord Christ.
Colossians 3:23–24

Chapter 1

The Connecticut River
July 1753

Constance Starling stood on the quay, the chain around her waist secured to a granite post. She cast her eyes toward the ship moored behind her—prison for the past six weeks. Or had it been seven? Mounted on the prow of the elaborately decorated merchant vessel, a figurehead of a mythological creature with the proud front of a horse, mane blowing wild, and the coiled tail of a seahorse, hugged the bowsprit. Bold and free, it mocked her. She had likely wearied the Almighty with her petitions for freedom, as she, too, was weary from uttering them. Yet she managed once more, "Lord, save me."

The heat of the sun beat down, moistening Constance's brow with perspiration, or perhaps it was fever. Her hat might have proffered some protection, but it had disappeared in the struggle that landed her in this frightful predicament. Then a cool breeze drifted off the river, providing a trickle of relief, and a subtle reminder that God was still with her.

Her stomach cramped from the meager portions of food on the long voyage from England, biscuits and water having been her only sustenance. Enough of neither. The slapping of the water against the hull of the docked merchant ship did nothing to squelch her queasiness. Her legs wobbled in rhythm and her knees buckled beneath her, throwing her into a filthy and rumpled heap on the rough, planked wharf.

Her captor yanked Constance up by the elbow, nearly pulling her arm from its socket. "Stand up, lass. You'll be good to no one, not even yerself, if ye can't even stay on yer feet. If I don't sell yer indenture, there'll be no hope for ye—you'll never survive another long journey."

The stench of liquor on Captain Smout's breath made Constance retch. Her eyes stung as she glared at him in defiance. She tried to swallow the lump forming in her throat, but it was far too parched to allow her to do so without pain.

The gruff man lifted a tarnished flask to her mouth and poured a bit of rum between her chapped lips. As it dribbled down her chin and neck, his ire rose. "For pity's sake. Drink up. You're worth little enough to me now, and you'll be no good to me dead." The liquid burned her throat and she spat it into his face, like water spraying from a whale's spout into the angry sea.

The captain hoisted his punishing hand in the air but another, far stronger, intercepted it.

"That is enough!" a brawny man twisted the captain's arm behind his back. "You will do as I say and leave her be." His stormy eyes sailed toward hers through the raging sea of his anger. For a fleeting moment the tempest abated, and she found safe harbor there.

"All right, mate. Easy now. I meant no harm." Smout tried to shake loose, but the man kept a firm hold. "Truce," Smout pleaded.

Her protector turned the captain around and relaxed

his grip. He stepped back and took a protective stance near Constance. All she could see was the hale form of this gallant man in brown breeches and a long, tan waistcoat. A queue of dark hair tied with a leather cord hung down upon his broad shoulders. "Release this poor woman," he demanded.

Her gaze darted back to Captain Smout as he began to speak again, a sly grin appearing through his burly gray whiskers. "I'm willin' to consider it. Let's say we negotiate the terms of her indenture."

Constance tried to keep her wits about her, to see what fate would come—though murky voices and blurred images swirled around her like a raging whirlpool pulling her into a deep abyss.

❧

Nathaniel turned at the sound of a faint whimper at his feet. He kneeled down and gently lifted the woman's head. A low groan escaped her lips and her eyes fluttered open, beckoning his help. He retrieved his engraved silver flask from his pocket and offered her a drink of water. She took several sips, and then her eyes closed once more.

Nathaniel gently laid her back down on the wooden boards, unsure of what else to do, and looked up at the churlish sea captain looming over them.

"I will take her off your hands, for a price." Nathaniel could hardly believe the words that spilt from his mouth.

"A price, aye?" The man chortled. "Ye think I don't have my wits about me? I'm the one who's selling her contract."

Nathaniel's mouth went dry. He thought to reach for his flask again, but it was nearly empty now. At last he mustered up a response. "She is worth nothing to you like this. I will take her as she is."

"She still cost me her passage. I'll get recouped for that at least. She's a comely lass, at least she was when she commenced the voyage. If'n she recovers she'll be worth a good deal," the trader said.

"She will be worth nothing dead. Let me get her some help."

"Nathaniel." The ever-deepening voice of his adolescent brother, a younger, leaner version of himself, yet already as tall, caught his attention. The lad's eyes held a look of confusion.

"Alden, there you are. I need your assistance."

Alden stared at the unconscious woman. "I see that. Who is she?"

Nathaniel's glare demanded an answer from the captain.

"Her name is Constance. Starling, I believe. But it's my name you ought to be concerned about." The haughty man stood straighter and clamped his ring-laden fingers around his lapels. "Magnus Smout at your disposal, owner and captain of the good ship *Fortuna*. I'm the one you're going to compensate."

Alden looked more confused than ever.

"Never mind him," Nathaniel said as he tugged off his cravat. "Give this a soak so we can cool her face. And fetch some fresh water if you can." He handed Alden his flask and the lad fled.

Nathaniel smoothed his hair back and tugged on his queue as he tried to think of what he could do next. He had little coin on him, perhaps a few shillings, having spent what he had on supplies. He certainly wasn't equipped with the funds a ship's captain selling a contract of indenture would accept.

Perusing the merchant ship, Nathaniel noticed the figurehead of a seahorse attached to the bowsprit. It was quite damaged, one of its legs broken and the other altogether missing.

"This is your vessel?" Nathaniel asked.

The man issued a proud nod. "That she is."

"And a fine-looking vessel at that. But I see your figurehead has met with some misfortune. 'Tis a shame. She won't get far without her legs." Nathaniel cocked his head and grinned.

Captain Smout grumbled. "A shame is right, though she did come by her wounds honorably and survived a dandy storm."

It seemed he cared more for his figurehead than the young lady lying unconscious there on the quay.

"Then you have found good fortune, Captain Smout, befitting your ship's name. I happen to be a journeyman figurehead carver. I apprenticed under Phineas Cushing, one of the best master carvers in the commonwealth."

"Indeed?" Captain Smout rubbed his beard.

"Indeed." Nathaniel lifted his chin. "I will barter the woman's contract for a full repair. I'll even give your figurehead a fresh coat of paint."

"Where is your shop located?"

"About ten miles downriver. Glassenbury." Nathaniel dared hope. The man was taking his bait.

"How are you traveling?" the captain asked.

"Another brother delivered us by means of his own brig on his way up river this morning. I mean to hire a conveyance for our return trip."

"It might take you half the day to get back. Why bother when I can deliver you in an hour's time—for a price."

The thought of boarding a ship with this unsavory curmudgeon incensed Nathaniel, and he despised the thought of putting Miss Starling back on that vessel. But Nathaniel had little choice—he must get the girl some help. Soon. He might find a doctor here in Hartford, but that he could not afford. 'Twas the best solution. Another hour and they would be home.

He exhaled. "Agreed. But you have to go down to Glassenbury for the repair. What is it to you to have us aboard?"

"It is worth your silver flask, I say."

Nathaniel gritted his teeth. "I cannot do that. It was my father's."

The captain extended his arm toward the sickly woman and frowned. "What's worth more to you? A sentimental token, or this young woman's life?"

Could this man not have one iota of decency?

A short time later all the legalities had been resolved and all were aboard the *Fortuna*. Contemplating his decision, Nathaniel leaned against a keg of rum, one of many that Smout's men had loaded into the hold below. What should have been an uneventful trip to Hartford for supplies had turned into a situation that could change the course of his life. He glanced at Miss Starling, who, after briefly wakening was now sleeping again. A thick braid of light brown hair draped over her shoulder. Unkempt tendrils clung to her dampened alabaster face. He studied her delicate cheekbones, an elegantly shaped nose, and the graceful curve of her neck. How could someone so lovely be subjected to such a fate?

His thoughts turned to his younger brother, uncertain of the kind of example he was setting for him today but grateful for his unquestioning assistance.

"You did well, Alden. You will make a good apprentice someday—you've a cooperative disposition. I am sure Uncle Phin would be glad to take you on when you complete your studies. But perhaps I shall take you on as my own apprentice," he teased. "I know, your heart is set on Yale. Dr. Hale seems to think you have the aptitude and disposition to make a good physician someday." As the eldest brother of four, Nathaniel had always been most concerned for Alden, who had had the least time with their late father. Nathaniel hoped his remarks would please his youngest sibling.

Alden looked over at Miss Starling and turned back to him. "You did the right thing, Nathaniel."

"You think so? I hope Uncle Phin will understand."

Alden shrugged his shoulders. "You had no choice. He'll come round. What will become of her, though?"

"Let us hope Mother can restore her to health. She is good with herbs. Then mayhap Miss Starling can be of help to her." All else remained a mystery.

Once aground at the shipyard, Nathaniel set to the task of getting his new charge to safety. "I will take her directly to the inn. You unload the supplies and bring them to the carving loft. At least I have a few days to prepare my explanation before Uncle returns."

Nathaniel lifted Constance in his arms. Barely awake, her limp form rested against his chest. He could feel the warmth of her feverish body through his garments. The sound of shallow breathing alarmed him all the more. She was getting worse. "Stay with us, miss. You will be in good hands soon."

Miss Starling's head drooped and her arm fell lifelessly, dangling at her side. Nathaniel's breath caught in his throat. "No, Lord."

Alden's eyes widened and locked with Nathaniel's. "Is she. . . ?"

Nathaniel gazed down at the unknown woman cradled in his arms and observed the rise and fall of her chest. "No. . .not yet."

Alden stood tall, his countenance resolute. "I'll go for Dr. Hale. He will know what to do."

Nathaniel only hoped there was yet time enough. "Make haste, Alden. Make haste!"

Chapter 2

Glassenbury, Connecticut, Connecticut River Valley
July 1753

Her fever has broken." Constance made out the muffled sound of a man's voice and tried to pull herself out of her daze.

"There now. You're awake." The warm smile of a woman, about the age her own mother would have been, greeted Constance as she attempted to focus.

An authoritative-looking man wearing a gray wig and spectacles stood beside her bed, offering his own greeting. "Welcome to Glassenbury, Miss Starling."

"Where?" she rasped.

"You are at my home, the Red Griffin Inn, at Glassenbury in the Commonwealth of Connecticut. . .in America," the woman said.

Connecticut. America. It began to come back to her. They had docked at Hartford. Captain Smout. Captain Smout. . .

Her eyes darted around the unfamiliar room. There was no sight of him. Could she be safe at last? But who were these new caretakers?

The woman wore a ruffled cap, with dark hair and wisps of gray peeking out from it. "I am Mistress Ingersoll, and this is Dr. Hale," she offered.

The man took Constance's wrist, felt for her pulse, and counted in silence. "Still weak but improving." He laid her hand back down on the covers and eyed her with concern. "Mrs. Ingersoll has been keeping vigil for some four days now. If not for her constant care and her prayers…well, let us just say you are in good hands, young lady."

Constance rubbed the soreness on her arm and noticed some circular-shaped bruises. She looked up in confusion at the doctor and then met Mrs. Ingersoll's kind but tired eyes, a familiar-looking blue gray.

"Dr. Hale is much to be thanked. That is from the cupping."

"To restore the humors, dear," Dr. Hale said. "The marks will fade in time."

"I'll put another plaster on her arm, if you wish, Doctor," said Mrs. Ingersoll.

The man nodded.

"Take a sip, dear. 'Tis meadowsweet tea," said Mrs. Ingersoll. "I shall have our maid, Lucy, bring you a caudle from the hearth. What you mostly need now is nourishment."

Constance took a sip and moistened her lips. "How did I get here?" she managed.

"That would be my son Nathaniel's doing. If he had not the good sense to get you away from that lowly captain of the *Fortuna*, who knows into whose hands you might have fallen. You owe my son a debt of gratitude, but that should be settled as you serve out your contract."

"Contract?"

"Of your indenture. He is your master now."

Though tears threatened, Constance protested. "I've only

one Master, and that is my Lord and Savior."

A deep voice came from the doorway of the bedchamber. "I'm afraid He is not the only one, Miss Starling." A stalwart young man entered the room, a parchment document in hand.

"Constance, this is my son. Nathaniel Ingersoll."

⁂

Nathaniel stood in the doorway, shifting from one buckled shoe to the other. He should have waited. The poor girl was still recovering. "Good day, miss. . .uh, I do beg your pardon, I will come back later." He retreated into the hallway.

"Stay," she croaked, albeit with an authoritative air.

He turned back and looked into the room, Dr. Hale peering up at him over his spectacles. "You heard the young lady. She requests your company."

Nathaniel arched a brow. *Requests or requires?*

"I will see to that broth now, if you would be so kind as to remain here until I return, Dr. Hale," Mrs. Ingersoll said.

"Certainly." Dr. Hale pulled a timepiece from his pocket. "Then I must examine her and be on my way."

Nathaniel assessed the peaked young woman propped up in the large bed in one of the unoccupied guest rooms. Her hair was now tucked beneath a cap, revealing the pleasant shape of her face. Her full lips formed a pout. Her large brown glistening eyes met his, beckoning for answers. He swallowed hard and shifted his attention to the doctor. "How is Miss Starling, Doctor?"

"I am pleased to find Miss Starling faring well, though she must not overexert. If you are asking to find if she is fit for work. . ."

"I am asking out of concern, as her mast—as the one responsible for her. I do, however, wish to discuss the matter of this agreement." He rustled the paper in his hand. "I believe she deserves to know, if she is up for it."

Constance dried her eyes and took in a deep breath, triggering a raspy cough. "Has it not occurred to you gentlemen that you may speak to me directly?" She sat more erect and pulled the bed cover up under her chin.

"In fact, Mr. Ingersoll, I would like to thank you for seeing to my rescue from the clutches of Captain Smout. But I fear he was successful in his goal of selling my indenture... unrightfully so. I was taken against my will and demand to be released."

Nathaniel felt as though an anchor dropped into his gut. What trouble had he wrought upon his family?

❧

Constance realized she was in no condition to be making such requests, but she must get these people to understand her plight.

Mr. Ingersoll shook his head. He looked up, dragging his hand over his hair as he spoke. "I assure you, miss. You are no prisoner here."

The intense expression that crossed his chiseled face and his sincere declaration almost convinced her of its truth. Perhaps he was, indeed, unaware that she had been spirited away from England and was not a redemptioner.

"Heavens, no," Mrs. Ingersoll said cheerfully as she reentered the room carrying some linen. "She is our guest. At least until we sort it all out." A maid followed her, carrying a tray of steaming broth. The young woman set it down with a reassuring smile and then took her leave.

Constance's captor—or rescuer—folded his arms across his broad chest. Cocking his head to one side, he addressed his mother. "You heard?"

Mrs. Ingersoll stepped toward Constance and took her hand. "That she has been brought to this country and indentured against her wishes and is now in our custody?" His mother's compassionate look fell upon Constance. "Have you any way that we can verify this, dear?"

"You have my word," Constance said.

The sound of a chair scraping against the floor announced Dr. Hale as he stood. "If you will excuse me, folks, it appears that you have much to discuss. I will be back in a few days' time. Please send for me if need be." Mr. Ingersoll shook the young doctor's hand and thanked him before he departed, receiving a warning in turn. "Be mindful that she is still recuperating."

Mrs. Ingersoll brought the bowl of aromatic broth toward the bed, but Constance held up her hand, halting the attempt when a wave of nausea overcame her. She squeezed her hand into a fist, willing the nausea to pass. With eyes closed, she took a deep breath and the queasiness abated.

The kind woman set the bowl back on the side table. "We will talk later."

"No. Please. It mustn't wait." She looked up at Mr. Ingersoll with pleading eyes.

His mouth drew into a grim line, but he gave her an affirming nod. "Tell us what happened."

❧

Nathaniel could hardly believe this fate that had fallen on Constance...Miss Starling, and himself. He listened intently to her account of the dreadful afternoon. She disclosed that she had been walking with a friend in the vicinity of a London port to deliver a gift of charity. When the sky gave evidence of an approaching storm, she and her companion had briefly separated to finish their errands in haste. Apparently then, Captain Smout's men accosted her and dragged her back to his ship to sell her indenture in America with the intent of earning a tidy sum for her passage. He forced her to sign the contract with a threat of starvation. She resisted for days, but at last relented for fear of her demise.

Now she lay fast asleep, with the promise that she would be cared for and given the opportunity to earn the funds for her passage back to England. No one should have to suffer such an ordeal, especially one so lovely. Nathaniel would honor this promise, even if it cost him everything he had. And most likely it would.

❧

"Lord we beseech Thee on behalf of this, Your child, to heal and restore her body, soul, and spirit."

Constance bolted up, heart pounding. She clutched her chemise close to her chest when she realized that a man in a dark suit hovered over her bed. His eyes flashed open, as did Mrs. Ingersoll's, Lucy's, and Nathaniel's.

"Am I dying?"

"Oh dear! I hope not." Mrs. Ingersoll placed her hand over her mouth to hide her apparent amusement. "We are praying to the contrary. Sorry to have alarmed you. This is Reverend Ashbel Woodridge, our minister."

"A pleasure to meet you, sir. Thank you for coming." Constance was moved by their thoughtfulness, yet she contended with her own thoughts. How could she ever repay them for their kindnesses? More so, how would she ever earn her freedom?

Chapter 3

After several days of convalescing, Constance sat at a small writing desk in the corner of the bedchamber, having penned two missives. She set the quill pen back in the ceramic inkpot, folded the paper, and applied the sealing wax. She hoped the letters would find their way back to England to inform her friend and her future employer of her whereabouts and seek their advice. If they could not help. . .well, she could not afford to think such thoughts.

She wandered to the glazed window and peered out toward the road. What lay in each direction? She had no concept of her location and was feeling restless after so many days lying abed. She surveyed the bedchamber once again, though every aspect of it was a permanent fixture in her mind's eye. The green-painted wainscoting with the hue of buttercups above. A wing chair upholstered in a paisley fabric. And the large full tester bed, covered with an emerald-green brocade fabric, evidence of this family's bygone wealth. Her strength was returning, and she must find a way to be useful and help repay them for their good graces and hospitality. They had even brought the minister here to pray for her, and that meant a great deal to her. Although if the Lord were truly watching over her, how could she be in this quandary at all?

A knock at the chamber door announced Lucy, who

entered carrying a gown. *Her gown.* Lucy laid the garment on the bed along with hose and garters and a petticoat Constance had not seen before. "The mistress had me launder and repair your gown, miss, and now that you are feeling better and have bathed, she sent some extra things for you as well," Lucy said.

Constance sorted through the items, including a dimity apron and short gown—suitable for housework. Was Mrs. Ingersoll expecting her to do chores at the inn to pay for her expenses? She had hoped that the mistress of the inn would not have to ask, as she had already decided to offer her services. Yet a contract still remained between her and Nathaniel. Would he require her services elsewhere? She picked up the clean gown and pressed it against her body.

"It is a lovely gown, Miss Constance," said Lucy as she tidied up the room.

"Thank you, though this is one of my plainest." Constance grew silent, recalling how the men grabbed her and tore her gown and grabbed her by the ribbons of her hat, almost choking her. The basket of food had spilled over the cobbled streets. "I was wearing it that day. . .it has a matching hat, a lace cap. . .they are gone now." As was her freedom.

"Now that you are faring well, we will move you to another chamber in the back of the house, in the garret over the kitchen lean-to. Mistress informs me that we are expecting extra guests and are in need of this room."

"Do you mean this is a guest chamber, not a family bedroom?" Constance asked.

"Indeed. You have been treated as a royal guest, for I sleep in the chamber off the kitchen, and they treat me as part of the family, they do. I've been with the Ingersolls for nigh onto eight years now, since I was a girl of twelve."

"Where does the family sleep?"

"The sons have rooms on the third floor, but Mrs. Ingersoll retains her room here on this second level."

"Three floors? What type of dwelling is this?"

Lucy laughed. "I forgot, you have not yet been about, inside or outdoors. 'Tis a fine home, some call it a mansion. Captain Ingersoll was a wealthy merchant who traded along the Connecticut River Valley."

"Was?"

"Ah, yes. The good man departed this world several years ago, and that is when it became the Red Griffin Inn. As the eldest, Nathaniel is the rightful owner. He inherited the house and property two years ago when he came of age at one and twenty, though he continues to let his mother operate the inn for her livelihood. He is a fine man, that Nathaniel." Lucy removed the vase of fading flowers that Nathaniel had picked from the garden. It occurred to Constance that she had not seen him for several days.

"As are the other boys. Boys, ha! They are mostly men now, except for Alden, who is yet sixteen. He and Nathaniel have rooms under the gambrel roof."

"And the others?" Constance asked.

"Jonathan is twenty and one, a merchant trader like his father. He is away a good deal, and when he is home he sleeps upstairs as well. But Micajah who's nineteen—Micah as they call him—is apprenticed to the baker and lives there."

"Will you help me dress, Lucy?"

Lucy's cheerful laugh filled the air. "That is what you are

used to, methinks. I can tell you are a fine lady. I've never been a lady's maid before, though I have assisted Mrs. Ingersoll and some of the dame guests when asked."

"Thank you, Lucy. I only hope to be as gracious as you have been to me."

⁂

In the keeping room, Nathaniel rested his elbows on the long oak table and stared at the contract of indentured servitude. Perhaps there was a clause he had missed that could sever the binding legal document.

"Let me take a look at that." Uncle Phineas took the paper from Nathaniel's grasp and sat down at the head of the table in the high-backed armchair. He took out a handkerchief and cleaned the lenses of his wire-rimmed spectacles before setting them on his bulbous nose. He mumbled aloud as he read through the bond. Nathaniel pushed back from the table, his chair scraping across the wide, planked floor. He stretched out his legs and stared at the flecks of sawdust on his shoes while his uncle perused the document. Dare he look up and partake of his Uncle's wrath? It would come either way.

"Whatever were you thinking?" His uncle looked up over his glasses, enunciating each word with impending judgment.

Nathaniel sat up straight. "I was attempting to save a young woman's life, sir."

Uncle Phineas frowned. "You did not count the cost of your decision."

"She did not cost much. I did not need to pay the captain more than. . ."

Uncle Phin interrupted. "Did you spend the money I sent with you for supplies?"

In truth, he had considered it, but instead. . . "I used my own coin and bartered the rest."

His uncle pulled a silver flask from his waistcoat and planted it on the table.

"My flask!" Nathaniel reached for it, but Uncle Phin clutched it underneath his arthritic but brawny fingers.

"Not now."

"How did you. . . ?"

"I stopped at Mosely's Tavern when I came in from my trip and encountered an ornery sea captain raising it up in the air as he was bidding his farewell. I immediately recognized it and followed him out. I had to make a good bargain to retrieve it. I'll explain the terms later."

Nathaniel's shoulders slumped as he heaved a deep sigh.

"You may have it again, but you will have to earn it back. In the same way you need to earn back my trust."

Nathaniel tossed his palms upward.

"I don't think you realize the burden you have put on this family. You've imposed a cost on your mother, on me, and on yourself. One that you cannot afford." Uncle Phin gripped the edges of the table and leaned in, rising slightly from his chair. "Have you even considered the payment to the doctor, her medication, the expense to this household to provide for the waif's needs—her clothing, food. . ."

Nathaniel's ire rose, but he restrained his tone as he spoke. "She can work for that."

"Now that she lives. For what? Your mother already has hired help. You cannot be giving things away if you want to be successful in your craft, in business. Your time. Your labor. Your possessions. . ." Uncle Phin slid the flask back into his coat pocket. "Everything has a price."

Nathaniel had heard the speech before. But this was a unique instance, and he had needed to make a fast judgment. Did he really err? "Is not this woman's life worth anything? I was compelled to do what was right. As my father taught me. As you have taught me."

Uncle Phineas huffed. "Right?" The frustrated man found his handkerchief again and wiped the perspiration from his brow.

Nathaniel waited for him to speak as the clock on the mantel ticked. And tocked.

"You will have to do the extra work on your own time."

"That is what I intended, Uncle."

"Your time and talent are valuable. You need to learn that lesson."

A lesson he had been learning for many years under his uncle's tutelage—and scrutiny— learning the art and magic of ship carving. What would his future hold now?

"How much did you say she cost?" Uncle Phineas grumbled.

Nathaniel exhaled. "Apparently, too much."

Chapter 4

Constance peered into the large, pleasant room with half-paneled walls. Rain tap-tapped against the paned window glass. The chill of dismal day was offset by a low fire crackling in the massive hearth.

Still, her heart froze at the hurtful words that fell upon her ears as she approached the room. It was not that she expected Mr. Ingersoll to value her, but since her parents' deaths during her childhood, she had often felt like a burden. After Uncle Chauncey's death, she had to depend on the kindness of her friend's family, and now this.

"Dear, do come in and sit." Mrs. Ingersoll entered the room behind Constance. Obviously she had not heard the men arguing.

Mr. Ingersoll looked up from the dining table at the end of the room where he sat in conversation with an older, stout-looking man. The older man's mouth drew into a tight line and he shook his head. He immediately stood.

"Is this how you treat a servant?" Phineas muttered, but loud enough for all ears to hear.

"This is my brother, Phineas Cushing. Phineas, please stand and greet our guest, Miss Constance Starling," Mrs. Ingersoll said.

"Guest, you say?" Mr. Cushing made an elaborate bow.

Constance glanced at Mrs. Ingersoll, who glared a look of warning at the pompous man. "Here, dear, sit by the fire. You mustn't catch a chill—you are still recovering, after all. I beg your pardon at my brother's unseemly attitude. He has recently returned from a long trip and is quite exhausted."

"Thank you, Mistress Ingersoll," Constance said quietly as she sat on the settee.

"Phineas, we are still trying to establish the role of this young lady. As for now, we treat her as a guest, and I will expect nothing less from even you," his sister chided. "There is no need to be such a crosspatch."

"By all means. Do forgive me, miss. From England, are you?"

"Aye sir. 'Tis a pleasure to meet you." Constance lowered her gaze and clasped her hands resting in her lap.

"She has gone through a terrible ordeal and is just now gaining her strength." Constance looked up and met Mrs. Ingersoll's kind smile. "I am so glad you decided to join us downstairs this evening."

Mr. Ingersoll spoke. "Uncle Phin, Miss Starling claims that she was taken against her will and put on that scoundrel's ship. He obtained her indenture against her will. She was from a respected family in England and was spirited away from all she knew and loved."

The man's wiry eyebrows rose, nearly touching the edge of his wig. "How can we know this is true? Even so, you paid for her indenture. By law she cannot be released from the contract until the terms are met and her freedom taxes have been paid. What of your future? And what kind of example is this to your brothers—especially Alden, who looks up to you so much? Before you take matters into your own hands, you should consult the rest of the family when your actions affect us all."

As if on cue, Alden entered the room. "You should have seen her, Uncle Phineas—she was almost dead. We saved her life." His face colored. "We, and the good Lord, with the skill of Dr. Hale, of course."

"Alden, decorum." The tall young man whipped his head around at his mother's sharp retort. Mouth agape, he laid eyes on Constance. "Oh. Miss Starling. You are looking well." Alden stepped toward his uncle.

"Pardon my interruption, please, but Uncle Phineas. . ."

"Alden, dear, we are in the midst of a discussion," Mrs. Ingersoll said tersely.

Mr. Cushing regarded his sister. "Let the boy speak, Dorothy. Alden, what say you about this affair?"

"Thank you, sir. Isn't it our duty to show Christian charity in a time of need?"

"This charity is an expense to the family that it can hardly afford, especially with your desire to attend Yale College. It is one thing to give when there is a surplus but quite another when there is not." Mr. Cushing then muttered loud enough for all to hear, "Why you cannot learn a trade like your brothers. . ."

"Please, Phineas, let us stay on course. You know Alden is going to study medical arts. We have already settled that matter," Mrs. Ingersoll said.

"I—I will work to repay you and will not leave here in your debt," Constance asserted through the oncoming tears she attempted to resist but to no avail.

Palm pressed to her face, Mrs. Ingersoll shook her head. "No wonder you have never married, Phineas. Please be more sensitive." She reached into her pocket and found a small embroidered handkerchief and handed it to Constance.

Constance wiped at her tears and sniffled. How had this trial come upon her? Only a few months ago she had been looking forward to finally moving on in her life after dealing with the aftermath of her uncle's death. The debt he left from his business failings had left her almost penniless, and she at last had accepted her lot. All was not lost. She had arranged employment as a lady's companion, and she could retain some modicum of respect in society. Yet now. . .

Mr. Ingersoll stood. "Enough of this. My judgment may have been poor in your eyes, Uncle Phin, and perhaps I was wrong to presume to rely on the good graces of this family. I promise to make restitution to all of you and further, to aid this unfortunate lady as far as it depends on me."

"Miss Starling." Mr. Ingersell held out his hand and helped Constance from her seat. Unlike the gentlemen of England, his hand was rough and calloused. Yet the warmth that exuded from his firm grasp proffered her the feeling of protectiveness and assurance—and something more? *Foolish thoughts.* She must keep her sensibilities intact. Mayhap her illness had addled her brain.

"Where are you going?" Mr. Cushing demanded.

"We have some things to discuss, in private."

"You can continue to say whatever is needed right here in this room."

"Nay, Uncle Phineas. This inquisition is over."

"I will speak to you about this later," the curmudgeon replied.

"Mother, have we anyone occupying the guest parlor?"

"Not at present, dear," she said.

Mr. Ingersoll gestured toward the door. "Miss Starling, please come with me."

Constance stood and gave a departing glance to her judge and jury. Although she had held her chin high during the encounter, when she met Mrs. Ingersoll's compassionate nod, she promptly lowered her head to hide the moisture forming again in her eyes.

"Across the way, please," Nathaniel said.

❧

As Constance crossed the front hall, she took a few deep breaths to regain her composure. Upon entering the parlor she faced a beautiful cabinet-top scrutoire and sighed. The writing desk was similar to the one her uncle had owned before it was sold off, along with the rest of his belongings. A hasty inventory revealed grander furnishings than those in the family hall. An ornate half tester bed, folded up on its hinges, stood against the far wall. Covered with lavish curtains and coverings of stunning crewelwork, apparently this bedstead on display was used for their most honored guests. Wallpaper, depicting a pastoral scene, covered the wall above the painted wainscoting, and the hearth wall was fully paneled. An oil painting of an impressive looking man in his middle years, resembling Nathaniel, hung above the fireplace.

"My father."

Constance startled when Nathaniel spoke.

"He would have dealt with this situation reasonably, as I hope to. Come and sit, and we will attempt to achieve that goal."

Nathaniel led Miss Starling to a small carpet-covered table. "I apologize for my uncle's demeanor. He is not usually so abrasive, though he is always very attentive to my mother's interests."

"And yours?"

"Yes, and mine. I am not sure if you know, but I apprenticed under him for years and am now a journeyman at his ship-carving loft. This did not please my father, who desired for me to follow in his footsteps. Yet, as I said, he was reasonable and eventually relented when Jonathan expressed a desire to follow his direction as a ship merchant on the Connecticut River."

"Miss Starling, I know little about you, only that you seem sincere." Nathaniel tried not to be distracted by the way her eyes glistened from the light of the fire as the evening drew nigh. "I wish to help, but I need to know how."

Miss Starling retrieved two letters from her pocket and set them down. "I would like to send these in the post, if I may. They are to my acquaintances in England, requesting their assistance."

"I'll see to it." He drew the letters toward his side of the table. "The post rider should be through again soon. Still, it will take three months before you receive a reply. In the meanwhile, we must come to terms with this arrangement."

"There is nothing to arrange, Mr. Ingersoll. I will work for my keep. I have little experience, though I shall do my part."

"You are not accustomed to much work then?"

"Our servants took care of my late uncle's estate. Though

I am adept at needlework."

"You will work for my mother. Perhaps you can help her with the mending and such." Though Nathaniel wondered what the *such* might be.

"Certainly, Mr. Ingersoll."

"There are more than enough men with the surname of Ingersoll in this house. You may call me Nathaniel. You should be addressed by your Christian name, as is fitting for a household servant. I would not wish to offend Lucy. She is dear to our family, and mother would box my ears if I upset her." Nathaniel grinned.

Constance gave a little laugh, and one of her delicate eyebrows rose.

"How else do you think she keeps four sons and an ornery brother in line? She puts up with precious little nonsense."

"I've seen." Constance smiled. "And what about the servants?"

"The ducking stool." Nathaniel issued a wry grin. He stared across the table at the comely woman before him, admiring the transformation at her expression of mirth.

The tall clock in the front entry chimed. This would be a long three months.

༖

Constance slid her hand over the Red Griffin Inn's roadside sign featuring a large hand-carved griffin. "This is a lovely sign. Surely it must draw attention to the inn." She looked at the stately crimson-colored clapboard house with rows of windows and impressive central stack chimney. "Though I imagine such a fine house draws enough attention on its own. Are all the homes in this area as grand?"

"Not all, though many are, especially here along the main street, Country Road." Lucy pointed north, to her right. "Colonel Thomas Welles has built a fine home up past the church for his son John and his soon-to-be daughter-in-law, Jerusha Edwards. She is the niece of Judge Pitkin of the Supreme Court in Hartford, you know. The Welleses own one of the shipyards down at Log Landing, before you get to the ferry and the tobacco fields. That is where Mr. Cushing's carving loft is."

Constance nodded, her gaze lingering down the road. "That is where Nathaniel works?"

Lucy turned left, shielding the sun from her eyes. "Yes, about a mile or so from here on the river."

Constance adjusted her borrowed straw hat. "It's close then."

"Yes. Country Road meets High Street up ahead. At the bottom of the hill we turn left onto Tryon Street, which leads right to Pease Lane. It's a pleasant walk down to the river. They specialize in figureheads, though they also do other ship carving. Sometimes other projects such as architectural features and business signs." Lucy turned and pointed above the double front doors. "Mr. Cushing created that broken-scroll pediment over the door."

"That is very nice." *Even if he is not.* Constance chastised herself for the errant thought.

Lucy placed her hand on the edge of the sign. "And this is Nathaniel's work. He made it for his mother a few years ago. The red griffin is from the Ingersoll family crest."

Constance tilted her chin. "He is very talented."

"Mmm. Yes he is. Handsome, as well." Lucy's coy smile

caused Constance to wonder what the young woman was implying.

Constance looked toward the rear of the property. "I think it would be nice to plant some flowers around the sign post. Might it be possible to transplant some from the garden out back?"

"Why don't we go take a look? I am sure the mistress will not mind. In fact, she will probably be quite pleased with the idea."

The two walked around the back of the property, and Constance marveled at both the fenced-in kitchen garden and the flower garden beyond.

"You may bring some in for the dinner table, if you wish," Lucy said.

Constance gathered a bouquet of the summer blooms and lifted them to her nose, taking in the fragrant scent.

Mrs. Ingersoll strolled toward them from the kitchen door. "Ladies, I do not mind your being friendly, though our patrons may not be if we are not ready for the midday meal. If you continue to eat the bread of idleness, our guests will have no bread to eat."

"We will be in by the by, mistress, after we collect some herbs for the stew." As the proprietresse went back inside, the pair went into the herb garden and cut sprigs of parsley, thyme, and rosemary. Lucy looked up from her task and said to Constance in a low voice, "We shall ask Mrs. Ingersoll about the flowers for the sign later this afternoon. . .when chores are done."

As Constance stepped into the kitchen, the smells of spices and smoke greeted her. From the ceiling beams hung dried herbs, salted meat, fowl, and cookware. A myriad of hooks, pots, and utensils filled the wall-sized hearth, where Mrs. Ingersoll leaned over tending the fire, humming a tune. A hymn, Constance thought. The woman looked up and smiled. "Those are lovely blooms. You will find a vase in the buttery along with the knives."

"Knives?"

"Yes, I thought you might begin by helping Lucy prepare the duck. Make sure you remove all the feathers."

❧

Constance stared at the headless duck sitting on the worktable in front of the hearth. She had never touched such a thing in her entire life. In England, all their meat and fowl had come from the butcher and was prepared by their cook. With knife in hand she proceeded to cut off a few of the tail feathers. There, not as difficult as she thought.

Mrs. Ingersoll passed by the kitchen door, peeking in. "Constance, dear, you must *pluck* the feathers out, not cut them off the bird. Lucy will be back in a moment as soon as she is done assisting me upstairs. Please try to have it done by the time she returns. Then she will show you how to carve it up."

Constance felt as though the heat from the fireplace set her cheeks aflame. She kept her eyes lowered, fixated on the mallard. "Yes, mistress."

But how exactly one plucked feathers from an unfortunate creature such as this she could only guess. With nimble fingers she tugged on one, but it did not release. Placing her other hand atop the bird, she tried again, exerting a little more force.

"Oh, dear. I saw mistress in the hall and she said I had better see how you are coming along." Lucy felt the duck between her hands and chuckled. "That bird will sooner come to life and fly away than you will have success that way. Why, you've not even dipped it yet to loosen its quills."

Lucy grabbed the bird and dipped it into a pot of boiling water hanging from a hinged rod inside the hearth. She retrieved it with iron tongs and placed it back on top of the table. A few moments later, Lucy demonstrated her pulling technique. "You shall find it much easier this way. Go ahead then." Under Lucy's scrutinizing eye, Constance gave it a try and removed feather after feather with relative ease. "There, now. You finish that and I shall return shortly."

"Thank you, Lucy. 'Tis new to me, these tasks."

Lucy shrugged and retreated from the kitchen, mumbling to herself.

At last the task was done and Constance tidied up the area to prepare for the next step. The poor bird lay naked on a platter. She took the bowl of colorful feathers of varying sizes and dumped them onto one of the small fires in the hearth. She took a poker from a hook and attempted to hasten their consumption. The smoldering feathers released a malodorous stench and smoke began to fill the space.

Mrs. Ingersoll and Lucy came rushing into the kitchen, faces filled with alarm. "That smell! Constance, what have you done?" Lucy inquired, fanning the smell away from her nose.

Their bewildered gazes instantly turned toward the smoky hearth. "What have you put in the fire?" Mrs. Ingersoll flapped her apron. "Open the windows, before the whole inn takes on that horrible smell." Constance scurried toward the two small windows and lifted the glazed panes. She then unlatched the door and a black-and-white cat skittered past her.

"It's the feathers, mistress." Lucy said, as she covered the blaze with ashes. It only made the smoke worse. Mistress Ingersoll coughed as she neared the hearth and aided Lucy in shoveling the disastrous lump of feathers into a metal bucket. Lucy retreated out the door toward the wood line to dispose of it. If only Constance's blunder could be so easily removed.

"The quills! We never dispose of those. They are used for Alden's schooling." Constance had never heard Mrs. Ingersoll raise her voice, but now the mistress of the Red Griffin Inn simply stared at her in anger. . .disappointment. . .sorrow. Tears sprung to Constance's eyes. Mrs. Ingersoll took a step toward her, and Constance tried to utter an apology, but her words were frozen upon her lips.

Mrs. Ingersoll wiped her hands on her apron and reached for Constance's hands. As she took them in her own, Constance noticed the contrast of the older woman's work-worn hands with her own, smooth and pale. "My hands were once fair as yours. Before my husband died, I had servants enough to run my home. . .when it was not necessary to keep it as a place of lodging." Mrs. Ingersoll's countenance softened as Constance's eyes met hers apologetically. "You needn't apologize for your inexperience, dear. But we must rectify the situation, as there is much work to be done in a busy inn such as this without having to take extra time to repair errors."

Constance wondered what other tasks she might muddle up, but at least she now knew how to pluck the feathers off a duck.

❧

"When are you coming home? She is trying mother's patience."

Nathaniel set his chisel down and looked up from the carving.

Micajah shoved a pasty into Nathaniel's hand. "You have been gone for days. Be glad I brought you some food from the bakery. Have you even been eating?"

"Enough." Truth be told, he fell asleep on the cot in the back room of the loft each night too tired to eat, especially since Uncle Phineas bargained with Captain Smout to do extra carving on his ship. He could not make sense of his uncle's actions these days. Yet, who was he to complain? His own behavior had him befuddled. Constance was ever present in his thoughts. He was drawn to her and could not explain the feelings that pervaded his mind. But now with the increased responsibility of an indenture contract with taxes to pay to set her free, he must focus all the more on his work. This, far easier while not in her presence. "Mmm. This is pretty good. But I suppose anything would taste good about now," he garbled as he munched on the sweet meat-filled roll.

Micah tossed a rag at Nathaniel.

"So how is it going at the bakery?" Nathaniel asked his brother.

"I'm not here to talk about that. Mother is worried about you. And Constance is trying Mother's patience. Lucy has to teach her everything, and mother is concerned that Lucy may leave us."

"Lucy will never leave us," Nathaniel said.

"Well, when Constance set duck feathers on fire the other day it put Lucy in a "fowl" mood." Micah cracked a grin.

Nathaniel almost choked on his pasty. "Really? I did not realize. . . ."

A laugh escaped Micah's lips, and then he sobered. "It is not only that. Mother is also worried about Uncle Phin. His arthritis is getting worse. She has a great deal on her mind."

"Aye, I've been concerned for Uncle. He never complains to me about it, but I have noticed my workload increasing on items that require more intricate carving. He is not as adept as he once was, and I know it bothers him." Nathaniel poured some cider from a jug and took a sip. "As for Mother, I never meant to burden her so. I hoped Constance might be useful, not a source of contention."

"The Red Griffin has not been the same since she arrived, Nathaniel."

Neither have I.

Chapter 5

Constance marched toward the shipyard recounting her mishaps. Burnt molasses. Scorched puddings. Broken pottery. Singed bed sheets. Angry guests. She could not even coddle eggs. When she timed them with the recitation of the Lord's Prayer, as Lucy had instructed her, she lost track of her thoughts and ruined them. Her prayer had turned real as she petitioned the Lord regarding her situation—praying for her own daily bread, to forgive those who trespassed against her, to be delivered from evil. Was her situation truly the Lord's will for her life?

Mayhap Nathaniel could offer some advice. The basket of food that Mrs. Ingersoll had given her to deliver to her son presented the perfect opportunity.

Constance arrived at Log Landing, the place where logs were floated downriver and collected for lumber to be used in building ships. The area provided an ample view of the Connecticut River. In the distance, she could see the shipyard's several buildings and the wooden skeleton of an enormous vessel. But in this quieter section, the building for Cushing's Ship Carving was not difficult to find. A bust of a figurehead was mounted to a shingled structure. She went inside and found that the lower level was a nautical instrument and clockmaker's shop. Behind the counter, a man stood with his back turned, and she noticed a girl sweeping the floor. "I am looking for the ship carver's shop." The girl smiled and pointed to a stairway.

Constance entered a loft at the top of the stairs. Immediately the smell of freshly cut wood assailed her, and she was surprised that she found it rather pleasant. Her eyes scanned the rustic-looking room, which she guessed spanned almost the entire second level of the building. Curls of wood shavings and sawdust littered the floor, some swept into piles. Ample light filtered in through several windows, illuminating a multitude of dust motes in the air. Carved displays hung on the walls as well as all manner of tools. Upon several worktables rested more tools with a variety of half-carved pieces, projects in the making. Bins of lumber and a large block of wood awaited the workers' skillful touch. A large wooden eagle was propped in the corner, and she marveled at its beauty. Was it the craftsmanship of Nathaniel or his uncle?

Constance set the food basket down on a dusty workbench. She picked up a rag and began to wipe the surface. She set the rag down, afraid she would disturb something or cause some kind of damage as she seemed to have a propensity for doing. Tears stung her eyes at the thought, and she buried her face in her hands.

A strong grip latched onto her shoulder and she jumped. When she turned she found Mr. Cushing standing there.

"I did not mean to startle you, miss. You are a timid thing."

The untrusting glare she returned to him would hopefully tell him that she was not, but instead tears streamed down her cheeks. She had never been one to cry so much, yet of late the tears seemed to frequently lie in wait.

He offered her his handkerchief. "There now, it is not all that bad, is it?"

She blotted her moist face, noting his attire was much different from the first day they met. His work clothes consisted of a blue-and-white patterned shirt, a worn waistcoat, and light-colored trousers. Gone was the wig, replaced by a Monmouth cap, and his weathered face was dotted with white stubble. "Would you really like to know, sir?"

"Yes, dear, I would. I would also like to offer an apology for being so harsh with you. It was uncalled for. My sister informs me that you are trying very hard to please her and do what you can to meet your goal of returning to England."

Constance sniffed. "She told you that?"

"Why, yes. And I have something to tell you as well. I have been investigating the matter of this Captain Smout and his transgression against you. The authorities have told me that if you can provide evidence of who you are and that your intent was not to come to the colonies as a redemptioner, that the indenture might be nullified. Further, it may be possible to bring charges against him and seek restitution."

"You have done this for me?" Constance beamed. "Mr. Cushing, how can I thank you?"

His gray eyes twinkled. "You can begin by sharing with me the contents of this food basket. Is it something you made?"

"Be grateful it is not. Lucy has prepared some pies and other foodstuffs for you and your nephew. I have no doubt that they are quite tasty, yet had I cooked them, that may have been another matter. I do not seem to be equipped with that particular gift."

Mr. Cushing picked up a small block of wood from the workbench. "We all have our talents, Miss Starling. And like this piece of wood, the carving process will reveal the design for which it was intended. I suspect you, too, will soon discover what you are fashioned for and how to best be of service."

"I suspect that you discovered this piece of wisdom through your own experience."

"Indeed I have, though I doubt it will take as long for you as it did for me before the design of your life takes shape." He winked. "By the way, if you are looking for my nephew, I believe you might find him hanging about somewhere by the river."

❧

Constance shielded her eyes beneath her straw bonnet as she tipped her head up toward the prow of the *Fortuna*. The ship was secured to the wharf alongside the river, and Nathaniel dangled from some sort of scaffolding off the bowsprit.

"Ah, good day, Miss Starling. Constance," Nathaniel called out to her.

"Good day, Nathaniel," she called back.

He put his paintbrush inside a pail that hung from a rope beside him. "How do you fare this pleasant day?"

"I am greatly improved, I am pleased to say," she said.

"Indeed?"

Constance smiled brightly. "Aye."

"I am happy to hear it." Nathaniel nodded with a smile of his own.

"Are you certain that you are safe up there?" Constance asked.

"I have done it a great many times and assure you the chains hold well." He glanced down to gather up his supplies. Was he coming down to see her?

Constance focused on the *Fortuna*'s mythological horse figurehead that Nathaniel had repaired and had been painting. "You have fixed her up quite well, restored her legs, and now she can gallop across the ocean."

"It would not be so easy for you." The unmistakable sound of Captain Smout's gruff voice hissing in her ear announced his unwanted presence.

Constance spun around. "Captain Smout."

He dipped his hat. "Miss Starling. 'Tis a pleasure to see you looking so well."

"Leave her be Smout," Nathaniel yelled down.

The incorrigible sea captain released a haughty laugh. "I dare say you are in a bit of a precarious position to defend this lady's honor, Mr. Ingersoll."

"Be careful, Captain, or I will paint your figurehead black!"

"Ha! We can't be having that, or my crew would have my neck. Bad luck that is."

Smout turned to Constance. "Just as you have been to me," he sneered.

He toyed with the ribbons of her hat. "Should have waited. You'd fetch me a greater fee now that you have some life in ye."

"I am warning you, Smout." Nathaniel cranked the scaffolding in haste and a rope came loose. The plank he sat upon tipped and he fell into the river with a splash.

"Nathaniel!"

Constance looked back at Captain Smout. "Help him!" The man was laughing so hard he began coughing. He obviously had no intention of coming to Nathaniel's aid.

Constance lifted her skirts and ran down the dock. She looked at the dark water but saw nothing.

❧

Nathaniel gasped for breath as he surfaced in the frigid river. He pushed his wet hair from his face and wiped his eyes. Constance stood on the edge of the dock, her hands pressed against her cheeks, framing her pursed lips. He swam the few feet to the dock and climbed up the side. She grabbed his arm to help him ascend to the platform.

He took in a deep breath, shook his head, and discovered his hair tie missing. His wet locks hung to his shoulders. "Thank you. It looks like this time you rescued me."

Her eyebrows rose. "Rescued? I fear it was my fault."

"Not at all. I shouldn't have been so careless." He looked around. "I'm glad to see Captain Smout has left."

Constance sighed. "As am I. Are you all right?"

He cocked his head. "A little embarrassed is all." He shook off a chill.

Constance looked down at her hand and saw her palm smeared with red. She gasped and stared at his arm. "You are bleeding!"

Nathaniel glanced down at his sleeve. He looked up at her concerned face, that beautiful face, and grinned. "Paint."

"Oh." Her face relaxed into a serene smile and she laughed softly.

Nathaniel's gaze passed over her. Even in what he recognized as one of Lucy's faded old aprons and borrowed gown, Constance was a vision to behold. Something about this woman exuded an inner beauty he was not sure she herself was aware of.

He glanced away, breaking the spell, and spotted a small bucket of water sitting by a post. He carried it back to her. "Hold out your hand."

Nathaniel trickled water over her upturned hand and rubbed her paint-stained palm with his thumb. He noticed the pale satin skin on the inside of her wrist and longed to touch that, too. His heart beat hard inside his chest. He thought he heard the soft sound of her breath catching. His eyes met her dark orbs and a little grunt escaped from his throat. His fingers trailed lightly down her fingers and back again, and he rubbed her palm again with his thumb. "That is better."

She looked down at her clean palm and pulled it back, holding it to her stomach with her other hand.

A breath swooshed through Nathaniel's clenched teeth. "I suppose I should get out of these wet slops. I am glad that I have another set of clothes up in the loft."

Constance's eyes wandered over him, and then she averted her gaze. Just as quickly she glanced up again, meeting his view. "I best be going."

"Constance. You never said what brought you here today."

"Why, you, of course." she said coyly. "You shall find a food basket in the loft, if there is any left. Your uncle found it first."

Nathaniel laughed as Constance turned away and headed back to the inn. His fall into the river must have addled his senses. He feared this Constance Starling was going to be his undoing.

Chapter 6

Nathaniel quietly entered the kitchen through the buttery door. He sneaked up behind his mother and planted a kiss on her cheek.

"You thought I did not hear you come in, did you?" She planted her fists on her generous hips and laughed. "It is high time you showed that handsome face of yours. I have been concerned about you. You are working too hard."

"I am doing what I must." Nathaniel sat down at the work-worn kitchen table. "Thank you for sending the food. Where is Constance, by the way?"

"Lucy took her to a public vendue to obtain some much-needed clothing."

"Oh?"

"The Hodges' daughter-in-law passed away, and their son is selling her belongings to help pay for the medical and funeral expenses and care of the new baby."

"'Tis a shame," Nathaniel said. "How is Lemuel caring for the child?"

"His mother is helping, and they have hired a wet nurse. He has moved back into his parents' home for the time being and has decided to let his house until he finds a new wife."

"A new wife?" Nathaniel wondered at the possibilities of him finding one here in Glassenbury.

"It would be best for him and the child," Mother said.

"Still, it is kind of his mother to help for now."

His mother puttered around the kitchen as she spoke with him. "I'm sure it is a happy burden."

"Mothers are a gift from God," Nathaniel said.

His mother walked over to Nathaniel and wrapped her arm around his shoulder and planted a kiss on his cheek. "As are their children. Even the grown ones." She chuckled.

"How will Constance pay for her new frocks?" Nathaniel asked.

"I sent her with a silver candlestick. Lemuel can redeem it at the silversmith's."

Nathaniel's voice rose. "That is too much."

"I felt led to contribute that to the Hodges to help in this time of need. The vendue was a good excuse, otherwise he might decline the gift."

"Mother, I am astounded by your generous spirit. Leave it to you to find a way to help the Hodges and Constance at the same time. And you have already done so much."

"The gift is not from me. 'Tis from the good Lord. All we have comes from Him."

The room grew quiet, and a gentle breeze drifted through the window. Nathaniel smiled at his mother. "You seem content today. I had been concerned that you were feeling upset."

"Is that what Micajah told you? He mentioned he had stopped by to see you."

Nathaniel yawned. "He said there was some difficulty."

"Yes, I suppose that is true. This has been a time of adjustment for us all." Mother grew thoughtful. "Yet the other day I was sitting in the parlor looking up at your father's picture. The Lord encouraged me with the remembrance of the time before your father and I were married. Jonathan Edwards came to Glassenbury, and we heard him preach. He said something that has stayed with me ever since, though of late I had seemed to have forgotten. He said, 'I assert that nothing ever comes to pass without a cause.' There is a purpose in all of this, and I thank the Lord for allowing our family to be a part of His plans."

Nathaniel nodded and considered his mother's words.

"Though she is not accustomed to much work and has little knowledge of household chores, Constance is really quite amiable and eager to help," Mother said.

"Is she learning?" Nathaniel asked.

"Yes, and it will prepare her to housewife someday." A slight grin spread across his mother's face.

"If you are thinking. . . That is not feasible. . . Not. . ." He bit into a molasses cookie and nearly cracked a tooth. "Ow!"

"Oh dear. Where did you find that? I thought that batch was given to the pig."

"I hope you soaked them first." Nathaniel grinned. "Did Micah make these? I heard he was going to supply the inn with the baked goods from now on."

"Yes, he is, and that will be a great help to us." Mother frowned. "I'm afraid that Constance baked that cookie."

"So, she is that bad, eh?" Nathaniel grimaced. "I think she added too much ginger."

"It is not as bad as all that," Mother said. "I am assessing her skills and trying to build her confidence by allowing her to utilize them."

"What can she do?"

"She is good at serving, though I think she is more accustomed to being served. Yet, she is very attentive to our guests' needs. And she enjoys gardening and putting fresh flowers in the guest rooms."

Nathaniel recalled the flowers that he had picked for her when she was ill. He hoped they brought her joy, especially now that he knew she was so fond of flowers.

"She also planted flowers around the sign out front. Did you notice when you arrived?" His mother planted her hands on her hips. "Nathaniel?"

"Um, yes, Mother?"

"The flowers around your sign. Did you see them? They complement it very nicely."

"I shall take a look."

His mother placed a plate of pumpkin bread and a cup of milk on the table for him. Then she walked over to the settle by the hearth and picked up a small stack of linen towels. "And Constance is especially adept at needlework." She pointed to the corner of the cloth.

Amusement filled Nathaniel's face. "A red griffin. She did this?"

"Yes. She suggested it herself. I have asked her if she might also label the bed linens the same for the laundress."

Alden tromped into the kitchen and grabbed a piece of pumpkin bread. "Hello, Nathaniel." He turned to their mother. "Has Constance returned yet? She promised to help me with my Latin lessons."

Nathaniel looked at his mother and the two began to laugh.

"Will wonders never cease!" Mother crossed her arms.

"What is so humorous?" Alden asked.

Nathaniel could not help but see that Miss Constance Starling had found a special place in his family's hearts. And if he were not careful, his heart would be lost to her as well.

⚘

Constance and Lucy walked down the tree-laden street on their way home from the vendue.

"It was kind of Mr. Hodge to offer to deliver the garments to the inn when he goes on his errand this afternoon," Constance said.

"You acquired a whole wardrobe. Petticoats, short gowns, long gowns, stays, stomachers, kerchiefs, shoes, even some gewgaws. The departed Mrs. Hodge had fine taste, and she was a very kind Christian lady."

"I am glad you found a few nice things as well." Constance adjusted her new cotton mitts. She admired the embroidery on the fingerless gloves. "Yes, all of the articles are very comely. Though, I must confess, I am not accustomed to wearing secondhand clothing. It is not that I am not grateful, as I am. . . . I am sorry." Constance buried her face in her hand and shook her head.

Lucy stayed her hand on Constance's arm. "There is no need to apologize. I understand what you are saying."

"Mrs. Ingersoll has been very kind to me, and I do appreciate everything she has done."

"I know you do, and she knows as well. She will be pleased to see that you have sufficient things to wear now. You even have a new gown for church." Lucy chattered on. "That Lemuel doted on his wife, but now he has so many expenses and has no reason to keep her wardrobe. There are no female family members nearby that would benefit from them. I imagine he could have kept them for a new wife, or mayhap he already has found one."

"Lucy Goslee, what are you implying?"

"Did you not notice his awareness of you?" Lucy teased.

"I only observed a man who looked disturbed to see his deceased wife's garments being auctioned off," Constance said.

"He could not keep his eyes off you, Constance. Mayhap he was contemplating a courtship."

Constance tilted her head toward Lucy. "I do believe you are either jealous or simply daft. But what of I do not know. I am in no position to consider marriage nor instant motherhood. I know nothing about babies or children."

"'Tis what mothers and mothers-in-law are for," Lucy said.

"The terms of my indenture do not permit me to marry," said Constance.

"Unless, of course, you were to exchange your bond for the bonds of matrimony." Lucy giggled.

Constance let out an exasperated breath and swatted her hand in the air. "Lucy! What in heaven are you implying?"

"You cannot tell me you have not noticed how handsome the Ingersoll men are. Fine men at that, Connie."

"I have not been called that since my childhood."

"Do you mind if I call you that then?"

"It would be nice for a friend to call me Connie. That is what my papa called me."

"Were you very young when your parents died? My

parents are both gone, too. That is why Mrs. Ingersoll treats me as her own daughter."

"My mother died when I was very small, and my father died when I was ten. That is when I went to live with my uncle and my aunt. Uncle Chauncey treated me very well, but when Aunt Silvia passed away, he was never the same. He became somewhat reckless in his business ventures and was taken advantage of by his partners."

Lucy shook her head. "Oh, Connie."

"When my uncle died earlier this year, his estate was absolved to pay his debts. My sole means of support expired, and I went to live with friends. I am—was—to be retained as a lady's companion for a Lady Bennington in Devon." Constance sighed and gathered her shawl around her shoulders. "I prayed most earnestly that God would provide for me. I never expected to find myself in this circumstance. On another continent. Subject to a master."

"A kindly master," Lucy said softly. "If you do not mind me saying, I detect some bitterness. Do you not appreciate what the good Lord has wrought?"

Bewildered, Constance stopped on the side of the road and faced Lucy. "What He has wrought? This? Here? Against my will?"

"But what of Thy will? Can ye not see the handiwork of God? In all things He works together for the good of those who love Him. Connie, doest thou love Him?"

Chapter 7

On Sunday, Lucy helped Constance dress then styled her hair with a crisping pin. This was to be her first time in church wearing the new garments she had received from the Hodges. If only she did not have to face Mr. Hodge wearing one of his dead wife's gowns!

During the service her mind wandered back to Lucy's question. "Doest thou love Him?"

In England, Constance dutifully attended worship services and said her prayers. In fact, she thought, her prayers had been more frequent from the time of Uncle Chauncey's death to this very day than they had probably been over her entire lifetime before. Yet, the idea of loving God seemed too personal, intimate. How did one love God?

She expected it was through works of service, and she thought of the years she had helped the needy by conducting obligatory charity work. But when she went to live with her friends after her uncle's estate was sold off, she found special joy in the acts of charity that she participated in with them. Their attitude showed their love of God. Constance tried to emulate the same, and her reward? She was kidnapped and forced into servitude. Did she love a God that allowed that to happen? Did He love her?

Uncle Phineas coughed loudly, bringing her attention

back to the service in time to hear Reverend Woodridge offer the benediction. "Now, may God who is able to make all grace abound toward you; that ye, always having all sufficiency in all things, may abound to every good work."

She pressed her hand to her chest as realization dawned. His grace. Even in the midst of her dreadful ordeal, God loved her, supplying her every need including settling her with a loving family.

Mayhap she could try again by acknowledging this grace and trusting that God would continue to provide for her and enable *her* to abound in every good work, just as Reverend Woodridge said. This would be her love offering to God.

❧

The congregation stood and made their way out of their enclosed pews. As Constance exited her row, a familiar face greeted her.

"Miss Starling, I believe." Lemuel Hodge took her hand and offered a slight bow. His mother stood nearby, holding the baby and smiling.

"Mr. Hodge. A pleasure to see you again."

He cleared his throat. "You look very becoming today, Miss Starling."

Constance smiled and glanced down. "Thank you, Mr. Hodge. It is kind of you to say so."

Lucy approached Mrs. Hodge and began doting on the infant. But Mr. Hodge seemed to barely notice Lucy's presence and attention to his baby. 'Twas a shame, Constance thought. Though plain, Lucy had a radiant smile and her demeanor was so sweet and kind. She certainly had extended extraordinary grace and patience toward her. Lucy was loyal and hardworking and, by the looks of it, adored babies.

"Was that one of my wife's gowns?" Mr. Hodge asked, drawing Constance's thoughts away from Lucy.

Constance did not expect this awkward inquiry and tried to keep her discomfiture from showing. "It is, sir."

"I am glad to see it of use." He stared at the gown, overly long, and blinked at the sound of his mother's voice.

"Excuse us, dear," Mrs. Hodge said to her son. The elderly woman handed the babe to Lucy and took Constance aside. "Dear, please don't be uncomfortable to be seen wearing these clothes. We are happy to see them be of use. My daughter-in-law's appearance contrasted very much to yours, so be not concerned. Many of the garments we gave you she had never worn. That *robe à l'Anglaise* is very attractive on you."

Constance looked over and saw Nathaniel heading toward them, looking so dashing in his blue coat, buff breeches, brocade waistcoat, and crisp, white stock around his neck. His fine silk stockings showed off his shapely calves. Suddenly she felt warm all over and fluttered her fan.

"Thank you, Mrs. Hodge. You are kind to put me at ease, but if you will please excuse me. . ."

She made her way past the congregants to the side door of the church. She exited and scurried around the back, where she leaned up against the white clapboards. A torrent of tears threatened to release, but she refused to succumb to them. Her feelings for Nathaniel were growing, and now Mr. Hodge was taking an interest in her, when Lucy would be a perfect companion for him and his child. Nothing seemed to be working out for her, despite the words of Reverend Woodridge. God's words. Oh, that she could trust them. She took several deep breaths to regain her composure and rejoin the others at the front of the church. She started walking around the building, but as she was about to turn the corner, she heard voices.

"Hodge, I see you have taken an interest in Miss Starling. Perhaps you are unaware that she is newly indentured to me."

"This I know," Mr. Hodge said.

"Then you also know that she is bound to me for the entirety of her contract, which does not permit her to have alternative loyalties. I hope you understand. If you have a mind to seek permission to court her, it will not be allowed," Nathaniel said.

"Perhaps you should let her speak for herself," said Mr. Hodge.

"As I have said, what my servant wants is inconsequential."

Constance could not believe her ears. Was Nathaniel really that callous? If he was, had she misinterpreted his subtle nuances? Or was he merely putting up a front for Mr. Hodge? She inched closer, staying close to the wall of the church, and could now see the pair standing near a tree.

Mr. Hodge chuckled. "Now, Nathaniel. I do not believe for one moment that you have become such a tyrant. I have never seen you so vexed, man. What is this about?"

Nathaniel let out a swoosh of air. "I am merely being protective of Miss Starling. It is my right. My duty."

"It is also your right to seek her for your own wife. That is what you want, is it not?" Mr. Hodge grinned. "While you contemplate that, let me assure you that I have already taken an interest in your mother's hired girl, Miss Goslee. She has taken to my young one so naturally, and I know her to be a virtuous and kind young woman."

Nathaniel patted him on the shoulder. "Pardon my foolishness, Lemuel. It pleases me to know you have your sights fixed on Lucy. She has been with our family for many years. A girl with such remarkable qualities is rare, and I have never seen a more cheerful and capable one. At least that is how I think of her, but I suppose she has come of age. I wish you both much happiness." Nathaniel extended his hand.

Mr. Hodge nodded with a large smile and shook Nathaniel's hand. He looked over Nathaniel's shoulder, catching Constance looking at them. She froze.

"Thank you. As for the apology, if she has heard all that we said. . ." Mr. Hodge pointed his chin in Constance's direction, "I think you ought to send it that way."

Nathaniel turned and his countenance fell. "Constance. I. . ."

She could not bear it. She clutched her silk skirts and fled.

❧

Nathaniel heard a sharp cry come from around the corner of the church. *Constance!*

He ran and found her fallen in a heap. He stooped down by her side. "Constance, are you hurt?"

She hugged her knees, her pretty stocking-clad ankles peeking out below her petticoats. He averted his gaze and noted her fabric-covered hat with her pretty brown curls spiraling down onto her shoulder. The hat remained tilted down, concealing her face entirely. Tiny whimpers were muffled beneath it.

He tipped her hat upward and lifted her chin with his fingertip. When her eyes met his, the hurt he saw there almost did him in. "Constance. . .I am so sorry."

Her lashes collected her tears and her lower lip trembled, yet she said nothing. He tried to steady his heart. If they were not at the church, he might very well take her in his arms and confess how precious, indeed, she had become to him.

"Can you stand?"

She nodded.

He rose and took her hands, gently pulling her to her feet. She stood upright, somewhat disheveled, her gown having collected an array of tiny sticks and leaves. He reached out to wipe a smudge of dirt from her jaw.

She slapped his face with her kid glove, sending his cocked hat to the ground.

Nathaniel rubbed the sting from his cheek. "I suppose I deserved that."

But before she could reply, a voice bellowed. "What is going on here?"

"You may ask him." Constance marched past Reverend Woodridge, leaving Nathaniel to fend for himself.

Nathaniel explained the misunderstanding, painfully recounting the conversation that he had had with Lemuel. It had been embarrassing enough when Constance had heard, but he was mortified to have to confess all to the minister. He knew Reverend Woodridge would expect full disclosure of the incident, especially after he saw a disheveled Constance slap Nathaniel, tears streaming down her face. Strangely, Nathaniel felt somewhat relieved to have unburdened his frustrations. But nothing subdued the regret he felt over hurting Constance's feelings.

When the family walked home from church together, Nathaniel trailed behind them in his misery.

Alden trotted back to join Nathaniel. "Brother, what keeps you? You are walking like an old dame. Come up and join me and Constance. She could use the company. It seems nothing I can say will cheer her."

"Alden, I fear if you cannot cheer her, no one can." *Least of all me.*

Chapter 8

The last light of dusk came through the small window of Constance's bedchamber as she lit the candle on the table by her bed. The narrow chamber with a slanted roof was plain but adequate and brightened by a pretty bedcovering that Mrs. Ingersoll had given her.

Constance sat on the edge of her bed and reached for *The Art of Cookery, made plain and easy: which far exceeds anything yet published* that Mrs. Ingersoll requested that she peruse. She opened the small book, determined to become more adept in the kitchen.

> *To the Reader. I believe I have attempted a branch of Cookery, which nobody has yet thought worth their while to write upon: but as I have both seen, and found, by experience, that the generality of servants are greatly wanting in that point, therefore I have, taken upon me to instruct them in the best manner I am capable; and, I dare say, that every servant who can but read will be capable of making a tolerable good cook, and those who have the least notion of Cookery cannot miss of being very good ones.*

But as the scent of the bayberry candle filled the room, Constance's thoughts drifted back to the events of the morning, and she let out a heavy sigh. She had suppressed her feelings most of the day, enough to make it through the afternoon's activities. Mrs. Ingersoll was in the habit of asking Lucy and Constance to join them for the family dinners on Sundays—so long as there were no guests at the inn that needed attention. Why did today of all days have to be one such day?

She wasn't sure if it was Reverend Woodridge's presence as he visited with the Ingersolls this afternoon, or simply the recollection of his poignant benediction, but Constance tried to take his words to heart to help her endure the day.

Yet, she knew she had failed miserably when put to the test in the incident with Nathaniel that occurred after the morning service. She was not sure what sin she had committed when she slapped him across the face, if any at all, though she did regret it.

After dinner he returned to the loft, with a gentle reminder from his mother not to work on the Lord's Day, but Constance knew he was also painfully enduring the day for his mother's sake. Once Nathaniel left, Reverend Woodridge invited Constance to sit with him on a bench in the garden to discuss what had happened during her encounter with Nathaniel.

Constance related the conversation she overheard Nathaniel and Mr. Hodge having and how hurt she had felt upon hearing Nathaniel speak of her desires as "inconsequential." To him, she was nothing more than a lowly servant. When Mr. Hodge had asserted that Nathaniel might wish to pursue her for himself, Nathaniel disregarded the comment entirely. The duel changed course, and the men proceeded to praise Lucy for her many virtues, which all the more illuminated the fact that Constance was lacking.

How different things were here in the American British colonies than in England, where gentlemen fought for her attentions. But when she all but confessed that she was falling in love with Nathaniel, somehow she sensed the kind reverend already knew.

Constance wondered how Nathaniel's conversation had gone with Reverend Woodridge this morning. The wise and compassionate man must be the keeper of many secrets. And she still had one of her own.

❧

The following morning, outdoors behind the carving shop, Nathaniel prepared the trunk of a tree that exceeded his nearly six feet, for the carving of a new figurehead. He scraped off a length of bark and stood. He braced his hands on his lower back to stretch and felt the perspiration through his loose-fitting shirt. He took a drink of cider and anticipated the forthcoming meeting that he and Uncle Phin would have with an important customer to discuss further details of the project. Nathaniel was relieved to at last be done with the work on the *Fortuna* and to return to his regular duties. But he was especially glad to be rid of Captain Smout. As much as he had complained about the man, Nathaniel could no longer imagine what it would be like if Constance Starling had never come to Glassenbury, even at the price of his and his family's convenience. *Lord, please help me to trust You for my decisions, right or wrong. And I pray that You will help Constance to trust You also. I am sorry for hurting her when You have entrusted her to my care.*

He stepped back to assess the huge piece of oak and wiped his brow. The prospect of commencing a new piece usually excited him, but Nathaniel's sense of ambition had waned. If only he had some inspiration. As he stared at the ground, he caught a flicker of something out of the corner of his eye. His gaze traveled the ground until it met a pair of ladies' shoes. Then his gaze continued to slowly ascend over a familiar skirt and apron, at last landing on the beautiful face of Miss Constance Starling.

Nathaniel tightened his lips and lifted his brow. Her lips parted as if to speak, but then she closed them again. She offered a shy smile.

"Constance."

"Mr. Ingersoll."

Their salutations tumbled over one another.

"Mr. Ingersoll?" Nathaniel cocked his head. "We are back to that, are we?"

"Yes, I mean, no. . . Nathaniel, please. I have come to apologize."

"My dear, Constance, I am the one who owes you the apology. I never meant for you to hear that conversation."

"Your true opinion of me was revealed, and I shall have to accept it."

"Not in its entirety." Nathaniel took a step closer.

Constance's head turned at some commotion by the river. Nathaniel turned to look and saw his brother's ship, with the figurehead of a bright red griffin, moored by the shore. "Jonathan! Come, let us go greet my brother."

Constance followed closely on his heels as they made their way toward the docks.

"Nathaniel!" Jonathan shouted.

The brothers embraced. "You were gone much longer this time. I hope your trip was a success." Nathaniel looked out toward the ship.

"Indeed, it was. I brought some cloth for Mother and some more spices. My crew is seeing to them now." Jonathan regarded Constance with curiosity. "And who have we here?"

Nathaniel glanced at Constance and back again at his brother. "Forgive me. Miss Constance Starling, this is my brother, Captain Jonathan Ingersoll."

Constance held out her hand. "A pleasure to meet you, sir."

"Indeed, the pleasure is mine." Jonathan turned his head and winked at Nathaniel.

Nathaniel's chest tightened. "Jonathan, Constance is a new servant at the inn."

Jonathan appeared confused. "Has Lucy left us?"

"No, nothing like that. It is a long story, one which I shall tell you about later if you will come back with me and help me hoist up a new tree trunk for carving." Nathaniel draped his arm over his brother's shoulder. "Let us go surprise Mother. She will be glad you are home in time for the fall muster on Saturday. She would not want you to get fined."

"Has she forgotten that I promised to take us all up the river to Hartford for the occasion?" Jonathan asked.

Nathaniel shrugged. "Mayhap. Well, let us go assure her that you are present."

Jonathan offered Constance his arm.

"Thank you, Captain Ingersoll," Constance said with a smile.

"You may call me Jonathan," he said with a roguish grin.

And now Nathaniel was not sure if he was glad his brother had returned or not.

"The family calls me Constance."

"I do hope you will be joining us on Muster Day, Constance."

"Of course she is. I will not allow her to miss it."

Constance craned her neck toward Nathaniel and shot him an angry glance. Mayhap he should take some lessons in charm from his brother.

❧

As they sailed up the Connecticut River toward Hartford, Constance marveled at the first signs of autumn, already displaying an array of color on the tree-lined shore. The reflection of God's glorious handiwork in the glistening water caused her to hope that her life would reflect God's love to those around her.

Nathaniel walked up and stood beside her.

"'Tis beautiful," she said.

"Beautiful, indeed." But Nathaniel was not looking up the long winding river. His eyes were fixed on her.

Constance sighed, and tried not to blush. "This journey is much more pleasant than my first."

Nathaniel leaned against the rail. "Forget about Smout. He is long gone by now."

"A fine morn," said Jonathan as he sidled up to them. He made an impressive-looking ship's captain. Nathaniel's younger brother matched him in height and build, though his hair was not as dark and his eyes were a hazel brown.

Jonathan looked out into the deep blue river. "The Nayaugs called the Connecticut River *Wahquinnacut*, meaning 'bear-of-a-long-river' or 'great river'."

Constance turned to him. "Nayaugs?"

"Indians."

"Oh." She nibbled the corner of her lower lip. She had heard about the Indians in America and wondered if they were still a threat to the colonists.

Micajah joined them. "Do not fear, Miss Starling. We have a ship full of militiamen at your service."

"I am glad to hear it, Micah." The three brothers made a dashing trio. And she found that she much preferred the attentions of this troop of men to the stuffy aristocrats in London's ballrooms.

She looked around at the crowded deck, of men dressed in makeshift uniforms and ladies in fancy dress and children playing together. Mrs. Ingersoll and Lucy were chattering away on the opposite side of the ship. "Where is Alden?" she asked.

"I believe he's bending Dr. Hale's ear," Nathaniel said.

"He will make a fine doctor someday."

"With thanks to you for helping him master his Latin," Nathaniel said.

Constance pointed up the river. "Look, more ships!"

"Yes, all of Hartford County is convening for today's Fall Muster," Jonathan told her. "Our regiment alone includes Glassenbury, Westhersfield, Middletown, and Kensington Parish. We normally muster on the village green, except when the entire regiment is gathered. Traveling the river is the most expeditious way to get there."

Before long they had arrived in Hartford. Nathaniel took Constance by the hand and helped her down from the ship onto the quay. She looked around and sighed. Nathaniel gave her an acknowledging glance and squeezed her hand ever so gently before releasing it to join his regiment.

The morning passed quickly as the women visited with one another while preparing the noon meal. Girls played with their hoops and dolls, while boys of all ages held stick muskets and practiced formations of their own.

The sound of fife and drum announced the parade. The Sixth Regiment Connecticut Militia marched by, garbed in a variety of colors, many in their hunting garments. Muskets hung from their shoulders, along with their haversacks and powder horns. Despite the motley uniforms, they presented an impressive assembly.

The Ingersoll men marched in unison with their company, led by Colonel Thomas Welles, a Glassenbury shipbuilder.

Mrs. Ingersoll pressed her hand to her chest. "This is Alden's first year and possibly Phineas's last. It pleases me to see all the men I love assembled here and looking so valiant."

"Hmmm." Constance nodded absently, but she had eyes for only one soldier.

❧

After a forenoon of drill and maneuvers, Nathaniel joined his brothers and uncle for a picnic with the family. They ate ham, poultry, squashes, beans, fruits, breads, puddings, and pies. New cider was served to all, as Mother would abide no rum.

The Hodges joined them under the shade of a large elm tree. Lucy sat jostling the baby in her lap, Lemuel beside her, being particularly attentive to both.

Mother looked at each of her sons and smiled. "You boys made a fine display on this important day. I am proud of all of you." Her eyes grew misty. "What is more, your father would have been proud to see his four sons ready to serve their country. We have much to be thankful for; we are living in times of peace. Yet it is good to know that we have such able bodies at the ready to protect us—my courageous young men." She smiled toward Mr. Hodge and Lemuel. "And that goes for the Hodge men, too. . .including that precious baby boy who will join these ranks someday."

As laughter filled the air, several colorful leaves floated onto the blanket, adding to the spirit of merriment. The spicy, sweet scent of cinnamon, nutmeg, cloves, and molasses tickled Nathaniel's senses as he lifted a piece of cake. "Thankful we are, as well, Mother. You outdid yourself with the muster gingerbread this year." He took a bite and licked his fingers.

His mother smiled and issued Constance a knowing grin. "You may send your compliment to Miss Starling."

Constance arched an eyebrow and smiled. A slow blush appeared on her face. "May I serve you another piece?"

"Please!" Nathaniel would eat gingerbread all day if it would make her happy.

After the meal the crowd gathered for artillery demonstrations, fistfights, footraces, marksmanship, and other competitions. Food booths and tents were set up, vending peanuts, cakes, and rum.

As the day wore on, Nathaniel hoped he would have a chance to talk to Constance about a matter of importance, though she seemed to have disappeared. She was probably chaperoning Lucy and Lemuel, as he noted the elder Hodges minding the sleeping baby.

Nathaniel wandered the green, and Jonathan caught

up beside him. As they walked along they talked, joked, and discussed the recent news from Jonathan's copy of the *Connecticut Gazette.*

Jonathan held up the paper. "Listen to this headline, Nathaniel—'Ship's Carver Enamored of Indentured Servant.'"

Nathaniel grabbed the paper from his brother's clutches and whacked him on the shoulder. Jonathan took off running and Nathaniel pursued, playing a game of cat and mouse. The two finally stopped, huffing and puffing. Jonathan's laughter roared. Nathaniel leaned over, hands on his knees, trying to catch his breath.

Jonathan stood and patted Nathaniel on the back. "Truly, Nate, I have seen the way the two of you look at one another. What is holding you back?"

Nathaniel grunted and pulled on his queue. "It is complicated—too much so, although I may have a plan."

A flash of Constance's cheery yellow gown caught Nathaniel's attention. "I refuse to be a pawn in your game, Nathaniel Ingersoll. I am not one of your little toy soldiers." Constance marched off.

Bewildered, Nathaniel looked at Jonathan. "How does this happen? She always catches me unawares, and at the most inconvenient times."

Nathaniel went after her. She had found refuge back under the elm tree, rejoining the family. It was obvious that she refused to budge.

His mother looked up at him. "She is obviously upset, Nathaniel. Whatever you have to say may be stated in our presence."

CARVING A FUTURE

"Very well, then." Nathaniel exhaled. "Constance, I only wish to release you from your indenture. I have an alternative arrangement that I would like to propose."

All gazes shot to Nathaniel faster than a lead musket ball and then ricocheted over to Constance. Then she whizzed off the blanket like a cannon on fire—straight into Jonathan's arms.

Chapter 9

L et her go!" Nathaniel demanded.

Constance spun away from Jonathan, embarrassed that she had run to Nathaniel's brother for safe harbor.

"Nathaniel, calm down," Jonathan ordered, releasing Constance and stepping toward him.

Nathaniel pulled back his arm and plunged his fist into Jonathan's jaw. The men fell to the ground and rolled about furiously.

Constance cried out. "Nathaniel! Stop! Jonathan, no!"

Micajah and Lemuel appeared, seizing the brothers and pulling them to their feet.

Colonel Welles approached the scene. "I trust this diversion is all in good sport, men?"

"Yes sir," they said in unison.

"Very well, then. I would hate to have to put you in the stocks." The colonel turned to Constance. "What say you, Miss Starling?"

Constance glowered at Nathaniel for a moment. "Mayhap this one."

Colonel Welles arched his heavy eyebrow.

"'Tis tempting," Constance said. "But you may leave him to me."

The colonel issued a warning scowl and then dismissed

himself from the incident.

"Let us leave Constance to her peace, Nathaniel. Jonathan," Micajah said.

"No. I mean, I should like to speak to Nathaniel now," Constance said.

"You are certain?" Jonathan asked.

"Yes. Thank you for your aid, gentlemen."

The troop marched away.

Nathaniel wiped the dirt and blood from his split lip with the back of his hand. Letting out a deep breath, he hung his head, his hair hanging loose. Then he glanced up with stormy eyes, waiting for her to speak.

Constance sighed. She took a few steps toward the nearby stone wall to hide her pending tears.

Nathaniel walked up behind her. "Constance, please," he said—his voice raspy yet seemingly sincere.

Constance turned and crossed her arms over her embroidered stomacher. "I will not abide an obligatory marriage. I refuse to take further charity—the union we already have is taxing enough. Besides, I am already betrothed."

Nathaniel worked his jaw. "To Jonathan?"

"Of course not!" *What was he thinking?*

"To whom then?" Nathaniel stood straighter. "I have not given my consent."

"If you must know, I have a previous arrangement to wed a Mr. Polsted in England. I am unavailable to be otherwise attached, and thus your consent is not required." Despite her protest, Constance's heart plummeted. She refused to cry. She had already spent too many precious tears since coming to Connecticut.

Nathaniel's countenance stiffened. "Constance, please. I had only hoped that you would remain and work for wages."

Had she misunderstood? Her resolve threatened to crumble, but she stood fast. "I assume that is an expense you can hardly afford, since you are trying to build your future. I have already inconvenienced you enough, Mr. Ingersoll."

Nathaniel removed his cocked hat and held it contritely in front of him. "Please listen. Lucy and Lemuel are to be married. She will be leaving her position at the inn, and Mother would like to hire you in her stead."

"She need not hire me—I am already her servant."

"If you accept this, it will relieve me of the expense, and it should be a great relief for you as well."

"What of the freedom taxes you must pay?" Constance asked.

"I will manage in due time," he said.

Constance tucked some errant strands of hair under her cap and straightened her hat. "I will continue to work to repay the expense I have already caused your mother, and you."

Nathaniel shook his head. "You confound me, Constance."

"It is simple, really. Did you not know? Your Uncle Phineas has offered to hire me on my day off to do some chores and grind some pigments for the paint at the carving shop. I refuse to be an expense to your mother, even if that means continuing to be a burden to you."

A new week had begun. Nathaniel stumbled out of the back room into the loft, tucking his shirt into his breeches.

"Good gracious, you look like a shipwreck," Uncle Phin growled.

Nathaniel grunted.

"Your mother sent you some leavings of ham and biscuits from this morning's breakfast. There is hot coffee on the wood-stove." Uncle often started the stove to take off the morning chill, even in the summer, despite how warm the loft became by the heat of the afternoon.

"Thank you." Nathaniel took his apron from a hook on the wall and wrapped it around his waist then poured a mug of coffee. Uncle Phineas seemed to eye his every move.

"When are you going to start sleeping at home in the comfort of your own bed? You would be better rested and ready for work in the morn." Uncle Phineas gathered up some tools and placed them by the grindstone. "That being said, I should like to have a word with you."

Nathaniel turned to grab a trencher of food and muttered under his breath. Uncle Phin may have been up since before dawn this Monday morn, but Nathaniel's day had just begun. He glanced at the small clock on a shelf. Half past seven—no wonder Uncle was champing at the bit.

A gouge clattered to the floor at Uncle Phin's feet, and he stopped peddling the small machine. "This grindstone is losing its power," he grumbled. But Nathaniel knew that Uncle Phineas had difficulty with the repetitive motion required to keep the grindstone turning. He had also noticed, for some time, that his uncle had been having increased difficulty holding the small-handled instruments with his arthritic hands.

Nathaniel picked up the tool and set it back on the workbench. "I will sharpen those later. I would like you to review the plans for the new figurehead with me, if you have a mind to." Hopefully that would distract Uncle Phin and help him to feel useful at another task.

"Indeed. Show me your diagram," the master carver said.

Nathaniel spread out the sheet of foolscap. His illustration depicted an image of a woman in a flowing gown, poised confidently under a bowsprit. "I plan to do scrollwork on the trail boards as her base, extending the design upwards toward the lower portion of the drapery of the gown. I have already calculated the angles."

Uncle Phineas rubbed his chin. "I inspected the form you have begun to shape. That is a fine section of timber you chose—methinks you will do fine with the one piece and not have to add to it. Let us hope he has not changed his mind and decided on a lion or a dragon." Uncle Phin flattened his lips.

Nathaniel slowly shook his head. "Oh, no. The contract stated a woman, and a woman he shall get."

"If you are going to inherit this business someday, you shall have to learn to please your customers."

"That I shall. Yet I will be clear on the parameters of my work beforehand, as you are. In return for a man's cooperation and funding, I will grant him a satisfactory and expedient product."

Uncle Phineas laughed and patted him on the shoulder. "That is what I wanted to hear."

Nathaniel squinted. "Did I hear you correctly concerning your plans for this business?"

"Indeed, you did." Uncle Phin looked Nathaniel square in the eye. "I cannot do this type of work forever. You have worked diligently with me over the past nine years, first as an apprentice and now as a journeyman. I would be pleased to pass this shop on to you, in due time. There is only one thing lacking."

Nathaniel listened intently, his heart filling with excitement. How long he had waited for this moment. Hoped. Prayed. Worked.

"You are ready to create your masterpiece, as I did, so that you can be recognized as a master ship's carver."

"Uncle Phin. I do not know what to say."

"Say you will."

"I will!" Nathaniel beamed with exuberance.

Uncle Phineas tapped his nubby finger on the diagram. "This will be your masterpiece, nephew."

Nathaniel smiled and shook his uncle's hand. "I will do my best to please you."

"That, you already do, Nathaniel," Uncle Phineas said. "You made a fine show with the regiment at the muster."

"What of my poor behavior? I fear I failed you all, once more."

"'Twas your own pride that altered the latter part of the day."

Nathaniel rubbed his aching shoulder and wondered if his brother had been injured, though Jonathan had said nothing on Sunday. In fact, they spoke little to one another yesterday, and he was thankful that Mother had been distracted enough by her guests not to notice. Though, mayhap she did.

Nathaniel looked out the window toward the river. "I should go apologize to Jonathan."

"You will have to wait on that. He set sail on the *Rivier Handelaar* at dawn." Then a twinkle appeared in Uncle

Phineas's gray eyes. "I remember what it was like to be young and in love."

Nathaniel grinned. "Uncle Phin, you never mentioned that before."

"It is a thing of the past. I lost my chance at love because of my own pride. Beware of that. 'Tis the only reason that I mention it."

Nathaniel looked down at his scuffed leather shoes and kicked some wood shavings on the floor.

"No need to be so downcast. You might still have time to redeem yourself with Miss Starling."

Uncle Phin headed for the stairs. Then he turned back. "Clean yourself up. Captain Cyprian Andruss is coming by to discuss the figurehead he commissioned. I shall be here with him this afternoon."

❧

Nathaniel looked up from his carving to see Uncle Phineas, accompanied by the ostentatious captain attired in a maroon suit trimmed in ruffles and lace. The captain removed his fancy three-cornered hat and perched it under his arm.

"Good day, sirs." Nathaniel brushed off his apron and walked over to greet them.

"Captain Cyprian Andruss, as you recall. My nephew, journeyman carver Nathaniel Ingersoll. He will carve the figurehead and nameboard for your new barque. We have a fine piece of oak selected for you."

"Capital! I have seen some of your handiwork, young man, and admire your talent." The stout gentleman eyed Uncle Phineas. "Cushing, you will be overseeing the project, I presume."

"I oversee all work at my shop, but I have every confidence that Nathaniel's work will exceed your expectations."

Captain Andruss surveyed Nathaniel stem to stern. "Very well, then. Now, what have ye in mind?"

Nathaniel brought out his sketches and showed the wealthy merchant the preliminary drawings, which were received with all manner of "mmms" and "ahhhs."

Then Captain Andruss wandered toward a window, looked out on the water, and mused aloud. "I see it now. . . a beautiful maiden facing the sea, embracing all obstacles, surviving all storms, calming the seas—"

The captain turned as Constance appeared at the top of the stairs. She stepped into a stream of light from one of the windows, which encompassed her in a heavenly glow.

"It is she!" Captain Andruss approached Constance. He walked around her, inspecting her, as if she were the finished product itself. "Have you ever seen such beauty?"

"Certainly not, sir. She cannot. I am sure we can find another model." Nathaniel had not expected that his pledge regarding how to deal with customers would be so soon put to the test, though he feared that this supercilious gentleman was accustomed to getting his own way. "Surely this young lady is of unmatched beauty. Do you not agree?"

Nathaniel cast Constance a furtive glance. "Yes. . ."

"Then, it is settled. The figurehead will be carved in her image."

❧

Constance's confused gaze darted from Nathaniel to Mr. Cushing and back again to the captain. She could not escape the feeling of another impending abduction. "I beg your pardon, sir, I should like to be consulted in this matter."

"Forgive my exuberance, young lady. Captain Cyprian Andruss, at your service." The man took her hand in his and kissed it almost humbly. "I only mean to borrow your likeness, miss. 'Tis too sweet not to share with the world. And what is your name, dear?"

"Constance. Constance Starling."

The captain threw his hands into the air and offered a broad smile. "What providence! My ship is named the *Constant*."

"It is?" Mr. Cushing asked. "I thought your new vessel was yet to be named."

"It is named now!" Captain Andruss turned to Nathaniel. "I hope you will carve the sign and gild the letters, as is fitting. Now, let us settle this issue at once." He clasped his hands behind his back and widened his stance, ready to issue his orders.

The captain continued with the ruminations that Constance had overheard when she had ascended into the loft. "Her hair is blowing in the wind, her eyes looking toward the future, with flowing hair and fair bosom."

Not that! Constance had seen figureheads before with women partially clad above the waist. If he was implying— she drew her arms over her chest, pressing her palm against the muslin modesty piece tucked into her bodice. Her eyes darted toward Nathaniel, and he seemed to sense her discomfiture as she nibbled her lower lip.

Nathaniel planted his hands on his hips. "Captain, if I may be so bold. Miss Starling is a lady."

Captain Andruss's face turned crimson. "Oh, I did not

mean. . ." He let out a nervous chuckle. "Miss Starling, I simply would like the honor of having Mr. Ingersoll carve your beautiful face and form into the figurehead for my new ship. When I set ashore in England, one and all will be in awe of the angelic sentry at my helm." He addressed Nathaniel and Mr. Cushing, to gain their support. "It could be good business, gentlemen."

Mr. Cushing looked at Constance. "It is up to you, my dear."

Constance contemplated the captain's words. "England?"

"Why yes, miss. I will return there before I embark on my voyage to the West Indies."

Constance tilted her chin. "Then I would like you to consider my plight, and mayhap we can come to some terms."

"You have my attention," Captain Andruss said.

"A short time ago I was taken from my home in England aboard the *Fortuna* and forced into indentured servitude here in America. I have been under the protection of Mr. Ingersoll and serving his family. Yet, he has recently offered to release me from my contract." She glanced toward Nathaniel for affirmation that his offer held true, but he remained silent, his gaze intent. "Moreover, I have no means to obtain a passage back to England. Although Mr. Cushing has been kind enough to offer me additional employment—and thus my visit here today—I am certain that a ship's passage is well beyond my means in the foreseeable future. If Mr. Ingersoll will still consent to release me"—her eyes flitted toward Nathaniel—"I would like to barter with you, Captain Andruss. You may use my image for your figurehead if you will pay my freedom taxes and provide me with a safe and comfortable passage to England."

"Then it is agreed. Mr. Ingersoll will release you from your indenture and I will pay all necessary fees. It will further be my pleasure to provide your passage back to England."

Constance smiled and sighed great relief. "Thank you, Captain Andruss." Her eyes moistened. She was going back to her former existence—and away from Nathaniel.

Chapter 10

Constance regarded the massive piece of timber which hung at an angle from a large beam with the aid of a heavy chain and pulley. Roughly hewn, she could neither imagine it as a tree nor as a ship's ornament, much less one that would look like her.

She had come early so that she could tend to some chores, but Mr. Cushing told her that was no longer necessary. He had hired a boy since she now had another occupation as the model for the figurehead. He had forgotten that she would be coming, however, and had made an appointment with another customer.

"I will be back momentarily." The old ship carver grabbed his coat and hurried off.

As Nathaniel approached, Constance felt a fluttering sensation in her chest. How could someone in a faded linsey-woolsey waistcoat look so handsome? His light blue eyes contrasted with his dark brown hair, and she had to resist the urge to remove the small wood shaving that was stuck there.

"Since you have come, why not stay and we can get started?" he asked.

Constance glanced down at her unkempt short gown and worn petticoat. "I am not properly attired."

Nathaniel grinned. "It matters not. At this stage I

only need to do some preliminary sketches and make some markings."

Constance assessed the wood. "It is very large."

"Yes, she is over six feet tall, though some are even larger, depending on the size of the ship. That is why it is important to draft the correct proportions." His eyes crinkled. "You will stay?"

"Yes, I shall."

Nathaniel stacked several crates in a steplike fashion. "Would you please climb up here? I would like to have you pose in the proper position."

Nathaniel offered her his hand, assisting her as she climbed upon the platform he had assembled. His strong, warm grip sent a startling sensation up her arm. "Please stand on this crate and take a right step up onto the next crate. Do you have your balance?"

"Yes."

He continued to hold her hand and with careful steps moved around and faced her. "Now your other hand, please. I am going to step backward behind you and pull you toward me at the proper angle. Is that all right?"

Her eyes widened. "Will I fall?"

Nathaniel chuckled. "Not at all, and if you should, I will catch you."

"Are you sure?" Constance asked.

"Do you not trust me?"

"Yes, Nathaniel Ingersoll, I trust you with my life."

"That is good to know." Nathaniel grinned. "Ready?"

Constance nodded. Nathaniel gently drew her arms back, causing her to lean slightly forward.

"Now, you may drop your hands to your sides."

He stepped back to assess the results. He stepped closer again, and as if it were a tool, he held his outstretched finger at the base of her neck and gently guided it to an upward tilt. And he did not even ask—nor did she mind.

He walked away and sat down on a stool and began to sketch, glancing up at her intermittently. A few times he got up and went to the timber and made some markings, returning again to complete his sketches. Constance admired the passion he seemed to have for his craft.

Nathaniel returned to her platform. "You may relax now. I hope that was not too uncomfortable." He took her by the hand once more. "Here. Let me help you down."

Constance stepped down from the upper crate to the main platform and turned, finding herself face-to-face with Nathaniel. His gaze would not let her go.

"Constance," he whispered. He took a slow, deep breath and swallowed.

Her breaths were shallow and mingled with his as he leaned toward her. He traced her neck and the curve of her jaw with his featherlight touch. His eyes never left hers. . .until he backed away. "Forgive me, I believe you are already spoken for."

⬜∞

Several awkward weeks passed by, and Constance rarely caught sight of Nathaniel. He worked the span of daylight, and if he did come home to eat or sleep, somehow he managed to avoid her, save briefly passing and seldom uttering a word. Constance worried that he was working too hard and prayed for him to remain well and able. Would the carving be done soon?

When might she find the opportunity to tell him that she really was not betrothed? She had refused to marry William Polsted, her uncle's insidious business partner, despite the cad's threats and insistence that they had a binding agreement. If not for Nathaniel's strange behavior on Muster Day, she might never have even mentioned it, yet it was the only weapon within her reach. *Father in heaven, I beseech Thee, please grant us all the freedom only You can provide and help us to follow Your will. Amen.*

One afternoon, after delivering a basket of food, Lucy returned from the carving shop with a message from Nathaniel. He requested that Constance come to the loft so she could pose for the carving. Might this be an opportunity to set things right? "Will there be a chaperone, Lucy?"

"You are needing a chaperone now, aye?" Lucy giggled. "Be not concerned. Methinks Mr. Cushing's new boy is there."

When Constance arrived, a boy passed her on the stairs and announced that he was on his way to chop some wood. What could she do? Nathaniel was expecting her.

As she stepped into the loft, she beheld the figurehead and went near. The sculpture had an elaborate scrollwork base and precise detail to every flowing curve and niche. The beauty of the figure that emerged from the bulk of ordinary wood nearly made her cry.

❧

Nathaniel stood at a workbench honing a curved gouge. As he looked down at the tool, the sound of Constance's sighs rose above the sound of the friction. He angled his head and peered at the demure Miss Starling as she inspected the hanging figurehead.

Constance's eyes met his, and if he was not mistaken, she blinked back tears. But why? He was trying to give her the respect she deserved and would not let his feelings for her complicate her life further.

"What is your impression?" he asked.

"It is difficult to compliment something that is in the likeness of one's self."

"Then compliment the craftsman," Nathaniel said with a wink.

Her pretty brown eyes glistened. "It is wonderful."

Nathaniel dipped his chin and eyed her earnestly. "Truly?"

Constance looked back at the sculpture and then again toward him. She placed her index finger on her chin. "One thing seems to be lacking."

Nathaniel chuckled. "You mean the face?"

"Yes." She patted her cheeks and smiled. "It seems that if I have one, this effigy must as well."

"The very reason I asked you here today." He set his honing strap down and stepped toward her, tool in hand. "Now that I have carved the drapery of the gown, I need to study your hands, your face, and hair."

He carefully removed her cap and arranged her hair over her shoulders, the silky locks slipping through his fingers. She smelled of autumn flowers and spices.

And just as the shape of a beautiful lady emerged as he released the figurehead's shape from its prison, he hoped with all that was within him that he could find a way to draw from Constance the love he knew she had inside for him.

"Are you to sketch me again?" she asked softly.

"Yea, though first there is something between us that

must be reconciled. You need to know that the burden I carry concerning you weighs upon me greatly. . . ."

"This you have said."

"But there is more."

❧

Constance and Nathaniel turned to the sound of someone running up the steps. Alden burst into the loft trying to catch his breath. "Uncle Phineas sent me for you. There is a visitor at the inn, and he says it is of utmost importance." His eyes widened. "It is the magistrate. He says it concerns Constance and Captain Smout."

The trio hurried out and boarded the wagon that Alden had driven to Log Landing and traveled in haste to the Red Griffin.

Mrs. Ingersoll greeted them with a knowing smile and ushered them into the parlor. The white-wigged magistrate sat at the table with Mr. Cushing, who promptly stood and made introductions. "The Honorable Judge Wiggins, Miss Starling. And my nephew, Nathaniel Ingersoll."

Constance greeted the magistrate with a curtsy, mortified to have left her cap at the loft. "Do sit. We have good tidings," the magistrate said.

The impressive gentleman continued. "I have consulted with Judge Pitkin of the Supreme Court at Hartford regarding the matter concerning your indenture. . .your abduction, rather."

Constance's heart leaped at the acknowledgment of the terrible injustice that had befallen her. Yet now she could hardly believe her good fortune—God's providence. Her eyes roamed about the room, meeting many heartfelt expressions.

Nathaniel nodded and offered a taut smile.

"Captain Magnus Smout of the *Fortuna* has been jailed for kidnapping and awaits sentencing," Mr. Cushing interjected.

"You see, when Mr. Cushing requested an investigation of your situation, we learned that several others had also petitioned the courts with a similar complaint," Judge Wiggins continued. "Captain Smout had also sold the indenture of other passengers against their wills at locations along the Connecticut coast and up the Connecticut River."

"I know there were other passengers aboard the ship, but I was kept in a secluded cabin. I never knew what became of them." Constance winced with concern. "Will they be freed as well?"

The judge clasped his hands on the table. "Yes, they shall. But there is something else."

Mrs. Ingersoll reached for Constance's hand, trembling in her lap. "What is it, sir?" Constance inquired.

"Captain Smout confessed that an unsavory gentleman named William Polsted was his accomplice, the mastermind behind your abduction. He claimed that Polsted sent you away when you refused to marry him, with the intent of appropriating Chauncey Starling's unresolved assets. Apparently your uncle's estate is of greater worth than you may have been led to believe. Word has already been sent to London for Polsted's arrest and imprisonment at Newgate."

Mrs. Ingersoll squeezed Constance's hand. "Praise be the Lord."

Constance sighed. "Indeed." It was all so much to take in. But at last she was free.

Free.

The figurehead for the *Constant* was nearing completion. Once it was painted and mounted on the ship, she would sail for England. Tears flooded Constance's eyes. She could hardly bear the thought of leaving those she had grown to love and serve with joy, yet she knew she had to reclaim her life. And by virtue of Nathaniel's lack of encouragement in the matter, she knew that, sadly, it did not include him.

❧

Nathaniel anxiously watched Uncle Phineas inspect the finished figurehead mounted proudly under the bowsprit of the *Constant* and awaited his verdict.

Uncle Phineas grabbed Nathaniel by the shoulders and gave him a broad smile. "You have done a remarkable job, Nathaniel. 'Tis a masterpiece indeed!"

Nathaniel returned the manly embrace, latching on to his uncle's forearms. His heart soared. "Thank you, Uncle Phineas. I learned from the best."

"You make a fine master ships' carver."

Nathaniel exhaled and donned a great smile.

"I would like to congratulate you by offering you to partner with me in my business." Uncle Phin turned and pointed.

Nathaniel's mouth dropped open. Nailed across the carving shop was a new sign—CUSHING & INGERSOLL SHIP CARVING. "I am deeply honored, Uncle Phin."

The men shook hands, and then Uncle stuffed his hand into his coat pocket. "And I have a little something else for you." He winked.

Nathaniel accepted the silver flask that had belonged to

his father and swallowed hard. "Thank you, sir."

"I trust you will take good care of that now, nephew." Uncle Phineas slapped him on the back. "Come along, your mother has a fine dinner cooking in the hearth."

As the pair walked out of the shipyard, Nathaniel looked back at the figurehead—a vision of loveliness, so like Constance. Though no longer betrothed, she would soon be gone. But her image would be forever ingrained in his mind and on his heart. If only she had room in her heart for him. He glanced at Uncle Phineas, limping along beside him, and wondered what his uncle's life would have been like had he given love a chance. Was it already too late for Nathaniel?

❧

Wrapped in her cloak, Constance stood on the quayside on the chilly October morn, as mist rose from the river. Soon she would board the *Constant*—reminding her that God was her only constant in this world—but once she embarked Captain Andruss's ship, her life would change forever. England was an ocean away and so, too, her dreams would be.

She had said good-bye to Lucy last night and rejoiced with her that her wedding banns had been read. Lucy would soon be married, with a family of her own. Yet, parting from the Ingersolls was so hard that Constance could hardly bring herself to say farewell, except by means of a letter.

Constance faced the three-masted barque, admiring the intricate workmanship mounted on the prow. The brightly painted figurehead, fashioned in her likeness, was an image of a brave and free woman—just as she had become. A thought dawned—that not only was she free to leave Glassenbury, but she also was free to remain. And why not? Mayhap the Lord had brought her here to stay. Why she had not considered this until now she knew not, though the very realization of what the Lord had wrought in her life by allowing her to come here inspired new hope in her heart. Might that she would, she could freely offer her love to Nathaniel, if only he would accept it.

Autumn leaves rustled on the wharf, and the sound of rapid footsteps drew near.

"Constance! You are still here."

'Twas the sound of Nathaniel's voice. He attempted to catch his breath; his hair hung loose; and stubble darkened his jaw. "What think thee of the figurehead?"

"It is sublime," she said, her smile demure. "Magnificent, in fact."

"Thank you, good lady."

"How did you complete it? You never called me back to finish your drawings."

"Constance, my dear, I believe I have every lovely detail about you etched upon my heart."

"'Tis kind of you to say."

"'Tis my masterpiece—you were my inspiration. What shall I do if you go?"

"You said I am a burden."

"You are God's masterpiece and no burden to me. All that I carry is the love I have for you, waxing brighter even now, deep within my heart." Nathaniel moved closer. "I am confident that God had a special plan in bringing us together. Miss Constance Starling, I ask you not to leave but to stay and become my beloved wife."

Tears of joy streamed down Constance's face. "Oh,

Nathaniel. I love you and could never leave you."

As the sun began to rise, light filtered through the trees, casting its glow upon the river. Nathaniel took Constance's hands, drawing her into an embrace. Woodsmoke lingered on his garments, and she could feel the warmth of his body. He kissed her neck and buried his head in her unplaited locks, whispering, "I have always loved you, Constance. And I always shall. Come home with me, and together we will carve a future."

Muster Day Gingerbread

The following recipe is taken from *The Art of Cookery made plain and easy by A Lady*, 1747 (Hannah Glasse was discovered to be the authoress in the 19th century).

To make Ginger-Bread. Take three quarts of fine flour, two ounces of beaten ginger, a quarter of an ounce of nutmeg, cloves, and mace beat fine, but most of the last; mix all together, three quarters of a pound of fine sugar, two pounds of treacle, set it over the fire, but do not let it boil; three quarters of a pound of butter melted in the treacle, and some candied lemon and orange peel cut fine; mix all these together well. An hour will bake it in a quick oven.

Muster Gingerbread
(A modern version for you to try.)

⅓ cup shortening
½ cup brown sugar
½ cup molasses
1 egg
2 cups flour
1 teaspoon baking soda
¾ teaspoon ground ginger
¾ teaspoon ground cinnamon
¼ teaspoon ground cloves
¼ teaspoon salt
½ cup water, boiling

Cream shortening and sugar until very light. Add molasses and egg, beating well. In a separate bowl, stir together flour, soda, spices, and salt. Add to creamed mixture alternately with boiling water, beating after each addition. Bake in a greased 8 x 4 x 2-inch loaf pan at 350° for about 50 minutes. Cool a few minutes before removing from the pan, and wrap. This cake mellows and tastes best the next day.

Author's note: The treacle mentioned in the first receipt, as recipes were then called, is molasses. Muster Day gingerbread, sometimes called Training Day gingerbread or simply muster gingerbread, was usually prepared as a loaf cake. I discovered a variation of this recipe that was rolled out and baked as a cookie.

Muster gingerbread was traditionally washed down with rum after militia training, though I recommend a nice glass of apple cider or fresh milk.

Carla Olson Gade has been imagining stories for most of her life. Her love for writing and eras gone by turned her attention to writing historical Christian romance. She is a member of American Christian Fiction Writers and Maine Fellowship of Christian Writers. An autodidact, creative thinker, and avid reader, Carla also enjoys genealogy, web design, and photography. A native New Englander, she writes from her home in beautiful rural Maine where she resides with her "hero" husband and two young adult sons. You may visit her online at carlagade.com.

TRADING HEARTS

by Amber Stockton

Dedication

To my husband, for willingly assuming the *Mr. Mom* role so I can meet my deadlines. To my readers, for your support which enables me to continue doing what I love.

Chapter 1

Connecticut River Valley
October 1754

I believe this is the last of what you requested, Mr. Yancey." Jonathan Ingersoll set the final crate in the back of the shopkeeper's cart, nodding to two of his crew to return to the ship. He thanked the good Lord for this substantial order to go with the other orders he'd filled today. It would tide him over during the coming winter months when the frozen river made his normal trade route impassable. Trade hadn't come easy lately. He turned to face Yancey only to see the man had moved to the side of the cart.

"Hmm," the shopkeeper replied, sounding distracted.

"Is there something amiss, sir?" Jonathan knew the order was accurate. He'd double-checked and verified it himself. But the man's wrinkled brow and pursed lips made him second-guess his careful calculations.

"No, no," the man finally said. "Everything is in order." He held up a pouch cinched closed with a cord and dropped it into Jonathan's hand, the coins inside clinking against each other. "You are a good man and an honest trader, like your father before you." Covering Jonathan's hand—coin pouch and all—with his own, Yancey gave a nod. "I am certain you still feel the loss of such an honorable man. But it is a pleasure to continue doing business with your family."

"The pleasure is mine as well, Mr. Yancey." Jonathan withdrew his hand and turned toward the wharf. His father had taught him everything he knew. How could he not honor him by continuing in his trade? No time for melancholy thoughts, though. He had a schedule to keep, and the tide waited for no one. "I shall return after the spring thaw," he said.

"Headed back up to Glassenbury?"

Jonathan looked over his shoulder. "Yes, I am."

"Keep a watchful eye on the water levels up that way," the shopkeeper said. "The shoreline, as well, where the river narrows." He grabbed hold of the horse's reins and turned the cart toward town. "We have had some unseasonably heavy rains of late, and there have been reports of swollen riverbanks."

"It will remain uppermost in my mind," Jonathan replied, tucking the coin pouch into the leather satchel at his hip. "I shall instruct my first mate and crew likewise. You have my gratitude."

Without any further word, he and the shopkeeper parted ways. Jonathan made haste down the path to the river's edge, where some of his crew waited. As the seaman rowed the launch toward the ship, the *Rivier Handelaar*, Jonathan stared at his awe-inspiring vessel. His crew was among the best to be found. They worked in rhythm as well as the ebb and flow of the daily tides. And his ship stood like a beacon in port, beckoning to all who gazed upon it. From the red griffin figurehead at the stem that Uncle Phineas had carved, all the way to the stern, every mast, sail, deck, and hatch gleamed to perfection. It told all who beheld the Dutch fluyt, this belonged to a successful merchant tradesman. That man was once his father. Now it was Jonathan, and he intended to do everything within his power to continue the notable legacy.

After accepting the hand of his boatswain as he crested the rail, Jonathan made his way to the upper deck.

"What is our next destination, Captain?" his second mate asked, ready to give the orders to again set sail.

Yancey's words rang foremost in Jonathan's mind as he looked upriver. Once again, the steady droplets of rain fell. The gray clouds and precipitation had been a constant companion for several weeks. For a brief moment, Jonathan considered making port right there in Saybrook. But he might as well push as far north as possible.

"Let us press on toward Selden." Jonathan pointed to the mark on the map his second mate held splayed out in front of him. "We have several deliveries there," he said, tapping the dot, "and lightening our load will undoubtedly be a benefit to us as we enter into the swollen waters farther north."

Shouts rang out, commands floated on the air, and all crew on deck scrambled to heed the orders. Every man knew his duty and did it without complaint. In fact, they seemed to thrill to the task. Yet another reason to thank the Almighty Lord for the favor granted to him and his ship. The sails caught the damp, chilly breeze, and the ship made its first jerk as it headed for the mouth of the Great River.

Two hours later, with their most recent round of deliveries made and customers satisfied, the ship continued on its way toward Glassenbury. Each mile brought Jonathan closer to home. He could almost smell the fresh bread his brother Micah baked, and the aroma of his mother's onion pie tantalized his taste buds even without the actual presence of the fare. No matter how long he was away from the Red Griffin Inn, or how often he had to travel his trade route, the welcoming warmth of home called to him and made each journey that much more satisfying. Only two more stops this day before he could genuinely give the orders to make way toward their home port.

"Captain," his second mate called. "You might want to come have a look at this."

Jonathan made haste to the bow, his trained eyes taking in the scene before them. Yancey had made no mistake in his warning to take heed of rising waters. They were less than a thousand yards from the next village, and what he saw ahead signaled significant danger. He knew the shoreline of the Great River in this segment like he knew his own ship, and it was much wider than normal. To the left and right, where familiar trees usually stood sentinel over the banks, the murky water now encased their trunks, hiding the tall grasses from view.

Howling wind whistled through the branches and across the deck. Darkness descended on them in an instant, and the ship was tossed against the choppy water. His crew scrambled on deck, holding tight to the rigging and adjusting the sails in an attempt to maintain control. A jolt nearly threw Jonathan off balance.

Oh no! They had scraped the shallow river bottom. He mentally judged the distance to the shore. They were too close. Another jolt and another scrape. He had to do something fast, or they *would* run ashore. There was no way they could fight the current and remain in the center of the river.

"Chambers!" he hollered above the ominous winds.

The first mate rushed to Jonathan's side, slipping on the soaked deck and righting himself. "Yes, Captain?"

"We need to make port now. The winds are too strong, and the tide is hurling the ship to and fro. We cannot risk pressing through this." Jonathan looked off to the right, where the flickering lanterns in front of what appeared to be a quaint inn fairly beckoned to him. "There," he said, pointing toward the faint outline of the building. "We will anchor the ship and take refuge at that inn."

"Right away, Captain." Chambers saluted and barked out the orders to the crew.

Twenty minutes later, soaked to the skin and fighting against the blustering winds to maintain his footing, Jonathan and a third of his twenty-seven crew members approached the front of the inn. It might not be the Red Griffin—his home—but with its whitewashed front and painted black shutters, at least it appeared clean. He shivered. At this point, anything offering a blazing fire would be a welcome sight.

Lifting the brass knocker, Jonathan gave the door three swift raps. A moment later it opened, and a petite yet sturdy maiden greeted them with a warm smile that traveled from her delicately bow-shaped lips to her shining gray eyes. With her ruffled cap slightly askew and several tendrils of wheat-colored hair escaping the confines of her single braid, she looked a great deal younger than what he presumed her age to be. The aromas of beef, baked ham, and what smelled like onion pie assailed his nostrils. His stomach rumbled in response, earning a charming giggle from the maiden before him.

Sweeping off his hat and tucking it beneath his arm, Jonathan bowed. "Good evening, miss. My name is Captain Jonathan Ingersoll, and I command the *RivierHandelaar*. The flooded river has forced us to lay anchor about two hundred yards south, and this dismal rain has us all soaked through. My crew and I would be in your debt for a hot meal, if you have it to spare."

The young girl curtsied and swung the door open wider, gesturing with her arm in a sweeping motion toward the main room of the inn. "Do come in, Captain Ingersoll. My name is Clara Marie Preston. My father is the proprietor. Welcome to the Higganum River Inn."

Jonathan stepped aside and allowed the first wave of his crew to precede him. He glanced over their heads into the main room. They weren't the only ones to whom this inn had beckoned in this dreary weather. His men would have to eat in shifts and most would likely have to sleep in the hammocks below deck.

"I invite you to choose your tables from those available," Miss Preston said once they were all inside, "and I will notify my father of your arrival."

Jonathan touched the cuff of the maiden's sleeve, and she paused midturn.

"Did you need something more, Captain?"

"Is that perhaps onion pie that I smell?"

"Yes." Miss Preston smiled. "I baked it myself this afternoon."

As the maiden walked away, a grin came to Jonathan's face. Based upon how the skirts of the simple dress fell around Miss Preston's feminine curves, he'd been fairly close to the mark in his conjecture on her having attained at least ten and seven years. And she could bake the very pie he considered to be his mother's best dish. This meal just might be the next best thing to eating at the Red Griffin.

Taking a seat at the nearest table, he allowed his gaze to roam the room. So much of the decor reminded him of the Red Griffin. Well-scrubbed floors were dotted with bright rugs. The furnishings showed obvious signs of wear, but they appeared to be of good quality and well cared for. Flickering flames from the chandeliers hung from the beams above cast an ethereal glow about the room. The teasing aroma of that baking ham hung in the air. A scent like that would entice every weary traveler within ten miles to seek lodging at this establishment. If they had to be forced ashore earlier than planned, at least the resulting destination was one possessing a great deal of appeal. . .in more ways than one.

❧

Clara peered out from behind the swinging door leading from the hallway to the main room, her eyes scanning the occupied tables. When her gaze landed on the handsome captain, her breath caught in her throat. He certainly cut a dashing figure, from the polished black boots and fawn-colored breeches that hugged his long, muscular legs, to the broad shoulders encased in a fitted, navy overcoat, every button fastened and gleaming. That brought her to his face, where the rain-glistened brown hair was tied back in a queue, and high cheekbones gave way to warm, hazel eyes that had caught her attention the moment she opened the door. Well, that, and the rather loud rumble emanating from the captain as soon as he smelled the food cooking.

He sat at a table at the far edge of the room, leaning back in his chair with a nonchalant air, taking in the room with measured observations. Clara self-consciously smoothed her hands down the front of her apron and reached up to check her wayward tendrils. A whoosh of air escaped her lips as she felt the loose strands of hair around her ears and cheeks. She must appear a sight, for certain. Tucking as much as she could back into her braid, she then inhaled and slowly released her breath.

"Clara." Her mother's voice sounded from behind, making Clara straighten. "Have you discovered the number of gentlemen accompanying the captain for the evening meal, and what meat they would prefer?"

"No, Mama," she called over her shoulder. "I am on my way right now."

"Very good, my dear. Our guests need our attention. We do not have time to dawdle. Please also determine how many will be requiring a bed for the night. I am certain we cannot provide rooms for them all, but we shall do our best."

With another deep breath, Clara pushed through the swinging door and headed straight for the captain. As her eyes met his, a congenial smile formed on his lips. Had she imagined it, or did he immediately look her way the moment she stepped into the room? The way he watched her as she approached certainly made that reality a possibility. He seemed very aware of her every move, and Clara couldn't decide if that excited or unnerved her.

When she stood just a few feet from his table, Captain Ingersoll greeted her with a nod. "Miss Preston."

Clara bobbed a quick curtsy. "Captain Ingersoll." She folded her hands in her apron and shifted from one foot to the other. "Mama has asked that I inquire after the meal choices of your crew and how many might require a bed for the night."

The captain leaned back in his chair and smoothed his thumb and ring finger down the sides of his mouth. "Ah yes. I suppose it would be helpful if we told you what we would like to eat, for I am certain you cannot divine our thoughts."

The mirth in his eyes and the teasing slant of his lips drew out an answering grin from Clara. My, but he was charming. And if she didn't miss her mark, he knew it as well. Quite a dangerous combination but appealing nonetheless.

"Well, do allow me to set your mind at ease. My men will take a healthy serving of whatever you have readily available or in abundance. And only six or seven of them will be sleeping here tonight. The rest of us will bunk down on board the ship."

The rest of *us*? Clara's shoulders fell. Did that mean he wouldn't be staying at their inn? She had hoped to see him for longer than the evening meal. It didn't appear as if that would happen, though.

"After all, I cannot leave my goods and merchandise unattended, especially in this weather. Who knows what unsavory sorts are lurking about the river, waiting for the opportune moment to strike."

Merchandise? Goods? "Oh! Are you a merchant trader?" she asked.

"As a matter of fact, I am. Just like my father before me."

Her brother, Samuel, was a trader, too. Before his accident, anyway. But he was in town tonight. And considering his attitude of late, perhaps that was a good thing. Then again, maybe it would benefit him to talk with Captain Ingersoll. Perhaps the captain could help.

"Clara!"

Clara turned to see her mother standing in the doorway, an expectant look in her eyes and a stern expression on her lips. Oh! She'd done it again. She must see to the matter at hand. They had a room filled with waiting guests.

"Coming, Mama!" she called in return, pivoting on her heel.

"Miss Preston?" the captain beckoned softly. She again looked in his direction. "Do forgive me for keeping you from your duties. Please," he said, gesturing vaguely toward the expanse of the room, "see to your other guests. I am certain to be here for quite a spell and intend to make good use of your inviting fire."

She nodded, unable to voice a reply. That last statement filled her with such delight. And she was impressed by the captain's need to apologize, even though he had done nothing wrong. She could easily while away the hours enjoying his company. Oh how she prayed the evening would last far longer than usual.

Chapter 2

Just as Clara had prayed, the hours seemed to lengthen. Although she tried to resist it, her eyes continued to seek out Captain Ingersoll throughout the evening meal. And almost every time, she caught him watching her as well. The wind continued to howl outside, and the rain pelted the windows, presenting a cold and dismal landscape just beyond the sturdy walls of the inn. But inside, the fire blazed, and despite the weather, the resonant chatter from the guests lent a cheerful air. And the warmth creeping up Clara's cheeks was from more than the heat in the fireplace.

Not long after they finished eating, the guests retired to one of the other public rooms for continued diversion. Clara and her younger sister, along with two servant girls, kept them supplied with cups of steaming tea, hot cocoa, or water, as well as a selection of delectable pumpkin bars, applejacks, and orange-spiced scones. She made certain to be the one serving the room the captain had chosen.

Clara now stood at the preparation table, staring at the wall in front of her. If someone had told her that morning how her day would play out, she never would have believed them. The good Lord and good fortune certainly smiled down upon her with the rise of the river and from the moment Captain Ingersoll knocked on their door.

"Clara." Her mother's voice interrupted her musings. "Are you going to stand and stare at that wall for the rest of the night, or will I benefit from your assistance in preparing additional sweets for our guests in the other rooms?"

Clara straightened and blinked several times. Adelaide Preston was nothing if not hardworking and generous. She expected her children to be the same. Clara had to bring her mind back to the present. There was work to be done, and she needed to be aware enough to complete it. The precious time she wanted would only slip away from her with her daydreaming.

"I'm here, Mama. Tell me what you need me to do."

Mama passed a large, wooden bowl down the kitchen table to her. "Separate the flour into equal portions for the mixing bowls. When you are finished with that, you can move on to the sugar." She turned to give directions to the other servant girls in the kitchen.

"Mama, can I help, too?"

Clara's ten-year-old sister, Molly, missed the step down into the kitchen from the hallway and stumbled into the room. Nine-year-old Garrick was right on her heels and braced himself on the doorpost to keep from knocking her down. At one time or another, every Preston child had worked at the inn. But now Clara's oldest brother and older sister were married, living in the village proper. And Samuel had returned to the inn just a few short months ago.

"Garrick, you can go find your papa and help him with whatever he is doing. You are more than ready to start taking on more responsibility."

"What can I do, Mama?" Molly clasped her hands

in front of her and looked up at Mama with an angelic expression. Clara's heart warmed at the sight.

"You, my little angel," Mama said as she tapped Molly's pert nose, "can help me cut pieces of cheesecloth for these canisters."

Mama often said children were a sign of the good Lord's favor and blessing. And she at one point had a houseful. Clara hoped she'd be equally blessed when the time came for her to have a family. As she sifted through the flour and portioned out equal amounts for each bowl, her mind once again drifted to the captain.

How was it that she had never before encountered him or made his acquaintance? Their inn sat in a very noticeable location, and it had always been a popular resting spot for many a weary traveler. As a merchant trader, Captain Ingersoll no doubt traveled the waterways from the mouth of the Great River at Saybrook up north to where the waters became impassable by the larger ships. From the way he carried himself, he was not new to the trade. So why then had he only just tonight appeared at their door? Perhaps if she found a way to listen to more of the conversation in the room where he sat, she could learn the answer to her question.

The moment the next batch of scones was ready, Clara snatched the tray and rushed from the kitchen. After taking a moment to compose herself before bursting into the parlor, she stepped through the doorway with calm assurance, doing everything she could to make certain her racing heart could not be detected. As soon as she approached, Captain Ingersoll looked up and smiled. She smiled in return. He lifted the empty tray from the table in front of him and took the full one from her, placing the empty one in her hands.

Charm, confidence, grace, and a servant's heart. The captain was amassing an appealing list of qualities. His easygoing manner and awareness of others reminded her so much of Samuel—before—and that made him seem all the more familiar to her. Stepping to the side table, Clara retrieved the water pitcher and filled the empty cups, moving to pour tea and cocoa next. A low tone caught her ear as she approached the settee.

"Have you heard the news of General Washington?" one of the inn's guests asked of the captain.

Captain Ingersoll held up his hand and inspected his fingernails. "Do you mean in regard to the two battles against the French at Fort Dusquesne and Necessity?"

The man nodded. "Yes. Are you aware of what is to happen next?"

The captain crooked one corner of his mouth. "From what I have learned, the Duke of Newcastle has been in negotiations in the months since those two battles took place. I am not certain what has taken him so long, but I hear tell he has finally decided to send an army expedition not long after the new year."

"And Major General Edward Braddock has been chosen to lead the expedition."

"Major Braddock?" The captain leaned forward, resting his forearms on his knees. "Wasn't he just granted the colonelcy of the 14th Regiment of Foot last year?"

"One and the same," the other man replied. "It seems he has served Britain well, and as a major general, was the obvious choice. I cannot help but wonder what King Louis

XV is going to do should he learn of Britain's plans."

The captain's face grew grim. "Let us pray he does not discover those plans, or any attempt on Britain's part to thwart the French will be destroyed. And it could drastically affect my trade success along the river, should the French shipping industry be attacked."

Their conversation volleyed back and forth for several more minutes, but Clara's primary interest in the news of the battles was how the situation might affect them there in the river valley where they lived.

"So tell me, Captain," the man she had identified as Mr. Coulon said, "how is it you have never made port near this little village prior to this evening?"

Clara stopped in her tracks. This was exactly what she wanted to know. Now she could hear the answer to her unspoken question.

Captain Ingersoll leaned back against the settee and folded his arms across his chest. "In all honesty, I cannot say for certain one way or the other. In fact, when my first mate alerted me to the peril of the risen waters through this area, it was the first time I had actually taken notice of the existing village flanking the river."

"But from what I have gathered in what you have shared this evening," Mr. Coulon pressed, "you have been traveling this section of river for several years, even before you assumed control of your father's ship. Were you not aware of this village even then?"

Clara had asked herself the same thing not long after learning Captain Ingersoll was a merchant trader. Ships could only venture so far along the river, and they all frequented the ports in Saybrook on their way out to the ocean and other ports along the shore. So, why not Higganum or Haddum?

The captain shrugged. "Unfortunately, beyond the fact that I had no cause to make port in this area, as none of my current customers reside here, there is no other answer to your inquiry. And I do not believe my father had cause to trade here either, or I am certain I would have remembered stopping along the route." He uncrossed his arms and rested his hands on his legs. "If I had to make a conjecture, I would say the residents of this village and the residents nestled in this little nook have been trading with other merchants or getting their supplies from a trader along the post roads. There are far too many towns along my route for me to possibly service them all. But I am available to all who make a request of me."

So, that was it. And the explanation made perfect sense. The captain was right. He could never fulfill the needs of everyone along the trade path of the Great River. But perhaps now that he had stopped here and made some acquaintances, he would see fit to return and offer his services. Clara would have to speak to Mama and Papa at the earliest opportunity to discover who provided them with their supplies.

"Now, if you will excuse me, Mr. Coulon"—the captain's voice broke into Clara's thoughts—"I believe I am going to partake of the heat from the fireplace in the great room. The stove here is sufficient, but there is nothing quite like the heat from a fire to warm you through. And despite the length of time my crew and I have spent inside, there remain areas of my clothing that are not yet fully dry." He stood. "The fire is sure to remedy that."

The captain was about to head in Clara's direction! That meant he would pass directly in front of her if she did not move from where she stood.

Coulon waved his hand in the air as a dismissal. "Of course, of course. Thank you for your engaging conversation, Captain. I do hope to see you again sometime."

"And I you, Mr. Coulon, if for no other reason than to discuss the ramifications of Britain's military actions in the Ohio Valley and France's response. I have a feeling this is only the beginning."

A moment later, Captain Ingersoll closed the distance from the settee to the doorway in four long strides. Clara could do nothing but watch him as he approached, unable to avert her gaze or find anything else to occupy her attention. The captain commanded attention no matter where he stood, and his effect on her was doubly compelling.

He paused as he stood in front of her and smiled down, the flecks of green in his hazel eyes shimmering with mirth. Had he somehow discovered her attraction to him? Or was the delight she saw borne of genuine kindness and respect for the service she provided? Based upon how he had treated every person who had served him this evening, Clara assumed the latter.

"Miss Preston, might I presume upon you to bring me a fresh slice of that bread you served with the meal earlier this evening? And some butter as well, if you have it at the ready?" He placed his hand just below his ribs. "I must confess, that was the best bread I've tasted since I last enjoyed a loaf baked by my own brother, Micah."

Clara beamed. Little did he know she was the one who

had baked that particular loaf. "Thank you, Captain. I shall be certain to notify the one who baked it and share your appreciation." She preceded the captain through the doorway and turned in the direction of the kitchen. "Please, do make yourself comfortable by the fire. I shall have a warm slice with butter brought out to you there."

The captain raised his hand and bowed. "You have my undying gratitude, Miss Preston."

❧

Jonathan watched Miss Preston disappear into the darkened hallway alongside the public sitting rooms. She had been quite attentive tonight. As she saw to each table and each guest, her winsome smile and pleasant attitude only added to her quality service. He enjoyed the liberty of observing her from a distance most of the evening. And the other guests seemed rather taken with her as well. Not that it surprised him. Her beauty flowed naturally from within and bubbled out as it brought joy to others.

He turned and continued on his way toward the stone hearth on the opposite side of the great room. He passed in front of the broad staircase leading to the rooms on the upper floors and walked by the desk where he had earlier signed the register. A shelf behind the desk caught his attention. How had he missed that before? Even the light from the candles in the chandelier made the items adorning the shelf stand out.

He took a few steps closer and peered at each glass figurine in turn. Whoever collected these had an affinity both for fine craftsmanship and the wild animals of the great outdoors. In fact, he had only seen such delicate work performed in one town along the ocean coastline. He had two similar figurines on board his ship at that moment. One was intended for his mother, but the other he had purchased on a whim with no specific recipient in mind at the time. Now he knew why. And he had to retrieve it.

Once he had the glass animal in hand, he made certain the ship was secure and returned to the inn. He would be back on the ship all too soon, but only after he enjoyed what he could of the warm fire before spending the night in the cold and lonely captain's quarters.

As soon as he entered the inn, he glanced toward the hearth and saw a piece of bread with a dollop of butter beside it on the plate. Miss Preston had done as she'd promised. He only regretted not being there when she delivered it. . . if she had been the one to do so. Of course, judging from the way she appeared wherever he chose to sit, he had no doubt it *had* been Miss Preston who provided him with the additional bounty.

But he had a greater purpose to attend to. After casting a careful look about the room to make certain no one would see his actions, Jonathan stepped behind the desk and stood in front of the shelf. He carefully withdrew the swan figurine from the pouch at his hip and placed it on the shelf in an empty spot near the end. Taking two paces backward, he admired how well the swan blended with the other figurines nestled there. The lack of dust on the collection showed its owner took great care to keep them polished. Yes, this figurine had found a new home.

Nearly half an hour later, Miss Preston returned to collect his empty plate and refill his cup one more time.

"Thank you. The bread was just as delicious as the first

taste I had, and the hot tea has sufficiently thawed me to the core."

"The pleasure has been mine, Captain Ingersoll."

Miss Preston bobbed another curtsy and graced him with a genuine smile as well. A smile that had a greater effect on him than all the tea he'd drunk that evening. She left him then, walking toward the parlor. Jonathan returned his attention to the dancing flames in the fireplace, stretching his hands toward the warmth.

"Oh!"

The sudden gasp made him twist around to the source of the sound. As he and Miss Preston had been the only two in the main room, it took but a second to identify the reason. There she stood, holding the figurine he'd placed on the shelf only moments before.

"How beautiful," she exclaimed, running her finger along the delicate curves of the swan's neck and back. "It is simply exquisite."

Jonathan watched her marvel at the newest addition to her collection. He'd had an inkling she would be the owner, and now that he knew for certain, he found an even greater pleasure in knowing what he'd done. Should he admit to being the party responsible? Why not? What did he have to lose? He stood.

"I thought the same thing when I first saw it in the shop window in New Bedford, Massachusetts."

Miss Preston spun to face him, her hand going to her chest. "Captain Ingersoll? This was yours? You're giving this to me?"

Even from this distance, Jonathan could see the sheen of

unshed tears glistening in her eyes. It was all he could do not to go to her, but propriety kept his feet firmly planted on the wooden floorboards.

"Thank you," she said and sniffed. "Thank you very much."

Jonathan dipped his head then raised it and met her gaze from across the room. "Miss Preston, this time, the pleasure is all mine."

He didn't know what else to say, but it was obvious no further words were needed. Miss Preston replaced the swan in its new spot and backed away toward the parlor, bumping into the wall on her way. Other young maidens would have rushed from the room after such a blunder, but not her. Instead, she shrugged, a most beguiling and sweet smile gracing her lips, as she once again left the room.

The blustery wind howled just beyond the windows, and Jonathan shivered involuntarily at the thought of venturing outside once more to spend the night on his ship. The rain had ceased hours before, yet the cold remained. But just thinking of Miss Preston and her charm warded off the chill. The memory of the way she cherished his gift would stay with him for a long time to come.

Chapter 3

Clara pressed the brief missive to her chest and closed her eyes. Although saddened when she ventured downstairs this morning to find the captain and his crew already gone, pleasure immediately replaced the sadness when she discovered he had left this note. She had read it so many times, a tiny hole had formed in the crease. Unable to resist, she unfolded the piece of paper and read the note again.

Dear Miss Preston,

I am sorry I will not be here when you awaken, but we rose early and discovered the waters had receded sufficient enough for us to be on our way. As we suffered a delay yesterday, we felt it imperative that we make haste in continuing on our journey. But rest assured, that delay was made quite enjoyable by your presence and your family's service, and I cannot imagine any other delay I might wish to repeat than one which would bring us back to your inn.

Although the coming winter months will soon make passage along the river impossible, I will continue my trade via wagon cart and do my best to return by whatever means necessary before the spring thaw. In the meantime, I trust the newest addition to your figurine collection will take my place until I can return.

Yours sincerely,
Captain Jonathan Ingersoll

The captain had left a brief note for Mama and Papa, too, but it lacked the personal touch he'd included in his note to her. It was equally as cordial, and the sentiment echoed what he had written for her alone. Nevertheless, she enjoyed reading between the lines and interpreting a deeper meaning, even if he hadn't intended one. Most would call her foolish. She didn't care. Captain Ingersoll's note was hers to keep and hers to interpret as she wished.

"I do believe, Mr. Preston, our daughter has become smitten by a certain dashing captain who joined us last eve."

"Yes, Mrs. Preston. I would have to concur with your assessment." Her father paused. "I do wonder, though, how she will serve our guests if her eyes are constantly watching the front door for this gentleman's return."

"Perhaps," her mother continued, "we should relegate her to the kitchen in order to remove the temptation."

Clara glanced up into the amused faces of her parents. "Mama, Papa. You do not need to speak of me as if I were not present in the room." Nor did they need to restrict her duties in any way. "And I assure you, I am perfectly capable of seeing to our guests without distraction. You have no need to be concerned."

Mama reached out and placed her hand over Clara's. "Oh, we were not concerned, my dear. At least not more for the guests than we are for you." She patted Clara's hand.

"However, this is the first time your father and I can recall you being so enamored." Mama smiled. "We always knew this day would come, but we cannot help but wonder. Why this man?"

Papa snapped his fingers. "It is the uniform, is it not? Even I must admit, a man in uniform commands attention."

Clara shook her head. Oh how she loved her parents dearly, especially their penchant for the occasional lighthearted banter. "Captain Ingersoll is not the first seafaring guest we have had at our inn over the years. Nor is he the first in uniform. And I am certain he will not be the last."

Mama nodded. "This is true. But why this captain?"

In her mind's eye, Clara brought back the captain's image. Every detail, right down to the tiny scar on the lower left side of his angled jaw. Even now, the depth of his hazel eyes and his self-confident grin drew her like a mouse to molasses. And she would willingly endure the sticky situation for another opportunity to speak with him. All of a sudden, the captivating eyes blurred, only to be replaced by the expectant expressions on her parents' faces. Now, what was it Mama had asked?

"I am not certain I can answer that question, Mama." Clara leaned her forearms on the registration counter in front of her and shrugged. "What I do know is the captain possesses a quiet strength and inner peace that fascinates me. In the brief moments I had to observe or speak with him, he demonstrated kindness, genuine concern for others, and an awareness of everything and everyone around him." She straightened and turned to retrieve the glass swan he'd given her last night then faced her parents once again, cradling the figurine in her palm. "He had a way of making me feel special, of looking for that one thing that would say he noticed me, and doing it without hesitation."

Papa pressed his lips together. "Now, those are good reasons to be enamored of someone. They are admirable qualities to possess. No doubt about it." He propped an elbow on the counter. "Of course, his family's reputation and the stellar integrity his father possessed do not hurt his prospects either."

Family reputation? Clara set the swan on the counter in front of her. "Are you saying you know Captain Ingersoll, Papa? That you have met his father?"

Mama cleared her throat. "*Knew* the elder Captain Ingersoll, Clara dear. He passed away several years ago."

Captain Ingersoll's father was dead? And he had been a trader, too? That meant the captain had followed in his father's footsteps and probably even taken over his ship. Oh, how difficult that must be—to live everyday on a ship serving as a reminder that his father was no longer with him. Clara's heart went out to the captain.

"And now," Mama continued, "I do believe this is my cue to take my leave and return to the kitchen. The midday meal is not long off, and there are several items on the menu which need my attention." She reached out and gave Papa's arm a loving squeeze, sliding her hand down and touching her fingertips to his. "You two have a nice little chat."

Papa watched Mama walk across the room and disappear behind the swinging door to the central hallway. Even after all the years they'd been married, the love he felt for Mama shone in his eyes. Mama's, too. Neither one of them made any attempt to hide it. Clara prayed daily she would find someone to look upon her with the same level of affection.

"Yes, I did make the acquaintance of the elder Captain Ingersoll on more than one occasion." Papa turned to face her, leaning again on his elbow. "We did not engage in any business transactions, as I had already arranged for the delivery of our goods from another trader. However, there were a handful of times when he would take a meal with us, or I would encounter him in the village as he made deliveries."

"So, there was a time when the Ingersoll ship did trade with the people here in Higganum?" From what Clara had learned last night, the captain had never stopped here. But now she was learning his father had. Perhaps he'd done so when the captain had been too young to accompany his father.

"Oh yes. In fact, about fifteen years ago, he was responsible for the majority of trade conducted via the Great River's waterways."

"What happened?"

Papa looked up and narrowed his eyes. "I am not one hundred percent certain, but I believe another trader arrived and was determined to overtake the business Captain Ingersoll had established with the villagers here."

"But how could he do that? Wouldn't the captain have agreements with those villagers? And wouldn't it be rather difficult to steal a customer?" Clara didn't even know who this other trader was, but from Papa's tone of voice as he talked about him, the trader couldn't be half the man the captain's father was.

"As I said, I did not know the elder Captain Ingersoll

well. However, from what I can recall, this other trader began to falsify the captain's reputation and sabotage his trade agreements through attacks on the captain's character. I do not know how the trader accomplished it, but he must have had other men working for him. And it was a devious yet carefully orchestrated plan. Before long, many of the residents in the villages began to believe the lies and shifted their loyalties to the new trader."

"But that was not fair to the captain. He had done nothing wrong." The incident might have happened a little after when Clara learned to walk, but it still incited a great deal of anger inside of her. She clenched her fists and gritted her teeth, regardless of how unladylike she might appear.

Papa chuckled at her reaction and covered her fist with his hand. "You are correct. The captain *was* completely innocent of all charges against him. But that didn't change the minds of the villagers. This other trader had so effectively besmirched the captain's good name, continued trade with Ingersoll was out of the question."

"Oh, that was truly awful." Clara frowned, trying to imagine what it would be like to have someone lie about her in such a manner. And for what purpose? The guaranteed trade of a few tiny villages? It hardly seemed worth all that trouble.

"Yes," Papa agreed, squeezing her hand as she relaxed her fist. "But, from the reports of the dispute, no matter what that other trader said or did, Captain Ingersoll remained calm. Rather than verbally rebutting the falsehoods, he continued to do trade and conduct business as he had always done. And he never once raised a hand to the other trader or called the man out for his actions." A pleasant expression crossed Papa's face, as if the incident he recalled brought back fond memories. "When the time came to cease his dealings with the villagers here and remove this port from his route, the captain did so without a word. Any other man might have engaged in a round of fisticuffs or possibly even returned devious intent with an equally devious action. Instead, the captain walked away, his integrity still intact."

"That must have been extremely difficult for him." Clara could only imagine what she would do if that had happened to her. "But thank you, Papa, for telling me. I can see where this captain," she said, touching the glass swan, "gets his noble character. He comes by it honestly."

Papa nodded. "Yes. He does. And now you see why I said earlier that the character traits you mentioned were good reasons to become enamored of someone." He smiled. "If this Captain Jonathan Ingersoll is anything like his father, he is welcome at our inn anytime."

Clara smiled, feeling the effects all the way to her eyes.

"Now, that is enough stories for today. As your mother often says, this inn will not run itself." He grinned and reached out to trace a finger down Clara's cheek. "Besides, I have a feeling we will be seeing this captain again very soon."

As Papa headed outside, Clara paused and stared at the swan again. She carefully replaced it on the shelf and ran her finger across the arched back. Oh that her father's words would come true.

Chapter 4

Jonathan's crew strained against the frigid waters of the river. They had resorted to making use of the sweeps in order to navigate in the still winds. And the oars were even used on occasion. In the shallower areas, ice had already begun to form. It wouldn't be long now before the entire river was too frozen for ship travel. But he said he would do his best, no matter what it took. And he intended to do just that.

Three hours after leaving Glassenbury that morning, the town of Haddam came into view. Higganum was a little farther down. As his crew maneuvered the ship toward a place where they could make port, Jonathan's spirits lightened at the thought of seeing Miss Preston again. It had only been three weeks, but right now that felt like an eternity. He was over the rail and descending the ladder to the launch before his crew had even dropped anchor. Let them tease him. Jonathan didn't care. After all, he paid their wages. They would do well to remember that when the urge to mock him came upon them.

He rushed from the shore the moment his boots touched land, his long strides eating up the distance. Only a few more steps and he'd be knocking on the front door. But just as he set foot on the bricked stoop, the painted door swung open wide and there stood the young lady whose image had been uppermost in his mind since the day he left.

"Captain Ingersoll," she greeted with bright eyes and a smile. "How delighted I am to see you again."

Jonathan regarded Miss Preston for a moment before he spoke. Something about the fair maiden captivated him. Perhaps it was her guileless nature or her winsome smile. Maybe even that glimpse of her engaging personality he'd caught on his first visit. Whatever it was, he was glad he had come. If only he could prolong his stay. But the river wouldn't wait. He had to get the *Handelaar* to the South Cove at Saybrook and docked for the winter.

He swept off his hat with a flourish and bowed. "Miss Preston, as promised, I have returned." He glanced up at the gray clouds, threatening snow. "And once again, I am accompanied by less than desirable weather," he said with a grin.

She giggled. "It is not within your power to control the weather, Captain Ingersoll, but one does have to wonder about the good Lord's affinity for bringing you here under such dreary conditions."

"It is only to better accentuate my bright presence."

This time, she laughed. "When juxtaposed against the backdrop of bleak and gray, how could it be anything but?"

Jonathan pressed his hat to his chest and feigned offense. "You wound me, fair maiden. What must I do to return to your good graces?"

Miss Preston lowered her lashes and tucked her chin against her chest. "I dare not say, for it would be presumptuous of me to do so."

Ah, a sense of humor *and* modesty. Two quite admirable traits. Jonathan extended his hand. "Then, would you do me the honor of accompanying me outside for a spell? Do be certain to wear your wrap. It is rather chilly out here."

She glanced over her shoulder where her mother stood watching their exchange. A silent nod from the matriarch communicated her approval. Miss Preston reached for her wrap, but when face-to-face with him again, she hesitated. He turned and offered his elbow to her. She eagerly accepted.

With her hand tucked securely in the crook of his arm, Jonathan led her down the brick path toward a stone bench beneath a towering sugar maple.

"Shall we?" He extended a hand toward the bench. She sat and tucked her skirts beneath her, folding her hands in her lap.

The faintest of breezes stirred a few wisps of hair against her cheek. Jonathan started to reach out to tuck them behind her ear, but he closed his fist instead. That would be far too forward. A moment later, she took care of it for him, tugging at a lock of hair as it rested across her shoulder.

Jonathan had the feeling it was up to him to start the conversation, but what should he say? Yes, he was the one who had invited her to join him, but beyond that, he hadn't thought of much else. Talk of traveling his trade route or sailing his ship to Saybrook would likely not be of much interest to her. Perhaps he should talk about the inn. With the Red Griffin Inn run by his mother, that was a topic he knew well.

"So, tell me more—"

"What is it like, living—"

They both laughed as their words tumbled over each other's.

Jonathan gestured for her to continue. "Please."

Clara dipped her head then returned her gaze to his. "Your life on board a ship for most of the year affords you a certain advantage. I have overheard bits of conversation between Papa and several guests, along with my brother Samuel, that have piqued my interest, but they tell me their affairs are not for a young lady's ears." A beguiling pout drew Jonathan's eyes to her lips. "I do not wish to pry, but I am fascinated by what little I do hear and long to know more. And you spoke with one of our guests at your last visit about a Major Braddock, so you must be aware of what is happening."

He had best tread carefully, both in his errant thoughts and on this subject. As her brother and father said, much of the life of a seaman as well as military talk was not meant for maidens to hear. And he did not wish to anger either of those men in her life. But if he said too little, he would risk disappointing this very attractive young lady. Neither outcome held much appeal.

Jonathan shifted his attention back to her eyes and away from the more engaging area of her lips. "Tell me first how much you already know about the life I lead and the developments to the west."

Clara chewed on her bottom lip and gazed over his shoulder. He took advantage of that moment to observe her. Waves of wheat-colored hair were gathered with combs and fastened under a lappet cap. Eyes the deep gray of the wet sand along the cape near Saybrook hinted at wisdom beyond her years; yet, at the same time, her manner bespoke a youthful innocence that increasingly intrigued him. He presumed her to have nearly attained her eighteenth year but not quite. If more, then the men of this town should be brought to question for not seeing the beauty before them.

The object of his scrutiny shifted her focus and caught him staring. A becoming blush stained her cheeks, and she averted her gaze. Innocent indeed. A characteristic he found both refreshing and appealing. Unable to resist, Jonathan gave a light touch to her cheek. The warmth in her eyes chased away the embarrassment, but the doe-like innocence remained.

"Do forgive me. I must apologize for causing you discomfort. Please share with me what you know, and I will endeavor to supply the necessary facts to satisfy your curiosity."

His young companion brightened, and her enthusiasm once again took hold. "Over the years, Papa and Samuel have often spoken of the many ships that lay anchor in the harbors at the mouth of the Great River. I have only had the good fortune to see them once, many years ago. From the way they speak, the community there is fairly teeming with the latest information, commerce, and industrial developments. It all sounds so exciting. But here"—she made a general sweep of the property where the inn sat—"I am like a bird in a cage, seeing the world, yet unable to be free enough to explore it. What little I do know, I gather from the conversations of the guests at our inn."

Jonathan nodded. "I can see how your life might seem constrictive, but consider the diversity in the guests you meet every day. I would hazard a guess that you know more than the average villager."

"Perhaps. I do know there has been talk of the developments in the Ohio Valley and as far north as the

St. Lawrence Valley. I understand the dispute over who owns the land beyond the mountains has led to the animosity with the French, but I am unclear about how all of these recent events interconnect."

A sweet face paired with an intelligent mind. That was a combination Jonathan didn't often encounter in the women he knew.

He took a deep breath and exhaled. "Basically, both the French and the English claim all the lands from the Alleghenies west to the Mississippi River. While the area along the St. Lawrence River has also been under dispute, the Ohio Valley has recently become the main focus of this conflict."

"Papa says the Ohio Territory is beautiful. From his description, I can almost see it—majestic rolling hills and valleys with glimmering crystal streams, how the rising and setting sun casts color and shadow across the landscape, and all of it stretching as far as the eye can see."

Not only intelligent but a poet as well. He must learn more about this charming lady.

"Such a vivid imagination you possess," he said with a smile. "The problem is the French claim they discovered this land, while we English claim it is ours by charter and by our alliance with the Iroquois."

Clara pursed her lips. "If this land is as valuable as it is beautiful, any man would be foolish not to want it for his own." She tracked the progress of a lone brown leaf as it fell to the ground. "This land here, west of the Great River and east of the Hudson, has a beauty all its own. I would gladly fight for it if someone challenged me to its ownership."

Jonathan straightened, astonished to have found such a kindred spirit. She had no idea how much he longed to find someone in whom he could confide; someone who didn't have an obvious vested interest in the militant developments. Because he often associated with fellow seaman, trade customers, and the occasional riffraff he encountered in various taverns, Jonathan hadn't met many beyond his own brothers who could hold a passable conversation with him. Never in his wildest imagination would he have expected to find such compatibility with a young lady here in Higganum.

Clara's attention remained with the single, dead leaf, and she didn't seem to take note of his pause. "That is the exact source of the dispute," he murmured. "If the French have their way, we English will be confined to this narrow space between the Atlantic and the crest of the Alleghenies. On the other hand, if we have ours, the French will be hemmed within a small portion north of the St. Lawrence."

The sudden flight of two late-migrating swallows overhead caught their attention. When the birds flew into a nearby pin oak, a squirrel chattered in protest. The birds only flapped their wings, chirped a few times, and remained where they landed. Accepting defeat, the squirrel scampered down the trunk. Bounding over to another oak, he raced up it to resume his previous activities. Clara shared a smile with Jonathan at the little animal's antics before bringing their conversation back to the matter at hand.

"Why cannot England and France simply come to an accord on this issue?"

Jonathan sighed and shook his head. "In my opinion, greed is the force that blinds them to any compromise."

Impulsively, Jonathan covered Clara's hand with his then quickly withdrew it, conscious of propriety. She didn't seem to notice, or at least showed no signs that she did. No need to cause her undue distress by making advances that would be seen by a guest at the inn or either one of her parents. Better yet, they should move from this somewhat secluded spot.

"Will you walk with me?" He rose and extended his elbow.

She stood and again placed her hand in the crook of his arm. The pressure of her touch sent his mind wandering in another direction, but he quickly reined in his thoughts. It was enough to handle, simply escorting such a lovely young lady around the property.

Once they reached the path leading to the back of the inn, he continued. "Our current situation is tenuous at best," he said. "Hostilities have risen to an alarming level. England continues to launch attacks against the French, but we are suffering more loss than gain."

Clara turned her attention to him and furrowed her brow, as if attempting to piece together everything she knew and had learned. "We have been aware of the disputes, but we have had no awareness here of how critical the situation has become." She pointed past him, where the sails from his ship could be seen through the barren trees. "Not even our trade or the cost of goods has been affected as of yet. Colonel Washington's journal published in the *Maryland Gazette*, where he shared the details of his July encounter with the French near the Great Meadows, was our first indication."

Jonathan nodded. "The French commander and nine of his men were killed, which led to the colonies rallying in fear of the French threat. And as you overheard from my last visit, we should be receiving support soon from England. None of the bloodshed has trickled this far east, and for that, many of us are extremely grateful. But if this conflict continues to escalate, as I fear it will, it will not be long before we are unwillingly drawn into the midst of it all." He pressed his lips together then relaxed them. "If I had to hazard a guess, I would say this coming year will be critical in the decisions that are made regarding the potential for war."

Jonathan returned his attention to Miss Preston's face. Lines furrowed across her brow, and her mouth was pressed in a thin line, upsetting her delicate features. She seemed so vulnerable at the moment. How could he tell her he had to leave? That his ship and his crew awaited his return? But he had no choice.

He pulled his arm away and reached inside his coat for a note he'd penned, but in his haste he pulled out other papers with it. The pages fluttered to the ground at their feet. "Miss Preston, I must go."

"Go? But must it be so quickly?"

Biting her lip, she bent to stop the scattered papers from blowing across the grass in the breeze. He hastily dropped to one knee to help. As they reached at the same time, they bumped heads.

Brilliant. He was as couth as a drunken sailor. Hoping a smile would soften the abruptness of his announcement, he got to his feet, rubbing his head ruefully. He bent to take her hand, and she straightened to stand before him, regarding him gravely.

"Forgive me, Miss Preston. But, as you can see from the

condition of the river, the ice is already forming." He quickly took back the other papers and left her with the note. "If I do not make haste toward Saybrook, there will be irreparable damage done to my ship."

She clutched the note to her bosom. "And that would cause undue hardship on your trade business as well."

Jonathan nodded. "Yes. So you see why I cannot tarry." She started to respond, but he stayed her words with his hand. "I have enjoyed every moment of our conversation, and I do not wish for things to end here. But I cannot guarantee my availability during the coming months." He took a breath and prayed for courage, nodding toward the lone page she held. "I have written my request in that note to your father, but now I am asking you as well. Might I have permission to call on you after the spring thaw?"

"Yes, of course," she answered without hesitation.

"And would it be presumptuous of me to ask that you write?"

Her lashes swept downward, and a light pink colored her cheeks. She raised her gaze once more to meet his. "It would please me to have your permission."

In spite of knowing that spring was nearly five months away, a thrill lifted his spirits. He reached into his coat for a pencil, but before he could find it, she thrust one into his hands. He raised one eyebrow in question.

She colored prettily. "I keep a pencil with me at all times."

Jonathan knew the significance of what he was about to do, but he could no more resist than he could deny himself food and water. Already he felt the absence of her company at the thought of the long, solitary journey back to Glassenbury after he secured his ship. He quickly scrawled his address onto one of the papers, tore it free from the full page, and placed it with the note he'd penned, praying she'd write.

Clara held tight to the two pages from him, their hands barely brushing. She glanced down at the address he'd given her. "I shall write at the earliest opportunity."

Jonathan lifted her hand to his lips and brushed a kiss across her knuckles. "And I shall eagerly await the receipt of your letter."

He forced himself to turn and stride in the direction of his ship. Unable to avoid a final look, he glanced back over his shoulder to find Clara watching him.

She held the papers to her chest, and sadness softened her features. He gave a cheerful wave and tore his gaze from her as his measured steps put more distance between them.

Although hesitant to admit it, he left a part of his heart behind.

Chapter 5

Clara raised the tambour on her escritoire and reached for the quill lying next to the paper. She dipped it in the inkwell and started to write.

Dear Captain Ingersoll,

This will likely be the final missive you shall receive from me, as the spring thaw is nearly upon us. I have greatly enjoyed the written exchange we have shared these past few months, but it pales in comparison to knowing you will soon be here again. I am pleased to learn of your many successful ventures during the winter with your cart and horse, although I am certain it lacks the thrill of sailing aboard the Handelaar *and navigating the waters of the Great River. Perhaps upon your return, I might experience firsthand standing on board your main deck and receive a tour of your ship.*

Business has slowed, as expected, here at the inn, but we have not been for want of a consistent flow of guests. As I shared earlier, many of them have been integral in keeping me informed of the happenings beyond this river valley. I appreciate you sharing what you have learned as well, despite the grim nature of the news. It concerns me to hear of more soldiers crossing the land here in New

England on their way to the Ohio Valley, but from what you wrote, the increased activity and need for supplies has been good for your business. So how can I not at least be happy for you?

I anticipate the coming spring, knowing the thawing of the river will not only breathe new life into the bleak landscape and bring forth the colorful blooms, but it will also allow you to travel the waterways once again. You are no doubt anticipating that moment with greater expectancy than I. But until that day comes, I shall continue to watch and wait for your return.

Fondly your servant,
Clara

After reading it over once more, Clara folded the note and sealed it with melted wax then pressed a stamp with her initial into it. The courier from the village would arrive tomorrow, and her letter would be on its way. She prayed the captain would receive it before he departed for Saybrook to retrieve his ship.

"I cannot fathom why you would continue to correspond with this Captain Ingersoll." Samuel's voice held the predictable blend of disdain and bitterness as it always did when he spoke of what once was his life. "Knowing what you do about the merchant trade business."

Clara pivoted on her stool to face her brother, who stood in the doorway. He took several labored steps into her room, leaning heavily on the cane that had been his constant companion for almost a year, and stopped right in front of her.

"Father told me about your affection for this captain." His eyes narrowed and his eyebrows dipped into an angry point. "How could you possibly allow yourself to develop feelings for this man when he could very well be one of the traders responsible for the attack on my ship?"

Clara wanted to jump to the captain's defense, but that would only anger Samuel further. And she had no intention of succumbing to his cynical bait. Despite Captain Ingersoll's many merits, Samuel responded with retorts of how no trader could possibly be that virtuous.

"Samuel, you do not even know if Captain Ingersoll and his ship were anywhere in the vicinity when you were attacked." At least she hoped he hadn't been involved. Everything she knew about him gave rise to his innocence, but what if she was wrong? No. She couldn't be. "As I recall, you were the one to say his normal route and location at the time failed to line up."

"That does not mean he is innocent of being involved in some way. I was well on my way toward establishing a rather successful venture in this region before those men attacked me. It stands to reason that he might be in league with those who wanted to see me stopped." He shifted his weight to his good leg and gestured at the sealed note. "Tell me, what do you really know of this man beyond what he has told you himself?"

"I know what Papa has said about his father and the integrity he no doubt passed on to his son. And I know from the brief time I spent with him that he could not possibly be connected to any of the men you seek."

"Well, I am not so certain," he growled.

"Please, Samuel." Clara reached out and touched his injured arm. "I promise you that this captain is innocent. If you would take a moment to step outside of your anger at your circumstances, you would see that."

He yanked his arm away from her and glared, animosity and disapproval fairly shouting from his expression. "What I see is that you have completely disregarded what has happened to me and allowed your emotions to muddle your sensibilities. You care more about this. . .this nobody trader," he said with disdain in his voice, "than you do your own flesh and blood."

Now he was being simply absurd as well as ill-mannered. "His name is Captain Jonathan Ingersoll, and as he has done nothing to you. He deserves your respect."

"I do not care about his formal name or about your defense of him. You say he has done nothing wrong. I say that has not yet been proven." Samuel pinned her with his intent gaze. "And until this matter is fully resolved, you would do well to avoid men like him. Do you not realize the potential danger in which you have placed yourself?"

"But Samuel, that is what I am trying to tell you. There is no danger." Why was he being so bullheaded and narrow-minded about this? Even Papa had given his consent to the forthcoming courtship. Surely that should make a difference in her brother's mind. "Captain Ingersoll is a man you can trust. I promise you. And if you would take a moment to absorb everything I have told you, you will no doubt find that I am correct in what I say."

"There is nothing you can say that will change my mind." Samuel threw back his shoulders and thrust his chin into the air. "Perhaps I should have a talk with Father about all of this. See if he feels the same about your relationship with this man once he hears my side of the story once more."

Furious at her how her older brother attempted to exert authority over her, Clara jumped to her feet and stood toe-to-toe with him.

"Captain Ingersoll has always been the perfect gentleman in my presence, and he has never demonstrated anything other than respect for everyone around him. In fact, he even asked after you in one of the letters he penned to me this winter."

Samuel broke their visual standoff and stared out the diamond-paned window. "And you no doubt supplied him with all the details of my sad and lonely state."

"As a matter of fact, no, I didn't," she countered. "Instead, I wrote to him about how much you used to love the sea and sailing and that maybe one day you will return to it, once you are able to truly put the past behind you." If only her brother could move beyond this hatred. It was eating him alive and poisoning everything he did or said.

"The only way I am going to put this behind me is if I track down and discover who did this to me," he said, gesturing to his leg and arm. "When that day comes, and I can mete out equivalent justice, *then* you can talk to me about sailing once more."

"Well, do not interfere with our relationship unless you have solid evidence to prove that Captain Ingersoll was involved. I do not want your venomous distrust of all seamen destroying what could become a permanent arrangement."

If Samuel had been younger, he might have cowered

beneath her anger, but at almost twenty-two, he had no reason to fear her. And by the look in his eyes, he was not about to allow his sister to speak to him that way...no matter the circumstances.

He jammed his index finger into his chest and stared at her. "*My* distrust? I am brutally attacked, my ship is burned, my potential future is completely destroyed, and *you* are angry at *me* for what I *might* do should I be present the next time this captain appears?" He huffed. "I am only looking out for your best interests and do not wish you to get hurt. You?" Samuel jerked his thumb toward the folded note. "You are only concerned with what you see and your own feelings. You do not even want to acknowledge the possibility that your captain might be less than what you perceive."

"That is not true!"

Samuel brought his face within inches of hers. "I dare you to prove it."

Clara knew she would never succeed with her brother if they remained angry at each other and allowed their emotions to get the better of them. She took several deep breaths and tempered her ire then pressed forward.

"I actually will not have to prove anything. And I know the captain is exactly how I perceive him. You will be able to see it for yourself the moment you meet him. The type of men who attacked you do not conduct themselves with the integrity the captain possesses. And when you realize this, you will also see that his intentions toward me are completely honorable. Even Papa has approved."

Her brother remained silent for several moments, his mouth rigid and forming a tight line as his eyes narrowed.

Clara shifted from one foot to the other. Maybe she was actually getting through to him. But then he stiffened and tightened his grip on his cane.

"We shall see who will arise the victor," he threatened, limping from the room faster than Clara thought possible.

It was like the story Papa had told her about Jonathan's father all over again. Only this time, the trader attempting to sabotage Captain Ingersoll was her own brother. And his reason wasn't to steal away customers. No. It was to thwart the captain's chances of success so his eligibility to court her would be diminished. Clara had to do something. But what?

※

Jonathan turned at the long shadow appearing in the doorway of the stables, and there stood his older brother. Jonathan nodded to the groomsman who readied his horse. Thank the good Lord he didn't have to tend to the animal himself. He much preferred the ropes of the rigging to the leather of the reins, but he rode when necessary.

"Ah, the day has finally arrived," Nathaniel announced. "The dismal winter is behind us, and you can again set sail for the high seas."

"I am not certain the high seas are what I would term the location of my sailing." Jonathan chuckled. "But I cannot deny the thrill in my blood knowing in just a few hours, I will see my ship again."

Nathaniel grinned. "Are you certain that excitement is not due to the young maiden awaiting you in Higganum?"

How could he deny it? Nathaniel, more than their younger two brothers, understood the pull of a lady's affection. His wife, Constance, even now worked with their mother overseeing the inn.

"Yes, you know me all too well, brother." He gave Nathaniel a sheepish grin. "I confess, the prospect of seeing Miss Preston again holds an equal measure of draw as returning to my trade route." Grabbing hold of the reins, Jonathan led his horse toward Nathaniel. "And how fares your bride these days?"

"Her time is nearly upon us." Nathaniel sighed and ran a hand over his chin, then from his chin to his hair, leaving several dark brown strands standing on end. "I am not certain who is more worried about the coming little one." Jonathan walked with him out into the bright morning. "And it is a good thing Mother is experienced in these matters, because it seems everything I do or say is the wrong thing."

"Have patience." Jonathan dropped a hand on Nathaniel's shoulder. "It will not be long now, and then you shall have the squalling bundle stealing your sleep at nights."

"When you state it in that manner. . ." His brother grimaced. "It does not hold as much appeal as Constance has intimated."

"Do not take my word on it." Jonathan laughed. "Remember, I have no more experience than you in these matters."

"No, but it might not be long before you do."

And with that, the sweet face of Miss Preston came to Jonathan's mind. He wanted to ride right now to Higganum to see her. His work had kept him far too busy for social calling the past few months, leaving his desire to see her that much stronger. But he must see to the *Handelaar* first.

"And if your face is any indication, that young lady will be unable to resist."

Jonathan grinned and dropped the reins to take his brother's hand between both of his. "From your mouth to the good Lord's ears. May it be so."

✌

"I have kept each and every letter you wrote in a bundle tied with twine in my writing desk." Clara pressed her hand in the crook of Captain Ingersoll's elbow as they walked the brick path in front of the inn. The first glimpses of color were just starting to peek up from the ground, and tiny green buds were right on the edge of bursting open. "Going back to read them helped the long, cold days of winter pass more quickly." She'd never been happier to see spring arrive.

"Yes." The captain chuckled. "The words in those letters did have a way of keeping me warm." He smiled down at her. "Although I must say, gazing upon your face again far exceeds the warmth gained from your words."

Clara felt heat from her neck to her cheeks. She glanced away from him. It felt good knowing his affection had developed at the same rate as hers during their separation. But where did that leave them now? He had yet to declare a formal suit, although he had hinted at it when last they spoke and more than once in his letters. Would he follow through with that today?

He grazed her fingers with his free hand. "You mentioned a little bit ago that you had something you wished to share with me." His soft voice compelled her to again look at him. "It sounded important. Is now a good time to discuss it?"

Perhaps, although Clara would much rather pursue the topic of courtship than discuss her brother and his nefarious plans.

"Yes." She sighed. "Better now, before something happens."

The captain halted, and the instant tug made her stop as well. "Is everything all right?" he asked. "You are not in any kind of trouble are you, Miss Preston?"

Clara looked up into his soft eyes, mostly brown this evening, and a part of her heart melted. "No, no. I am not in any trouble." She sighed again and closed her eyes. *Dear Lord, please give me strength.* "But you might be."

The light touch of his finger on her chin caused Clara to open her eyes, and she allowed him to raise her face toward his. "Miss Preston, please tell me what is amiss." He lowered his arm but placed his hands at her elbows, the warmth of his touch bolstering her enough to continue.

"You recall from my letters how I mentioned my brother and the brutal attack he suffered last year?"

"Yes." The captain nodded. "And as a result, he has been unable to sail since, blaming those men for all he lost."

"His bitterness has gotten worse, I am afraid to say." Clara's throat tightened and moisture formed at the corners of her eyes. No. She couldn't cry. Not now. She must get this out. Taking a deep breath, she continued. "Samuel came to me two weeks ago, ranting about you being involved and how I was not thinking clearly about my relationship with you."

He glanced to the left and right then gently turned her to walk with him toward a bench. "Please. Let us sit."

Clara obeyed and angled her body toward his as soon as he sat down.

"Let me see if I understand correctly." His brow furrowed. "Your brother believes me responsible in some way for his attack? How can that be? I knew nothing about it until you told me."

"That is what I attempted to explain to him, but he refused to listen. Instead, we exchanged a few heated words, and he ended the argument with a remark about seeing who would emerge the victor." Even now, Clara couldn't quite make sense of what her brother had said. She only knew it didn't bode well for the captain. "One thing you should know about my brother—he can latch onto something like a dog to a bone sometimes. And he will not let go until he believes the matter is settled."

The captain tapped his forefinger to his lips and lapsed into silence for several moments.

Clara wrung her hands in her apron, chewing on her bottom lip as she waited. She only needed a word from him, a single sentence that absolved him of any possible connection. Finally he spoke.

"You say he was attacked in June of last year?"

Clara nodded.

"My ship was north of Glassenbury at that time. Yet, he believes I am somehow involved?"

Praise be to the good Lord. The captain hadn't been nearby after all! But that didn't clear his name yet. "Yes, and Samuel is determined to prove it." The moisture in her eyes pooled, and a lone tear slipped down her cheek. She didn't want to see the captain hurt by her brother's blindness to the truth.

Captain Ingersoll reached out and captured the tear with his thumb then smoothed her cheek, pushing a few tendrils of hair behind her ear. The tenderness nearly caused more tears to fall, but she held them in check.

"If your brother is seeking revenge on his attackers, he is likely to lash out at anyone in the shipping industry, but especially other merchant traders, if he believes the attack was of a premeditated nature to destroy his business."

"So, what is there to do?" How she wished she could steer her brother away from the captain, redirect his ire at someone or something else. But that didn't seem possible.

The captain placed his hands over hers, where they rested in her lap, and leaned toward her, maintaining a respectful distance. Everything in his expression spoke of confidence. She had done the right thing, confiding in him, even at the risk of alienating her irrational brother.

"Allow me to make a few inquiries along my route, and we shall see what I can discover." He squeezed her hands. "Oftentimes a level head can discover the truth more easily than one who goes forth in rage."

"Thank you, Captain." Clara mustered up as much of a grin as possible and sniffed. "Telling you this has not been easy for me."

He smiled, a soft light entering his eyes and making the blue flecks more prominent. "I realize that, but I am glad you have trusted me enough to share it." He again touched her cheek, and she leaned against the pressure. "I promise, together we shall find the truth."

The truth. Would her brother accept it if it were found?

Chapter 6

Ah, Captain Ingersoll." Samuel approached from around the side of the inn.

Clara and the captain jumped to their feet.

"We meet again."

The tone of her brother's voice might come across as cordial, but Clara knew better. The captain took an almost imperceptible step closer to her and placed his hand at the small of her back. His touch soothed her.

She closed her eyes, praying her brother would conduct himself in a respectful manner. He had made it clear the other day, though, that he intended to ferret out the truth regarding the captain's potential involvement in the attack last year. And Samuel's dogged determination usually got him into more trouble than not. If he went too far, she might adapt that same resolve where the captain was concerned.

"Good evening, Mr. Preston," the captain greeted, his own cordiality sounding forced. "Are you out for a stroll as well?"

Samuel groaned. "Do not attempt to hide behind false pleasantries, sir. I know you have spent sufficient time in my sister's company this evening, and she has undoubtedly warned you about me." He raised his cane and aimed it in the captain's direction. "So let us dispense with the formalities, shall we?"

Captain Ingersoll nodded.

"Our father has already spoken of your intentions toward my sister, but I wonder if you have told her the truth about the work you do."

"Samuel—"

"No." Her brother shifted his eyes to look at her. "Clara, you deserve to know. And if this man possesses half the integrity you claim he has," he said, glaring at the captain, "he should have no trouble answering."

The captain pressed the lapel of his buttoned coat against his collarbone before meeting Samuel's gaze. "I will be more than happy to oblige, although I believe your sister is quite intelligent and aware of what I do. What exactly do you feel she should know that she might not?"

"To start, have you informed her of just how many days and nights you spend traveling the river at one time? Or that you might be gone for many days should you need to venture out into the bay and journey to some of the larger ports around New England to acquire supplies?"

"Mr. Preston," Captain Ingersoll said, speaking in measured tones, "given the time lapse between the visits your sister and I have been able to enjoy, I am certain the length of my absences is obvious. She is well aware of what she will be facing."

"And that does not bother me in the least, Samuel," Clara spoke up. "I am certain there will be more than enough work to be done to keep me occupied while Captain Ingersoll is away."

They were speaking in such future terms, as if it were a foregone conclusion that their relationship was going to take on a more permanent nature. He still had yet to officially declare his suit. Was the captain aware of how their words sounded, or was he only seeking to satisfy Samuel's interrogation?

"What about your activities when you lay anchor for the night? When you seek repast at a local tavern or seek to quench your thirst?"

Samuel was baiting the captain. Clara could see it. Why was he so bound and determined to find something that might paint the man in an unfavorable light? Had the attack so turned him against the merchant trade business, he wanted to make certain no one he cared for got involved in it?

"Mr. Preston, I will not lie to you." The captain glanced down at Clara. "Or to you, Miss Preston." He looked back at Samuel. "There are several members of my crew who make it a habit to visit every tavern that exists in the ports where the *Handelaar* stops. And I have, on occasion, needed to escort them back to the ship personally, sometimes carrying them when they have imbibed beyond their limitations." He flattened his palm against his chest. "But I myself have never once been too deep in my cups that I was unaware of my surroundings or required assistance to walk."

Samuel snapped his fingers. "So, you *admit* to drinking on occasion."

"I do not know of a single man who does not." Captain Ingersoll shrugged.

He had a point. Even Papa kept a small supply of sherry and brandy available for guests when they requested it.

"And which taverns exactly, have you frequented?" Samuel pressed.

"Mr. Preston. . ." The captain sighed. "If you are attempting to manipulate the facts to appease your desire to somehow connect me to the scene of your attack, you will not be successful."

"So, you refuse to name the taverns then. That must mean you are withholding something for fear of being discovered."

"Or it could mean I will not engage in theatrics with you when you are so bent on sullying my character."

"There would not be any way to sully it if you were truly innocent." Samuel raised his cane again and nearly jabbed it at the captain. "You have all but admitted repeated visits to taverns, yet you refuse to name the ones where you have spent some of your nights."

Clara wanted to speak up on the captain's behalf, but it was not her place. Not yet, anyway. Captain Ingersoll was handling himself rather well, all things considered. She was quite impressed. But just how long would her brother continue with this ridiculous tirade?

"Believe what you will, Mr. Preston," Captain Ingersoll replied. "I stand by my word."

"I intend to make certain our father knows the truth." Samuel pressed his lips into a thin line and inhaled rather loudly through his nose. "Perhaps then he will rethink his compliance with your intended suit of my sister."

Clara gasped. No! Surely her brother wouldn't go that far. The captain's hand at her back formed a fist. She opened her mouth to protest but stopped and looked up at him.

"Mr. Preston, you should be aware that I will not stand idly by while you bear false witness against me. For every lie you tell, I shall be right there proclaiming the truth."

Samuel narrowed his eyes. "So you intend to challenge me, then? You, Captain, are not worthy of my sister's affections."

Captain Ingersoll stiffened, his eyes darkening and his jaw tightening. "And you, sir, are a cad!"

Samuel took a step back at the captain's harsh words. Clara also stared. She could hardly believe Captain Ingersoll had gotten so upset. When her brother hurled his worst accusations at him and attacked his integrity, he remained placid. But threatening to cause division between him and Clara had obviously been the tipping point.

"Now do you see what I mean?" Samuel jerked a thumb toward the captain and glared at Clara. "He not only undoubtedly knows several of the other merchant traders whose ships were near mine the night of the attack, he also admits to sharing company with drunken seamen and has gone so far as to insult me in your presence."

Clara shrugged. "And how is that any different than what you have been doing to him these past few minutes? You have been attacking his very character and paying no heed to me."

"So you are going to take his side over your own brother's?" Samuel's fist curled around the top knob of his cane. "And I thought you had more sense than that. Clearly, I was mistaken."

"The only sense I have right now is to realize you are merely speaking out of your anger and making empty threats."

"A lot of good my threats will do. I have already—"

Jonathan cleared his throat. Clara and Samuel turned their attention to him.

"I believe it is best if I take my leave now and return to

my ship. It is clear my presence is a source of hostility, and I do not wish for family members to engage in an argument because of me." He reached for Clara's hand and raised it to his lips, pressing a soft kiss on her knuckles. "Miss Preston, I do apologize for any problem I have caused you this eve. Please forgive me and remember what I said." He spoke softly, his eyes communicating what his mouth could not, at least not in front of her brother.

Clara wanted to stop him, but she knew it would only cause further trouble. "I will," was all she said as she watched him walk off into the darkening dusk. This evening had certainly not gone the way she had imagined it would. Once she could no longer see the captain, she turned on her brother.

"How could you do that?"

Samuel feigned innocence. "I have not the faintest idea what you mean."

"Do not play those games, Samuel." Clara clenched her fists. "You know exactly what I mean." She waved her hand toward where the captain had disappeared. "How could you treat the captain in such a disrespectful manner? He has done nothing to you other than be employed in the business of merchant trading. And despite your personal vendetta, that is no reason to transfer all of your hatred onto an innocent man."

Her brother pressed his cane against the ground and moved it in a circular motion. "You saw it and heard it yourself, Clara. Captain Ingersoll refused to be honest."

"No, he refused to be baited. And I admire him for that. Any other man might have engaged you in a round of fisticuffs for your tainted accusations." Clara wanted to continue her lecture, but it would not reach a conclusion anytime soon. She sighed and shook her head. He might be acting unreasonable, but Samuel was still her brother. And she did not wish to say something she might regret or risk causing irreparable harm to their relationship.

"And just who would you like to see be the victor in such a duel?"

"Samuel," Clara groaned. "I do not even know who you are anymore. You have become so controlled by your vengeance, I can no longer see the real man underneath." She turned and glanced back over her shoulder. As much as it pained her, she had to say this. "Until you can make peace with all of this, I do not wish to speak with you again." And with that, she walked away.

"Mark my words, Clara," her brother called to her back. "I intend to impede your captain's trade business in every way possible until he either proves his innocence or confesses to being involved. The truth is going to be revealed, one way or another. You will see."

Yes, the truth would be revealed. And when it was, Samuel would be the one who would be forced to apologize. At least she prayed that to be so.

❧

Jonathan spoke to other merchants, ship captains, and seamen as he traveled his route. For the most part, what he learned didn't help him piece together the mystery of Samuel's attackers any more than the details with which Clara had provided him. The passage of time since the incident didn't help matters either. If only he had met Clara last summer, he might have been able to help more.

It had been weeks. Every time he found someone with

information, he would ask one question too many, and the party would all but clam up. He knew most of those who avoided him were being intentionally evasive or silent. And that usually meant fear of someone else. To complicate matters further, with every delivery he made or every conversation he had, Jonathan found himself defending his integrity and countering a passel of lies that had been spreading throughout the river region. He knew exactly who was to blame, but that issue would be resolved when he found the answers to his questions.

And perhaps those answers would come tonight.

Jonathan pushed open the heavy door of the dark tavern and cringed at the loud creak it made as it swung in on its hinges. He ducked and winced then peered into the dimly lit interior. No one even looked up at his entrance. He stepped farther into the room and scanned the tables. A tip from the barkeep at the tavern across the river had led him here. All he had to do was find the informant. The barkeep said he'd described Jonathan to the man, but how good was his description? Jonathan moved to the side and out of the way, praying this man would come find *him*.

"Pardon me." A gravelly voice spoke not two minutes after Jonathan found an inconspicuous place to stand and watch the room.

Jonathan turned toward the sound. A rather burly man stepped out from the shadows near the wall and gestured at the small, square table nearest them. He looked like any other seaman, from the unkempt beard and bandanna tied around his head to the motley mismatch of apparel ending in a pair of buckled boots. Only his doublet decorated with braids indicated he might have attained a position of rank. Jonathan took a seat across from the man.

"Did I hear you might be looking for some information?" he said, barely speaking above the din of other voices.

"As a matter of fact, I am." Jonathan wanted to lean forward to hear the man better but hesitated. Best to be cautious until he could gauge if this man could be trusted. He touched the scar on his left jaw. An overzealous mistake had given him that scar. He didn't intend to repeat the incident. "What have you heard?"

"I remember this man, this Samuel Preston you have been asking after." The seaman scratched his beard. "This would be what? Around mid-June last year?"

"Yes. That is exactly when the incident in question occurred."

The seaman looked to the left and right then leaned in close. "You did not hear this from me, but there is a small band of river pirates who sail on the ship *Dominion*. They run their operation under the guise of merchant tradesmen, when they are really on the lookout for any loot they can steal, pillage, or plunder. And it does not matter to them how they come upon this merchandise. If someone gets in their way, they dispose of them." The man again cast a look around him. "If what I hear about this Preston fellow is right, he got in their way."

At last! He finally had a lead, something with which he could approach the river authorities in Essex. Jonathan extended his hand, but the man didn't move.

"I hear you are supposed to have some payment for me?"

What else should he have expected? It wasn't as if the

man would readily give away his identity or make any effort to be cordial. The other pirates would string him up for something like this.

Jonathan reached into his satchel and pulled out a small purse of coins. He dropped it into the seaman's beefy hand.

"Now, you never saw me, and you never spoke to me."

"This conversation never occurred." Jonathan nodded. "You have my word."

Chapter 7

Clara straightened and pressed two fists into the small of her back as she arched and tilted her head to gaze up at the cloudless sky. She had already scrubbed seventeen bed sheets and three times as many towels. On the personal clothing items of their guests, she had lost count. Hunching over the washtub once more, she plunged the last of the shirts into the murky but soapy water then slapped it against the washboard.

"Clara!"

Mama's voice called from the kitchen, and Clara looked up to see her mother peer around the doorjamb a moment later.

"Would you come into the parlor as soon as you can make yourself presentable?"

Presentable? Why would she need to take additional pains with her appearance? Unless. . .

"Of course, Mama. I will be in directly."

She twisted and worked out the kinks in her spine. At last, a reprieve. And if Mama made a specific request for her to appear respectable, that could only mean they had a noteworthy guest waiting inside. She always made certain to be clean and satisfactory, but this time was different. Could Captain Ingersoll have returned? Would this be the moment when he made his courtship official? Only one way to find out.

Twenty minutes later, Clara approached the parlor, only to find the doors had been pulled almost closed. Mama stood just inside and peeked through the opening just in time. She pushed the door open far enough for Clara to enter then pulled them completely closed.

"Ah, Clara. How good of you to join us," Papa announced. "Please, come take a seat."

Clara's heart jumped when she locked gazes with Captain Ingersoll. He smiled, looking resplendent in his navy velveteen doublet with gleaming buttons, silk braids, and satin trim on the cuffs. His tricornered hat rested on his lap on tan breeches that disappeared into nearly knee-high polished boots. His hair had been combed and fastened with black cord at the nape of his neck. The captain had certainly taken great pains with *his* appearance. And now, Clara felt rather dowdy in his presence.

That was when she noticed that an equally well-dressed gentleman sat across from the captain in a chair next to Papa. Her brother Samuel stood near the stove, his arm propped on the mantel above it.

"Clara?" Papa spoke again. "If you please?"

The only available seat within respectable distance of those gathered was next to Captain Ingersoll. She quickly took her place, careful not to sit too close. What was all of this about?

Papa looked to Mama, who nodded and took a seat near the door. They obviously did not wish anyone to disturb them.

"Very well." Papa cleared his throat. "Now that we are all

present, let us not forestall the matter at hand any longer."

This sounded far more ominous than what Clara hoped to be the topic of conversation. As the unknown gentleman's dress resembled the captain's in many ways, and as Samuel had been invited as well, the matter Papa referenced must be connected to Samuel's attack.

"Judge," Papa encouraged. "You have the floor."

Clara looked at Captain Ingersoll, but his mouth remained closed.

"Thank you, Mr. Preston," the other gentleman said. "For those present to whom I have not been introduced, my name is Captain James Wells. I serve under Colonel John Austin and reside in the town of Essex as a councilman and judge for the Connecticut Assembly." He extended an open palm toward the captain. "Captain Ingersoll is responsible for my being here today, and the reason involves Mr. Samuel Preston."

At the mention of his name, her brother straightened, his injured arm falling from the mantel to his side.

"Father?" Samuel's brows dipped toward the center. "You were aware of this?"

"Mr. Preston," Judge Wells said, directing his address to Samuel, "no one but Captain Ingersoll is aware of what I am about to say."

Clara glanced sideways at the captain. To most, he might appear completely relaxed, but she noted the subtle differences. The way he tapped his boot on the rug. The way his fingers drummed on the edge of his hat. Even his shoulders stood more erect than usual. And then his neck. His Adam's apple bobbed several times, and his tongue darted out to wet his lips more than once. Whatever this judge had to say, if he did not hurry, Captain Ingersoll might say it first.

"Are you going to appease our curiosity, sir," Samuel asked, "or shall we all remain in suspense?"

Clara wanted to know the same thing, only she dared not voice it.

"Perhaps the first bit would be better if it came from Captain Ingersoll," Wells replied.

"I came to know Judge Wells," the captain said as he stood, "as a result of the inquiries I made regarding the attack summer last on Mr. Samuel Preston."

Samuel groaned low in his throat, but a glare from Papa kept him silent.

"It was not easy," Captain Ingersoll continued, looking at Samuel, "but I eventually managed to find the answers I sought, and that led me to the men who attacked you." The captain swayed forward. "From that point, it did not take long to assemble my men and infiltrate the crew of the *Dominion* while they celebrated rather boisterously in one of the local taverns in Essex. Their inebriated state made confining them quite easy."

"And that is where I became involved," Judge Wells added. "The captain managed to locate me and provide me with the details of his inarguably daring act, but I did not believe it until I stood on the deck of the *Handelaar* and witnessed the scene myself." He grinned across the room at the captain. "Every crew member of that river pirate band sat on board deck, their ankles and wrists bound, and gags in their mouths." He laughed. "I am still puzzled about how you managed such a feat, Captain, but the end result made my job far easier than it could have been."

"So I was attacked by a band of river pirates?" Samuel stepped away from the stove, using his cane as support. "Not merchant tradesmen?"

"That is correct." The judge nodded.

"And their ship, the *Dominion*. It is nothing but a ruse?"

"Again, you are correct." Judge Wells stood and approached Samuel. "I am aware of the many months you have spent seeking out these men who committed such heinous acts against you." He placed a hand on Samuel's shoulder. "But you were looking for the wrong men. At least in the wrong line of work," he added. "And you have Captain Ingersoll to thank for discovering the truth."

Samuel looked between the judge and the captain. His shoulders drooped, and his eyes lost all the fire that had been a constant companion to his pinched face these many months. Next, his gaze went to Papa, who nodded. Clara knew what had to happen next, but would her brother follow through with it? She prayed he would.

"Captain," her brother began with a sigh. "It appears an apology is in order, and it must come from me. I also owe you a great deal of thanks."

"I appreciate it, Mr. Preston." Captain Ingersoll dropped his hat to the settee. He extended a hand, which Samuel took, shifting his weight to his good leg. "And I accept your apology. I know how difficult this is, so I will not cause you to suffer any further." He raised one eyebrow and angled his head toward Samuel, a slight grin forming on his lips. "I will, however, ask that you set to right the rumors you have you been spreading regarding my business practices and ethical behavior." He gave Samuel's hand a single shake. "Otherwise, I might be forced to command my crew to mete out the same punishment they delivered to those pirates who attacked you."

Clara bit her lip to keep from laughing at the thought of her brother trussed up, bound, and gagged. It might do him good to sit that way for a spell, but it wasn't likely to happen. Mama, Papa, and the judge weren't as successful at containing their mirth. And although she couldn't see the captain's face from this angle, her brother must have read something in the captain's expression that told him the captain *would* follow through.

"I believe time spent at the pillory or a few dips on the ducking stool would also suffice," the captain added with a smile.

"You have my word," Samuel rushed to reply.

"Very good." Captain Ingersoll withdrew his hand and clapped Samuel on the back. "Now, there remains one more person to whom you owe an apology." He stepped back and both gazes landed on her.

Clara inhaled quickly. An apology? To her? But she hadn't been wronged. Not directly, anyway. A spark flashed in her brother's eyes but dimmed when he reached for his cane and took several steps toward her. She stood.

"Clara," he began. "I know my behavior of late has been reprehensible. And I said a number of things in anger that I now regret." He dipped his head. "I confess my wrongdoing, especially where the captain is concerned. It was not fair to you, placing you in the middle." He raised his eyes and looked at her, penitence reflecting in the eyes that matched hers. "Will you forgive me?"

Although a nagging part of her screamed to deny him his request, a still, small voice told her she should. He was her brother, after all, and despite his actions, he remained a good man. She had no doubt his guilt would be punishment enough. It was not up to her to levy judgment on him. The good Lord could handle that far better than she.

With gladness in her heart, she met his gaze. "I do forgive you, Samuel, and I pray the next time you are tempted to act in haste, you will learn from your mistakes, not repeat them."

He nodded but didn't reply. On impulse Clara embraced him and kissed his cheek.

"It takes a great man to admit his mistakes." She placed a palm against his chest. "I am happy to have my brother back."

Papa stepped forward then, his hands in front of him, pressed together at their fingertips. "I believe we have settled what we all gathered here to accomplish." He turned to Captain Wells. "Judge, I appreciate you making the journey to be here today. If you will find a seat in the main room, our staff will see you receive a hearty meal before you must return home."

The judge patted his stomach. "Now, that offer I will not refuse," he said with a grin, nodding at Mama, who pushed open the doors and allowed him to pass.

"Samuel. Adelaide, my dear," Papa continued, moving to stand next to Mama. "Captain Ingersoll and Clara have a few things to discuss. Let us adjourn and grant them some privacy."

Her brother turned to face the captain. "You do right by her."

The captain nodded. "I will make it my priority."

And with that, her brother and parents took their leave. Clara turned her head from the doorway to where Captain Ingersoll still stood and sat again on the settee. A moment later, he regained his seat, tossing his hat on a low table. With a twinkle in his eye and a crooked grin, he reached for her hands.

"Before I say what is uppermost in my mind, might I have your permission to address you by your given name?"

"Of course." It seemed like such a natural request. Clara was surprised he hadn't made it sooner.

"Very well. Clara," he said and paused, as if testing the sound of her name on his lips. "And I would like it very much if you called me Jonathan."

She could only nod, the tightness in her throat making it impossible to speak.

"I made you a promise when last we spoke. . .and I have now kept it," the captain said. "I know it might take some time before your brother fully trusts me, but at least he can lay his anger to rest and return to a life of normalcy." He brushed his thumbs across her knuckles, and she had to quell the shiver that threatened to travel up her back. "Now, that leaves the matter of us and a certain courtship I promised."

Again, Clara could not force any sound past the lump in her throat. She licked her lips and swallowed several times.

"I see I already have rendered you speechless." Jonathan grinned. "That makes what I am about to say much easier." He raised her hands to his lips and placed a lingering kiss on the back of each. "Clara, would you accept my suit and travel back with me to Glassenbury to meet my family? I have taken the liberty of asking one of your servant girls to accompany you as your maid. At last I heard, my older brother and his wife were about to have a baby. I would like for you to meet that newest addition."

Clara bit her lip then took in a few labored breaths. He had finally said it. Had finally done it. She was certain he had already approached Papa. Otherwise Papa would never have left them alone. Nor would he have been certain the captain had something to discuss with her. Now all that remained was her answer.

"Yes, Jonathan. Without a doubt, yes." She squeezed his fingers. "I would be honored to accept your suit."

"Splendid." Jonathan again kissed her hands, only this time they were quick pecks. "Now, after we tell your family you have agreed, I do believe we have a tour of a certain ship to take, and then we shall be on our way. Your mother has already begun to pack your trunk."

He had thought of everything. She could hardly wait to get started.

Chapter 8

Pain-filled screams reached Clara's ears the minute she placed her hand on the front door latch of the inn.

The baby!

She burst through the front door of the Red Griffin Inn without even waiting for Jonathan to accompany her. After scanning what she could see of the main floor, her eyes immediately landed on the staircase leading to the second level. But the screams came from a room to her right. So the baby had not yet arrived. With only a second's hesitation, Clara raced toward the sound.

As soon as she entered the room, the familiar scene met her eyes. A woman Clara could only assume was Jonathan's mother kneeled beside a woman who had to be Constance, a wet cloth pressed to her forehead. The matriarch wore a ruffled cap over dark hair streaked with silver. But the penetrating power of the blue-gray eyes she turned on Clara was mesmerizing.

"You are Miss Preston, I presume?" It was more a statement than a question, but Clara nodded.

"How can I be of service?"

"The pains came on rather sudden and they have lasted for a bit more than an hour now," the mother said. "I have already sent for the midwife."

173

Constance had a death grip on the sides of the bed frame where she lay. From the look and sound of things, the woman might not last until the midwife arrived. Clara felt compelled to do something. She'd seen many babies born at the inn. She'd even assisted in the birth of her younger brother. Of course, that was nearly ten years ago. Nevertheless, some things a person never forgets.

"Have you ever been present for a birth?"

"Yes, I have." Clara boldly took a step closer. "Several, in fact."

"As have I." Mrs. Ingersoll nodded. "And with that said, I am certain you realize the midwife might not arrive in time."

"What can I do to help?"

"I have already set water to boil and instructed one of my servant girls to bring a basin of cold water as well." Mrs. Ingersoll removed the cloth from Constance's forehead, dipped it in the cool water, wrung it out, and replaced it. "If you would not mind fetching the boiling water and bringing some fresh towels as well, I will begin preparations."

"Very well," Clara replied, turning to go in search of the kitchen.

"Take the second hallway on your left, just before the stairs," Mrs. Ingersoll called.

While she found a basin for the water, Clara also had two servant girls prepare some nourishment for Constance. As soon as the baby arrived, the woman would need something to help her regain her strength. Clara located the extra cloths and tucked them into the waist of her apron; then she grabbed hold of the basin and made her way back to the room, careful to avoid sloshing the scalding water.

Mrs. Ingersoll had rolled up her sleeves and surrounded Constance with an abundance of towels.

"Miss Preston, we must work in great cooperation with each other. Are you certain you are ready?"

"Yes, Mrs. Ingersoll. I shall do whatever you need."

"Everything is proceeding just fine, Constance." Mrs. Ingersoll placed a hand on her daughter-in-law's forehead and smiled. Constance returned a weak smile, her eyes half-closed and perspiration dotting her upper lip.

Clara closed her eyes. *Lord, we could use Your divine assistance this day.* And that was the last thought she remembered.

In no time at all, the squalling baby entered the world, and as far as Clara could tell, without complications. She raised her eyes to the ceiling and smiled.

"Heavenly Father, thank You."

"Amen to that!" came Mrs. Ingersoll's reply. She held the baby over a makeshift table by the wall, using the hot water to wash the newborn. A minute later, she swaddled the child and made her way back to Constance. "We never would have accomplished this without His help," she said, kneeling on the floor beside the makeshift cot which held the new mother.

Clara peered over the woman's shoulder. The infant squirmed and fidgeted within its confines. Only whimpers escaped the tiny lips as Mrs. Ingersoll settled the baby into Constance's waiting arms with a smile.

"Constance, you have yourself a healthy baby boy."

The wonder and the joy of life. A miracle. Constance was so peaceful, and the little boy knew his mother held him. What had begun as so much pain ended in wonder and delight. The circle was complete.

"If you do not mind, Miss Preston, I do believe an anxious father is waiting outside." Mrs. Ingersoll chuckled. "You might wish to let him know he is welcome to come in and meet his son."

Soon the entire family crowded into the little room. Clara had no trouble identifying Jonathan's three brothers. They all shared the same blue-gray eyes of their mother, and two of them also shared the dark hair. Jonathan and the one Clara assumed to be the youngest son had lighter brown, and only Jonathan had hazel eyes. He must have gotten them from his father.

"Although Miss Preston and I have already gotten to know each other"—Mrs. Ingersoll spoke up, causing the quiet conversations to cease—"perhaps now is a good time to exchange introductions?" She gave Jonathan a pointed glance, and he immediately responded.

"Ah yes." He moved to stand behind Clara and placed his hands on her shoulders. "Mother, I would like to introduce you to Miss Clara Marie Preston." Jonathan shifted to catch Clara's eye. "Clara, my mother, Mrs. Ingersoll."

He then went on to introduce each brother in turn. From the eldest, Nathaniel, to the third in line, Micah, and down to the youngest, Alden, each one of Mrs. Ingersoll's sons stood tall and strong. Clara could easily see the family resemblance, in more ways than one.

"Nathaniel," Jonathan explained, "works as a master carver at Cushing & Ingersoll Ship Carving down by the river." He pointed at the third brother. "Micah is an apprentice for the town baker, but he never lets us forget the dislike he has for the man. So, he spends as much time here as possible, providing our guests—and us—with delicious baked goods. And that leaves Alden. He will be entering Yale College in the fall, studying to become a doctor of medicine."

Clara looked at each brother in turn and then at Mrs. Ingersoll, whose eyes shone as she beheld her sons. Each one had established a reputable trade or pursued it at present. Any mother would be proud of that.

Replacing his hands on her shoulders, Jonathan then addressed his family. "Clara works at her father's inn in Higganum." He gave her shoulders a squeeze. "She does not know this yet, but I hope to bring her here to work with you, Mother, running the inn."

Here? At the Red Griffin? Running it? That would be a dream come true. She had always thought she would take over for Mama, but this prospect held far more appeal. Clara twisted her neck and gazed up at Jonathan from the corner of her eye, smiling. He winked down at her.

"There is just one problem." He looked again at his older brother. "You have owned the inn since you achieved your twenty-first year. And now, with your family, I could not possibly ask you to give up that right."

"I believe I can answer that," Nathaniel spoke up from the edge of the bed where he sat cradling his wife and newborn son. He reached behind his lapel and withdrew an envelope, extending it toward Jonathan. "You are aware Uncle Phineas passed on about a month ago."

"Yes." Jonathan withdrew two pieces of paper from the envelope and held them in front of Clara for both of them to read. She did not follow a lot of what was written, but from what she could decipher, his uncle had solved the dilemma already.

"As you will see from that signed document, Uncle Phineas left the house and shop to me, with the provision that you have ownership of the inn if you live here with your future wife and allow Mother to live here still. Alden, too, as long as necessary." Nathaniel nestled his chin against his wife's hair. "Constance and I will be moving into Uncle Phineas's house at the earliest convenience."

"So, it appears to be all arranged." Jonathan stepped from behind Clara. "Except for one thing."

The knowing grins on the faces of Jonathan's brothers and mother alerted her to what Jonathan was about to do. Still, she thrilled at the prospect and allowed him time to kneel in front of her.

"I suppose the answer is quite obvious, but for the sake of propriety, I must ask." Jonathan flicked his gaze up to meet hers and took her hands in his. "I realize I have only recently asked your permission to court you, but Miss Clara Marie Preston, will you do me the honor of becoming my wife?"

"Yes! Yes! A thousand times, yes!" As soon as he stood, she jumped into his arms. She could hardly believe it. Just this morning she'd conducted life as usual. Now, she would soon become Jonathan's wife and manager of a beautiful inn. The good Lord truly looked down upon them with favor.

"I have prayed for years," Mrs. Ingersoll said from the other side of the bed, "that each of my sons would grow to find and marry women of good character and possessing a strong faith." Tears glistened in her eyes as she looked first at Constance and then at Clara. "Two have done so. There remains but two more."

"And that may be a little while longer yet, Mother." Laughter rumbled in Jonathan's chest as he hugged Clara to him. He pulled back just enough for her to see the sparkle in his eyes. "At least I have performed my duty." His expression softened as he studied her lips. Clara smiled, inviting his touch. Locking her arms more tightly around his neck, she sealed their vow with the unconditional acceptance of their two lives soon to be joined as one.

"Very good," Mrs. Ingersoll spoke up once her son had stepped back. "Who would like a piece of my onion pie?"

Clara smiled at Jonathan, remembering when he asked about that the day he arrived at her inn.

"I would," they both said in unison.

Onion Pie

From *Art of Cookery Made Plain and Easy*
by Hannah Glasse, 1747

1 pound of potatoes
1 pound of onions
1 pound of apples

2 pie crusts
½ pound butter
1 oz. of mace
1 nutmeg, grated
1 teaspoon pepper
3 teaspoons salt
12 eggs
6 spoonfuls of water

Wash and pare some potatoes and cut them in slices. Peel some onions, cut them in slices. Pare some apples and slice them. Make a good crust and cover your dish. Lay a quarter of a pound of butter all over. Take a quarter of an ounce of mace, beat fine, a nutmeg grated, a teaspoonful of beaten pepper, three teaspoonfuls of salt, mix all together. Strew some over the butter, lay a layer of potatoes, a layer of onion, a layer of apple, and a layer of eggs, and so on, till you have filled your pye, strewing a little of the seasoning between each layer, and a quarter of a pound of butter in bits, and six spoonfuls of water. Close your pye and bake it an hour and a half.

Tiffany Amber Stockton has been crafting and embellishing stories since childhood. Today she is an award-winning author, speaker, and a freelance website designer who lives with her husband and fellow author, Stuart Vaughn Stockton, in Colorado. They have a daughter and a son and a vivacious Australian Shepard named Roxie. Her writing career began as a columnist for her high school and college newspapers. She is a member of American Christian Fiction Writers and Historical Romance Writers. Three of her novels have won annual readers' choice awards, and in 2009, she was voted #1 favorite new author for the Heartsong Presents book club.

OVER A BARREL

by Laurie Alice Eakes

Dedication

To my sister for letting me use her dining room table.

"Trust ye in the Lord for ever:
for in the Lord Jehovah is everlasting strength."
Isaiah 26:4

Chapter 1

Glassenbury, Connecticut Colony
October 1758

The barrel was too light. Under no circumstances could the keg Micajah Ingersoll dragged from its corner of his storage room contain a hundred and ninety-six pounds of flour. Less than half of that at an immediate guess.

Bending his six-foot frame, since stooping had become impossible thanks to a French musket ball wound in his right leg, Micah examined the lid of the barrel. No seal. The wax poured around the edges had been neatly cut.

"Who would sneak in here and take flour?" He spoke to a room empty of everything save the ingredients for breads and the occasional pie—flour and sugar, the sourness of the yeast starter and sweetness of apples, the tartness of dried fruits and the exotic perfume of spices in their locked chest.

The spice chest was the only lock in the bakehouse Micah used. He kept the shop open so townspeople could use the ovens, in the event he was occupied elsewhere and they needed to bake. Glassenbury residents had always proven to be an honest lot, leaving money on the counter for the consumption of firewood or any other supplies they used, with the exception of the spices too expensive and too difficult to obtain to share as he did a pound or so of flour. He had been known to share as much as five pounds in an emergency. Micah had his small inheritance from his Uncle Phineas. He didn't care about giving away a few shillings' worth of flour.

"But half a barrel and more's worth?"

With a sigh at the idea that he might have to start locking up the bakehouse while he slept the few hours of the night his leg and the Glassenbury baking needs allowed him, he tipped the barrel onto its side and started to roll it into the more brightly lit bakehouse to better examine the pilfered barrel.

A squeak emanated from inside the wooden staves.

Micah froze. Surely he was mistaken. Mice could be enterprising when they wanted food. Because of the quantity of flour and grains he kept on hand, he fed a veritable army of cats just enough to keep them near his business, but not enough they wouldn't hunt the local rodent population away from his supplies. In the past six months, he hadn't seen so much as one mouse dropping in the storage room or bakehouse, and in his entire life he had yet to meet the mouse who could apply a knife to a wax seal. Chew through it, most certainly. Slit it with the neatness of a tailor cutting out a shirt pattern, never.

There it was again, a squeak; a rustle now, too.

And a whimper?

"Egad." Micah dropped onto the lid of another barrel and plowed his fingers through his cocoa-brown hair. It tumbled loose from the black grosgrain ribbon holding it away from his face, and he lowered his hands to his leg, rubbing the right calf so obviously smaller than the left. Too obviously smaller than the left below his knee breeches. Despite the leg's shrunken muscles, the pain was absent most of the time now. Surely he had enjoyed enough sleep to not be losing his reason as happened to some other soldiers wounded in the war on the frontier.

No, more likely one of his brothers was playing some sort of trick on him, exchanging a barrel full of flour for a barrel full of rodents. A few dozen mice squeaking at once might come through the wooden sides like a whimper in the stillness of the predawn hours.

Not wanting to release the vermin inside the bakehouse, Micah struggled to his feet and gave the keg a push toward the outside door. He would roll the thing right down to the Connecticut River and then pretend to his brothers that he had experienced nothing odd during that night's baking.

A thump and a cry rose from within the barrel.

A bang of his heart sinking into his guts, and a groan of dismay rose from within Micah. No mice squirmed and scrabbled inside that barrel. It was something much larger—larger than a mouse anyway. Larger than a mouse and much smaller than his tall, broad form.

Feeling more lightheaded than ever, the surgeon's laudanum had made him, Micah tipped the barrel onto its end again. Another thump and cry slammed against his ears.

"Lord, please do not let me find what I think I am about to find." He shot up a prayer, perhaps the first one in months, and slid the blade of his ever-present knife between the edge of the barrel and the lid. The latter popped up on one side. Micah grasped it and tossed it aside. It clattered onto the floorboards with a resounding roll. His heart felt as though it clattered to somewhere near his boot soles as he saw exactly what he had prayed not to see.

Two large dark eyes gazed up at him. A wide pink mouth spread even wider and let out a shriek loud and piercing enough to frighten a bobcat.

Micah flinched. "How did you get in there?"

He gripped the edge of the barrel to stop himself from covering his ears before the cries deafened him. Better not to concern himself with the hows right now and stop the yowling before it deafened the entire town.

"I am not going to hurt you." He doubted the creature heard him over her own keening. He couldn't hear himself. "Will you let me pick you up?"

No response but more howls, perhaps even louder.

Hard-working Glassenburians were not going to appreciate this kind of a ruckus in the middle of the night. If these cries grew any louder, the British navy would be sailing up the river thinking the French and their Indian allies had managed to invade this far east.

No help for it. If he had any hope of quieting things, he must act.

He reached inside the barrel, fully expecting to be bitten, and lifted the little girl into his arms.

Yes, certainly a girl, complete with flowing dark hair, somewhat the worse for wear with its matting of flour, and ruffled petticoats and gown. Little was not such an accurate description. She was small enough to fit into the nearly two feet across and higher barrel, but she was sturdily round and beyond the toddling-about stage.

But not beyond the sobbing-in-gasping-bursts-too-staccato-to-be-comprehensible-words stage. Five or six years, surely.

He tried to comfort her against his shoulder. "Where did you come from, little one?"

Hiccup. Hiccup. Hiccup.

He patted her back. "Where is your mother?"

Not that a woman who would abandon her child in a barrel deserved to be any child's mother.

The girl pushed against him, showing him a red and tear-streaked face. "I—" Hiccup. "Want—" Hiccup. Hiccup. Gasp.

He needed his brothers Nathaniel and Jonathan or their wives. They had children. They would know what to do. But walking through the streets of Glassenbury with a sobbing child in the middle of the night would do nothing good for his reputation. Likewise, neither would taking her to his mother at the Red Griffin Inn.

He could not, however, let her continue to cry like this. Surely it wasn't good for her. He knew little of children. A bachelor, he had only a passing acquaintance with children save for his nieces and nephews and the one or two who came into the bakeshop to buy the family bread.

And then he had encountered a few on the frontier while fighting for the English army. The less he thought about them the better. They had never sobbed like this. They were quiet in their fear and grief. Far too quiet for children.

Nothing about this young miss was quiet. If anything, her howls grew louder with each passing moment Micah dithered about what to do with her. If the ruckus continued, he wouldn't have to think what to do with her—the entire town's worth of ladies would descend on him to discover what he was doing.

Or perhaps they would simply think his collection of cats

had decided to yowl at the new moon.

He would rather have an encounter with ten cats than continue to hold on to this child. She pounded on his chest with tiny and ineffectual fists and continued her incomprehensible tirade. "I want" were the only words that emerged comprehensibly.

"Yes, well, I want a few things, too," Micah muttered. "Like to know how you got into my barrel and where the flour went. Like what to do with you."

Above all, he would like to know how to stop her crying.

He began to walk. He recalled Constance walking one of her babies when it wept inconsolably. From storeroom to bakehouse, he limped around and around, from door, to ovens set into the hearth, and back to the door. Still she sobbed. Still she struggled against his hold. Still her wants proved unintelligible. He could guess—she wanted her mother. So did he, or whoever was supposed to be in charge of her—the irresponsible, unfeeling, unnatural creature that she must be.

Beyond the window of the shop, the night remained black enough for the grayish glass to reflect his progress, his unbalanced gait, the protesting child, the light from the lamps flickering with the breeze of his passing, or perhaps the exhalation from the child's wails.

He paused at the window, allowing his body to block the light inside so he could peer out. Surely something along the street would give him insight as to where to take the child.

The only hope for him was to take the girl to Mother. She would know what to do. As an innkeeper since their father's death, Mother knew how to manage people of all ages. One small girl would be no trouble for her.

He turned from the window—and caught a flash of movement from the corner of his eye. He swung back, nearly overbalancing. Nothing moved in the darkness now. Down the street, a lantern in front of the inn glowed, welcoming the weary any time of day or night. Outside his bakehouse, the street lay silent and still. Yet he had seen something, a flash of white like a face on the other side of the glass.

He headed for the door, an idea, a hope, warming inside him. Not until he rested his hand on the latch did he realize that the child had stopped wailing.

"Did you see it, too?" he asked her. "Is it your—"

No, he dare not ask her again about her mother. He didn't dare risk setting her off again. Besides, she hadn't been facing the window. She wasn't facing the window now. She stared at something behind him.

He turned and noted a tray of sweet biscuits resting on the counter. How foolish of him not to think of a sweet to quiet the girl.

"Do you want one?" he asked.

She nodded "Please."

One perfectly clear word from her. Clear and perfectly polite.

He closed the distance to the tray and handed a cinnamon-dusted biscuit to her. She crammed as much of it as possible into her mouth, chewed, swallowed, took another enormous bite.

The poor thing was starving.

A flood of tenderness washed over him as it did each time he found a starving or wounded creature. Abandoned, hungry, no doubt frightened to death of him, a person more than five times her size, and all he had thought of was his annoyance over the noise she was making.

"Let me take you someplace with food," he suggested.

Mother would have ham, bacon, eggs, and bread left over from the previous day. There would be nothing fresh today if he didn't get rid of the child and get to work.

The first biscuit had vanished. He gave her another one and headed for the door. If he could keep her quiet for the hundred-yard walk to the inn, all would be fine.

She began to sob the instant he opened the door to a rush of crisp, autumn air. "No. No. No."

Micah groaned. "Hush."

The girl cried louder as he turned from the bakehouse. The biscuits seemed to have given her renewed strength. Her wails sounded louder. Already a light bloomed in the ironmonger's shop across the way.

"Want. My. Momma." This time her words rang out as clear as bells warning of disaster. "Momma. Momma. Momma."

For a flash, Micah considered returning her to the barrel while he fetched his own mother. Then he simply felt like yowling for her to come to him, too.

Someone *was* coming to him. Footfalls clattered on the stone walkway. The light, quick footfalls of a female. One of the townswomen wondering what wild animal he had rescued this time, ready to lecture him on the dangers—

A hand grabbed his arm—hard. "Where are you taking my daughter?" asked a voice like a honey-coated razor.

Chapter 2

M y child." Sarah Chapman grasped the big man's arm with both hands. "Where are you taking my child?"

"Momma." Eliza ceased wailing and lunged toward Sarah.

She caught her child, staggered under her weight.

"Not so quickly, madam." The man stepped back, pulling Eliza out of Sarah's hold.

"But she is my daughter." Sarah tried to wrap her arms around Eliza again.

The act brought her into an uncomfortable proximity with the man, and she stepped back, trying to pull Eliza with her. Eliza began to wail again.

"You can see she is my daughter," Sarah cried above her baby's sobs. "Please." Her throat closed. Tears sprang into her eyes, and she blinked hard to hold them back. "Please let me have my little girl."

"You were not so concerned when you abandoned her in my storeroom." The man took another step back, forcing Sarah to follow or let go of Eliza. "And I do not see in the least how she is your child."

"She called me momma." Sarah lost her battle with tears. They poured down her cheeks, likely streaking the dirt and flour smudged over her face.

Raven-haired, brown-eyed Eliza favored her deceased father in looks, if not in temperament, a complete contrast to blond-haired, green-eyed Sarah. Sarah had more than once been mistaken for the girl's nursemaid rather than mother.

"You left her in my storeroom." The man enunciated each word as though Sarah were a mooncalf and couldn't understand him otherwise. "No mother would do such a thing."

Sarah dashed the corner of her shawl across her eyes. "She would if she were afraid of having her harmed."

"Indeed." A world of doubt and disdain rang from that single word, quiet yet audible past Eliza's sobs.

Words of explanation, of defense of her actions crowded into Sarah's mouth. Her lips refused to cooperate. They parted but nothing emerged. She could scarcely breathe, let alone talk. Her limbs shook, and her head felt stuffed with uncarded wool. Worse, they were no longer alone in the formerly quiet street. The flicker of torches grew brighter, drawing nearer.

"What is amiss here, Micah?" someone cried out.

Eliza began to weep again, not deafening wails this time, but deep, racking sobs. Sarah's arms ached to be holding her baby. She reached up to take Eliza away from the big man holding her, but he took another step back, let out a grunt as though of pain or surprise, and reeled back against the door of the bakehouse.

It didn't hold. His shoulder struck the wooden panel, sending it flying back against the wall, and he followed. With Eliza gripped in his arms, he couldn't catch himself.

Sarah lunged after him to grab her baby. She ended up with her arms around both Eliza and the man. At least as far around them both as she could reach. He was broad and not an ounce of it excess flesh. He couldn't be the baker. Bakers were fat, were they not? He felt like all muscle and—

She jerked away, her face heating despite the chill of the autumn night. "I—I am so sorry. I thought. . . I intended to. . . Please just give me my daughter, and I'll be on my way."

"Doesn't look like her daughter." The torchbearer stood behind Sarah, the light flickering over Eliza's pale and tear-stained face, and the man's chiseled features twisted as though in pain, his cool, blue-gray eyes belying any hint of weakness of body. "Stolen, do you think?"

"I do not know what to think." Micah fixed those autumnal-chill eyes on Sarah. His features smoothed out. "I think I should fetch the sheriff."

"No, please." Even as the words left her lips, Sarah knew they were a mistake, but she couldn't hold back the protest, which surely gave away her fear of being discovered.

Micah's eyes narrowed. "I think I should indeed."

"I will fetch him for you," the torchbearer offered. "He will be as angry as a hornet, being waked up in the middle of the night, but if she's stolen this child or something, she should be—"

"I did not steal her." Sarah was gasping with the notion of being separated from Eliza. "She calls me momma. You heard her." She fixed a pleading gaze upon the bakehouse man.

His expression didn't change. "Children are gullible. They can be convinced to call a body anything."

A wave of murmurs rose behind Sarah.

"I could just fetch your mother," someone from the onlookers suggested.

Laughter ran through the small crowd.

A shiver ran through Sarah. This man must have a formidable mother if someone suggested her rather than the sheriff. And yet another woman might see the mother and daughter bond between Sarah and Eliza, be convinced she told the truth.

"Do not disturb the sheriff," Micah said. "I will get an explanation from this lady before we decide whether or not to notify the sheriff of her presence." His face softened. "No sense in separating them if she is telling the truth."

"I am. Eliza, tell the man who I am."

Eliza took a long, shuddering breath and buried her face against the man's shoulder.

Sarah's own next breaths entered her lungs in constricted bursts. Her head spun. She grasped the doorframe and blinked against encroaching blackness.

"She's going to faint," someone called.

"No." Sarah steeled herself against the desire to collapse. Eliza needed her strong despite the fact she had not eaten for a day and a half. "I am not a weak female who faints."

"She looks half-starved." This was a softer, gentler voice, a woman's voice.

Sarah blinked and looked around. An attractive woman of late middle years approached the bakehouse doorway.

"I am Mrs. Drake, the ironmonger's wife." The woman smiled at Sarah. "Please come into our shop and let me get something warm into you."

Sarah wanted to hug the woman and cry, "Yes, yes, yes."

But the man called Micah still held her baby. She sent him a pleading glance and hated every second of the eye contact.

"Of course I will bring her," he said. "You scarcely look strong enough to carry her ten inches, let alone ten yards."

"I have carried her all the way from—" Sarah snapped her teeth shut. She was too fatigued and hungry to be able to speak without giving information away. She bowed her head. "Thank you."

"Come along, child." Mrs. Drake slipped her arm around Sarah's waist and guided her forward. "The rest of you go back to your beds."

"But your man is away, and we don't know if she is a thief or not," someone shouted.

"She's got flour all over her," another man said. "Like as not she's been stealing from the baker."

"I didn't steal—" Sarah sighed. "Not much anyway."

"What did you do with nearly two hundred pounds of flour then?" Micah asked in a tone too calm and quiet to be trusted as genuinely unconcerned about his stores.

Sarah brushed at the telltale white powder on her nearly threadbare skirt. "I got most of it into a sack."

"Huh." He drew his rather nicely arched brows together over a high-bridged nose. "And how did you manage that without making a mess?"

"I cleaned up. I wanted no trace. . . ."

"For the thief catchers?" Micah asked.

"Hush all these questions, Micajah Ingersoll," Mrs. Drake admonished. "Your mother would be ashamed of you for being so inhospitable."

"Mighty strange to me, madam, that she would take out

all that flour to hide her daughter in one of my barrels. She could easily have just put the child in the sack instead."

Too obvious a hiding place. Sarah wouldn't say that if she could avoid it. The clandestine implications of the situation would confirm his worst suspicions. Eliza had been directed to remain quieter than a mouse. But no five-year-old child could remain perfectly still, and movement was less noticeable in a barrel. Besides, the barrel was more solid, safer.

Eliza was quiet now. Too quiet, clinging to the man like he was a lifeline in the middle of a stormy sea.

"And why weren't you closer at hand, unless you intended to abandon her?" Mr. Ingersoll pressed.

Sarah flinched. Eliza burrowed more closely to him, probably convincing him that Sarah had meant her baby harm.

"I never intended to abandon her. Eliza, what did momma tell you?"

"Momma?" An edge formed in the softness of Mr. Ingersoll's voice. "You are from south of here, are you not?"

Sarah bit her tongue. More speech would only convince him he was right.

"Micah," Mrs. Drake scolded, "no more. Can you not see she is unwell?"

"She would be more unwell in the jail." Despite his remark, Mr. Ingersoll stepped into the street, pulling the bakehouse door behind him, and started toward the building across the way. He limped badly, poor man. No wonder he was so ill-tempered. He must be in pain from that leg and carrying Eliza, small as she was. He couldn't possibly lift those heavy barrels of flour. Though perhaps he could with those shoulders and arms, muscles bulging against his—

Sarah pulled up her thoughts. She shouldn't notice such things about a man, not with her husband barely a year in his grave. She fixed her gaze on the ironmonger's shop door and light beyond that promised warmth and perhaps shelter, if shelter were something God would grant her at last. He hadn't provided much thus far, sending her north in the autumn, colder and colder nights, barely warm days.

She shivered.

Mrs. Drake tightened her hold on Sarah. "You'll come straight through to the kitchen. A shop full of nails and hammers is no place to rest."

It smelled of iron, rust, and turpentine. Despite the glow of the lantern in the window, the tools and paints seemed to radiate chill.

Not as much as the blue gray of Micah Ingersoll's eyes.

If those eyes ever warmed, if his fine mouth ever smiled, he would be heart-stoppingly handsome.

Fortunately for Sarah's conscience, he did neither as he carried Eliza into the kitchen behind the shop and placed her on the settle with the tenderness of a mother laying her own child in its cradle. "Sleep there, little one," he said in a voice so tender Sarah's eyes burned. He then removed his coat and laid it over her daughter and turned to poke the smoldering fire into a blaze.

"You sit down, Miss—Missus—" Mrs. Drake frowned. "What is your name, my dear?"

"Sarah Ch—" She bit her lip. She should have a pretend name ready, but she had changed it in every town through which they passed between Virginia and Connecticut. She didn't think she should use any of them again, and her mind rang hollow from a lack of new ideas.

Which, naturally, made the suspicious Micajah Ingersoll even more mistrustful of her.

"Do, please, seat yourself, Mrs. Sarah." He gave her a mockingly deep bow.

Sarah wished she possessed the strength to stand, snatch up her daughter, and run to another hiding place. Her legs, however, wobbled, and she dropped onto the settle beside Eliza. "Are you all right, precious one?"

"I tried to be quiet, Momma. But that barrel rolled and rolled, and I thought I might be sick." Tears pooled in Eliza's dark eyes, and she popped her thumb into her mouth.

"That's all right." Sarah tugged the thumb free. "I didn't know the man would come to his shop so early."

"When do you think I bake bread? Sunrise?" Mr. Ingersoll slammed the poker into its stand and reached for a bucket of water standing beside the hearth. "Do you wish to heat this, Mrs. Drake?"

"Yes, but I'll lift it." Mrs. Drake bustled forward and snatched the bucket from Mr. Ingersoll. "I am still strong enough to lift water. You needn't hurt yourself lifting anything that heavy."

Despite his injured leg, Micajah Ingersoll was strong enough to move those barrels of flour. Mrs. Drake's remark must have wounded the man's pride.

A muscle jumped at the corner of his jaw, and he turned away, not saying a word. He didn't even look at Sarah, but crossed the kitchen to lean against the worktable, arms crossed over his chest. "While Mrs. Drake does her Christian duty and serves you tea, you can tell us why you placed your child in a barrel that had recently held flour and then left her behind."

Sarah needed the tea first. Her throat felt as dry as that barrel of flour. She swallowed and tried to speak. Nothing emerged. The kitchen fell silent save for the crackle of the fire and the splash of water gurgling into the iron kettle suspended from a hook to swing over the flames.

"I'm waiting." Mr. Ingersoll speared her with his gaze.

Sarah crossed her arms over her chest in imitation of his posture and tilted up her chin so she could meet and hold his gaze while she spoke the absolute truth. He would accept none of her truths cloaked in subterfuge. "I am a widow, a very wealthy widow, with a very bad man insisting he will have me to wife so he can get his hands on my plantation. He nearly caught us a few days ago, so I headed inland to get away. I hid Eliza in the barrel while I looked for a place to hide for the daytime. I—I did not know that you would come to work so early, or I would have gone elsewhere."

"Indeed." No expression changed the strong lines of Mr. Ingersoll's face. "Is that all?"

"Yes." Flour was too damp to describe the texture of her lips, her tongue, her throat. More like chalk not quite ground into powder. "That's all."

"A pity." Mr. Ingersoll uncrossed his arms and straightened. "Because I do not believe a word you said."

Chapter 3

Micah had read of more believable dramas enacted on the London stage than the tale this flour-daubed woman had just told him. Runaway widowed heiress indeed. With Mrs. Drake there frowning at him, he managed not to snort with derision, and he believed Sarah Ch-something as far as he could throw her, which, alas, was not as far as he could throw before he ran off to fight for the English army. Not that he was still as weak as he had been when he returned home. He was still not able to cut logs for fires, as could other men, as he didn't have the balance, but he was not weak in body or mind. And his mind told him that this woman before him, pretty despite her disheveled state, could not be telling the truth.

Yet the fear twisting her delicate features tangled a knot inside Micah. Fear of him sending her to the town jail as a thief, or fear of someone chasing her.

Ah, yes, the chasing part.

"I should amend my last remark," he conceded. "I do believe you are being chased. But by whom is the question. Perhaps you stole that child, or perhaps—"

"I never." Sarah surged to her feet. All color drained from her face and she swayed, flailed one hand toward the back of the settle.

Micah caught her hand and pressed it to the solidity of the wood. Despite its generally grimy appearance and flour caked beneath her nails, Sarah's hand felt soft beneath his. Soft and warm from the fire.

He snatched his fingers away. "Sit down before you fall down." His tone was harsh, in response to the tightness building inside him. "Mrs. Drake, I dislike imposing upon you, but if you have some bread for this...female, I will bring you a fresh loaf whenever I manage to get to my baking."

"Of course I have bread, and no need to replace it unless I come over to buy." Mrs. Drake fixed him with a sharp gaze. "It is nothing less than my Christian duty to feed the hungry."

Micah flinched at the barb.

"I do not wish to be any trouble." Sarah sank onto the settle again and covered the little girl's hand with hers.

The child's mother or not, she did hold affection for the girl. Only someone who acted on the stage could pretend that kind of spontaneous tenderness. Of course, she might have been playing some role for so long she had learned to act the part. The little girl looked nothing like her and, despite calling Sarah "momma," had not seemed particularly eager to go into the woman's arms. Still, if she was the girl's mother, he had no right to separate them. . . .

And the longer he dithered there in Mrs. Drake's kitchen, the later the bakeshop would open, the less money he would make, and the more annoyed with the female he would grow. He needed to find somewhere to put her. The jail made sense, and he would not have hesitated a moment if it were not for the child. A prison was no place for a little girl. Separating her from the only person she knew in town, mother or not, was also wrong.

He glanced toward the window cut into the wall across from him. Light bloomed in the eastern sky, far too late for him to not be at his baking. But not too late for Mother to be awake and bustling about the inn, preparing breakfast for the guests and supervising the maids to clean rooms or the myriad other tasks involved in running the family business.

"If you will ensure this female remains here," Micah said abruptly, "I will fetch my mother and see if she can take her in at the inn. There is that room Constance used a few years ago."

He referred to his now sister-in-law, who had been near death when his eldest brother, Nathaniel, bought her indenture papers and carried her to Mother for care.

Huddled before the fire beside the sleeping child, her hands wrapped around a mug of tea, Sarah Whoever needed care, too.

"I'd take her in," Mrs. Drake said, "but I have no space once my husband and sons return from bringing the supplies up from New York City."

"No one needs to take me in." Sarah's voice sounded weak with fatigue or perhaps defeat. "I can survive on my own a bit longer."

"I think not." Micajah limped to the door.

Mrs. Drake bustled forward and laid her hand on the latch, preventing him from leaving. "You are not going to get the sheriff instead, are you?"

"No, I am getting my mother as I said." Micah glanced toward the window. "I do not want to let her leave, but neither do I want a female and child in the jail."

"Please." Sarah struggled to her feet. "Just let me leave. I am sorry for the trouble last night. I—I am certain that. . . man is gone now, and I can be on my way."

Micah did not respond. He had announced his intentions, he would not change his mind or go back on what he said. Mrs. Drake knew him well enough to understand that and stepped aside at last, with a nod and a tight smile.

"Of course you will go to your mother," she said. "I never should have questioned it."

"And I will bring by bread later."

"Too much later," he muttered as the ironmonger's door closed behind him.

He strode through the morning, noting frost lying over the plants and the vapor of his breath clouding the air before him. Winter approached with a rapidity that never failed to remind him of that horrible winter with the army in the western hills, never warm, never dry, never enjoying a full belly. The bakeshop from which he had been a runaway apprentice sounded like heaven on earth then. At that moment, five years later, it still looked like heaven, with light glowing dimly in the brightening dawn and the promise of warm ovens and warmer fires.

First things first.

He traversed the block of buildings to the inn with its weathered clapboard and shining windows, smoke from the two chimneys puffing vapor against the rising sun, and aromas of frying bacon drifting through the doorway. He rounded to the rear, to the kitchen, and pushed open the door.

Mother; his sister-in-law, Clara, wife to his second-eldest brother, Jonathan; and two maidservants swarmed around the large kitchen with platters and jugs nearly flying from hands to tables and back to other hands that carried them through the doorway into the dining room. Micah stood in the doorway for a few moments, not wanting to interrupt the rhythm of the morning routine, waiting for someone to notice him.

Mother did first. She paused on her way across the chamber bearing an enormous ham. "Micajah, what are you doing here, and with empty hands? We need at least three dozen bread rolls."

"Your guests will have to do without until dinnertime." He glanced at the other females, now all paused to watch and listen to him. "I. . .have a bit of a dilemma here." He flashed a glance at the door to the outside, hoping she would understand he wanted to speak to her alone.

Being his mother, who had singlehandedly raised him and his three brothers for a quarter of his life, she understood at once and thrust the ham into Clara's hands. "Carve this up thin. I'll be back in a trice—perhaps." She followed Micah into the innyard to where sunlight had reached a patch of the kitchen garden. She paused with her hands on her hips and her face tight. "You are not telling me you are quitting the bakehouse, are you? You are not nearly well enough recovered from your wound to—"

"I am not running off again, Mother." He interrupted with a gentle smile. "But someone has run off, and I do not quite trust her story."

Mother's blue eyes sparkled. "Another one?"

"You mean like Constance? No. This one is not a potential bride for me or Alden."

"You cannot know that if you just met her."

"Mother, please." Micah suppressed his sigh of exasperation with his mother's constant desire to see her four sons wed and settled. "This woman, I assure you, is a bane, unlike Constance or Clara."

Mother's face softened. "Yes, they have been a blessing. But what of this female, and how did you find her?"

"She found me. Well—" Micah hesitated, organizing his thoughts. "I found her daughter, or the child she says is her daughter, but they don't look a thing alike. The child is dark and the mother fair."

"Golden hair?" Mother cocked her head. "And blue eyes, of course?"

"No, her eyes are green. A pale, bright green like spring gr—" Micah's cheeks grew warm in the chilly morning air.

Mother started to laugh. "Pretty, is she?"

"Perhaps she is, under all the dirt and flour." Annoyance left his voice harsh, his tone hard.

"Ah, so you are not attracted to her." Mother sighed. "I will keep praying."

"Do, please, Mother, be satisfied with having two of us married off already." He tried to smile to soften his words.

She did not smile back. "You, of all my sons, need a wife most. You concern me greatly since you came home."

"With all due respect, ma'am, I am naught for you to be concerned about."

Her gaze flicked to his leg.

He clenched his jaw then forced it to relax so he could speak. "You know no woman here wants a lame man for a husband; thus, I am looking for no woman to take to wife."

"The right—" Mother stopped and sighed.

They had endured this discussion since he returned home from Albany in the New York colony, feverish, close to having his leg amputated. All Mother seemed to think about was getting her four sons married to good, Christian women. Micah had seen the pity in the females around Glassenbury. He wanted none of that.

"This does not in any way meet your specifications," Micah said. "She has told me a tale like some drama out of London and acted badly at that. Indeed, she is the last sort of female I would take to wife, if I were in the market for one. Now then, to practical matters. . ."

Chapter 4

My mother will give you a place to sleep." Micajah Ingersoll stalked into the Drakes' kitchen and began to talk to Sarah without greeting.

Half asleep before Mrs. Drake's warm fire, her stomach full for the first time in a month, Sarah jerked upright at the sound of the baker's voice—a melodious timbre that should belong to a preacher—and banged her elbow on the arm of the settle. Her breath hissed through her teeth. "I was asleep." Sarah rubbed her eyes for emphasis. "What do you want me to do with your mother?"

"It is what my mother will do with you." His gaze skimmed over her. "Clean clothes and water perhaps will do as an introduction."

"Micajah." Mrs. Drake bustled in from the ironmonger's shop. "You know better than to talk to a lady that way."

"I'm sorry." He didn't sound as though he were. "I am in a bit of a rush. The baking is already hours behind."

"I will make up for it." Sarah stared at her filthy hands, the fingernails black with dirt and whitish gray with flour. "I can bake."

"Never heard of an heiress who could." Despite the words, a hint of interest sparked in his blue-gray eyes. "And if you speak truth, we may be able to work on an agreement.

What can you bake?"

Sarah dropped her gaze to her filthy fingernails again. "Cakes. Fine sugar cakes."

"I would be welcome of that for a special reason," Mrs. Drake said.

"Perhaps you would be interested, but I can't see too many others in Glassenbury thinking the cost would be worth the effort." Despite his words, Mr. Ingersoll's eyes still held a gleam of interest. "Of course, if they are. . ." He trailed off and bent to pick up the still-sleeping Eliza from the settle. "We must be on our way. I am losing money by the minute."

So money drove this man. He was angry with her because she was taking away from his baking time.

"I told you to let me go," she murmured. "You could have been about your baking without troubling yourself with me."

"And leave you to steal from my neighbors? I think not."

"I have not stolen—" Sarah sighed.

No doubt the bit of flour she had wasted convinced him she was a thief.

"Where does your mother live?"

"At the inn." Mr. Ingersoll headed for the door.

"She is a fine lady," Mrs. Drake said. "She will be kind to you."

"Not possibly as kind as you have been, ma'am." Sarah dropped the older woman a curtsy.

Mrs. Drake laughed. "I have never been curtsied to before. We do not hold much with that sort of thing up here."

No, of course they wouldn't. Sarah's cheeks grew hot, and she scurried after Mr. Ingersoll, her head down.

Sunlight tinged the horizon, burning through morning

mist. Sarah shivered in her now threadbare shawl and the gown that should be held out with several petticoats but now hung limp and a little too long over just one, as she had sold the others to buy what little food she could purchase with the pittance the once-expensive garments had gained her.

If Mr. Ingersoll could see the lace she had traded for bread, he would believe her an heiress. Or perhaps not. He might think she wore her mistress's cast-off clothing, as Sarah had once so blithely passed a mended gown or petticoat to her serving women. Serving women who likely now thought her tucked away in a home in town, while they took orders from Benjamin Woods's appointed overseer, and Woods himself chased after her.

Even the thought of the man's name, the image of his handsome but dissipated face in her mind, sent a shiver up her spine that owed nothing to the morning chill away from the warm fire. Striving to keep up with Mr. Ingersoll, she glanced around, certain she would see her husband's factor skulking in a doorway, an alleyway, ready to pounce. She knew she had seen him the previous day, coming after her himself, not trusting to an agent, so he could force her to be his wife without delay. Surely she hadn't been imagining things. That face, those black eyes, looked like no one else she had ever encountered.

She saw no lurking shadows of a man spying on her movements. He might not have followed her inland, up the river, to this town. He might have thought she would push north to Boston and her late husband's grandmother in the hope the woman would take her in for the sake of Eliza.

They reached a large clapboard house with the sign of the

Red Griffin swinging above the door without encountering anyone. Woodsmoke and the aromas of frying bacon drifting through the street announced that the townspeople were awake and readying themselves for the day. In the distance a bucket clanged, and a horse whinnied close at hand.

"We will go around to the back," Mr. Ingersoll announced. "I will not parade you before any guests who might be at their breakfast. This inn holds a fine reputation."

And she looked disreputable. Sarah understood that implication.

"Momma?" Eliza lifted her head from Mr. Ingersoll's shoulder.

"I am here, child." Sarah reached up to stroke her daughter's soft tangled curls. Her knuckles rasped against Mr. Ingersoll's jawline, a line of whiskers he had missed beneath his chin. An odd thrill ran through her at the familiarity, and she jerked her hand away, pulling Eliza's hair in the process.

The child cried out.

"I–I'm sorry." Sarah glanced around, feeling as though she needed a bolt-hole, a place to run and hide. Nowhere presented itself to her. Two horses being hitched to a wagon by a groom stood between her and the stable. Other buildings rose around the inn on three sides. Most important, Mr. Ingersoll still held Eliza.

He shot her an impatient glance. "Are you coming?"

"Yes." Sarah hastened to keep up with him.

They rounded the end of the building and a tall, well-favored woman of middle years emerged from a kitchen doorway on a wave of apple and cinnamon scent. "Is this they?" she asked Mr. Ingersoll.

"It is. More trouble for you, ma'am." He set Eliza on the ground. "Can you walk from here, little miss?" Again his tone held that tenderness that brought a lump to Sarah's throat.

Eliza giggled. "Of course I can walk, sir. I am not a baby."

"No, I expect you are quite old enough." He spoke to Eliza but shot Sarah a glance of returning frost.

Old enough for what? Sarah would not ask him. She didn't have the time to ask him. His mother glided forward, graceful in her black bombazine gown and snowy apron. "You know they're no trouble, Micajah. For shame you even saying so."

"We do not know that yet, ma'am." He straightened, his features pinching for a moment as though the action brought him pain. "I will be off to the bakery. No one will have any bread this morning." He strode away, fast, yet limping badly.

His mother gazed after him, her brows furrowed. "He works too hard for a man who hasn't yet recovered."

"I never asked for him to carry my daughter." Sarah stooped to gather Eliza close to her.

But Eliza had caught sight of a black-and-white cat striding from the stable and ran forward with a joyful, "Magpie!"

"No, Eliza, that's not—" Sarah started after her child but hesitated. Too many people rushing at a strange animal might make it flee, in which case Eliza would give chase. Or it might attack. Either way, Eliza would make a fuss and draw more attention to Sarah than she had already garnered in the past few hours.

"It will be all right." Mrs. Ingersoll laid a gentle hand on Sarah's arm. "She is a friendly cat."

"She looks like one Eliza played with in the garden at home."

"And where is that home, my dear?" Mrs. Ingersoll asked.

Sarah hesitated then decided she should be perfectly honest with this lady. If she could convince her, though her son had been dubious about the veracity of her words, Mrs. Ingersoll might be more willing to help Sarah get to Boston. Once there, surely she could pay her back.

"I came up here from Virginia, ma'am." Sarah wrapped her shawl more tightly around her shoulders and kept her gaze on Eliza now kneeling to pet the cat.

It rubbed its head against the child's hand as though enjoying itself.

"It is not a pretty tale," Sarah admitted.

"I expect not, but you are a very pretty young woman." Mrs. Ingersoll smiled. "Despite the grime. Would you like a wash for you and the child?"

"The child," Sarah said with cool dignity, "is my daughter. She has five years, and I have three and twenty."

"Ah, you wed when you were. . . ?"

"Sixteen, ma'am. My father died and Mr.—Mr.—" She sighed and bit her lip, reluctant to give her full name, but knowing she must to earn this woman's trust. "Mr. Chapman was my friend from childhood and had just come into his inheritance. He needed a wife. I needed a guardian, so we wed."

"And he has gone to be with the Lord?"

"Last September. He caught a chill."

"Which you are about to." Mrs. Ingersoll opened the kitchen door. "Do come in. I already have water heating. Your child's name is Eliza?"

"Yes." Sarah reached out her hands. "Leave the cat and come here, sweeting. We are going to have a wash."

"And an apple?" Eliza remained on her knees beside the cat, which had toppled to its side and rolled onto its back, all four paws waving in the air, claws sheathed.

"I want an apple," Eliza announced.

"Eliza, no, you mustn't. You must wait until someone offers you something."

"But I am hungry." The hint of a whine crept into Eliza's voice. "I want—"

"Eliza, enough." Sarah wanted to crawl into the hayloft with mortification. She offered Mrs. Ingersoll a tight smile. "I apologize for her poor manners. Before—before last month, I am afraid we all spoiled her. I thought... We thought...she would have a different sort of life." Sarah marched to her daughter and bent to pick her up. "You must listen to me, Eliza. I told you that."

Eliza's lower lip puffed out.

"Do not cry. Remember what I said when we ran away from the bad man?"

Eliza's lip quivered, but she scrambled to her feet and took Sarah's hand without a word. When Sarah rose and turned to Mrs. Ingersoll again, the woman's eyes had narrowed in speculation much like her son's, without the coldness.

Sarah wished she could stick out her lower lip and pout and weep like a child. Perhaps stamp her foot, too. Nonsense. She knew God was punishing her for living a life of leisure, doing as she pleased and showing little heed for how the nursemaid and other servants spoiled the beloved daughter of the house. They liked Sarah well enough. She was kind to them and didn't ask too much; however, Eliza was everyone's pride and joy. Only a son of the family would have brought more joy to the plantation. Sarah was paying for it now, with Eliza and she being too poorly acquainted as mother and daughter for anyone here to believe her claim of maternity. And thus they didn't believe anything else she said either.

"I was spoiled, too," Sarah admitted.

"Let us make you more comfortable," Mrs. Ingersoll responded. "Then you may tell me your whole story, and I will make my own decision about whether or not I believe you tell the truth."

"Because your son does not?" Sarah did not move toward the door in the older woman's wake.

Eliza tugged on her hand. "Please, Momma? I smell apples."

"Hush, baby." Sarah did not go toward the house. "Is he going to have me put into the jail?"

"Not yet." Mrs. Ingersoll opened the door to the inn, and a wave of fragrant warmth spread into the yard. "He's acquiring the *London Connecticut Gazette* first to see if you fit the description of any runaway servants."

"I am not and never have been a servant," Sarah insisted.

"Even if this is true and, judging by your hands, I suspect you are telling the truth, he has suggested that we keep the child close here at the inn while you help in the bakery."

"What?" Sarah could scarcely breathe. "But she is my daughter."

"Aye, so she is." Mrs. Ingersoll nodded, the ribbons adorning her cap fluttering in the morning breeze. "So you will not be running away without her. If you do, then we shall know that all you've said is an untruth."

Chapter 5

Micah's mother brought Mrs. Chapman to the bakehouse three days later. Micah had seen her every evening when he took his meal with Mother and often Jonathan and Clara, too. She conducted herself in a quiet and composed manner and avoided Micah's eyes, though if someone spoke to her first, she responded to them, and even greeted the inn maids by name. To Micah, she said not a word, as he pretended she wasn't there—a rude action, he knew and his mother and brother pointed out—but he couldn't help himself. Mother must not gain ideas of matchmaking with this female about whom they knew nothing. Simply because the previous week's *Gazette* said nothing about a runaway servant or wife did not mean the notices simply had not arrived in Connecticut yet.

And she was just too fine to look at for his comfort. Dressed in a clean black gown and apron, her face and hands scrubbed clean, Sarah Chapman was a much different looking lady than the vagabond who had rushed up to him in the street in the wee hours of the morning. Beneath a bleached cap, her hair shone as gold as an English guinea, and her complexion glowed as pale and smooth as a pearl. In truth, she was more than simply a pretty girl. She was beautiful, and his heart skipped a beat or two before he got it under control and focused on his brother.

After the second day of Mrs. Chapman's presence, Jonathan and Nathaniel took Micah for a walk along the river. They ignored the protests of their womenfolk. Neither of Micah's elder brothers believed him incapable of a walk, though he sometimes gritted his teeth against the pain caused by having to keep up with them.

"Why don't you trust her?" Jonathan asked. "Clara says she's quiet and gentle—"

"And scarcely pays attention to her child," Nathaniel broke in.

"Which is why I don't trust her to be telling us anything other than a faradiddle," Micah said, gazing at the undoubtedly icy water of the river and thinking how its chill would soothe his aching leg. "Constance and Clara are always talking to or at least looking after the little ones. Mrs. Chapman scarcely seems to know her child."

"They do things differently in the southern colonies." Nathaniel looked thoughtful. "It would seem like proof that she is an heiress if servants did all the work."

"Not a wife for you then." Jonathan clapped Micah on the back.

He snorted. "Tell that to Mother."

The brothers laughed.

Still, Micah began to observe Mrs. Chapman more closely, especially when little Eliza joined the family in the big inn kitchen. When they prayed, Mrs. Chapman took the little girl's hand. Often, she stroked the child's forever-tangled curls, and sometimes she gazed upon Eliza with a tender glance that put odd notions into Micah's head, such as how much he would like a wife who gazed upon their children as though they were a wonder.

In that first week of being near Mrs. Sarah Chapman, Micah began to believe that she was the girl's mother after all, and had not stolen her from her rightful home and merely convinced Eliza to call her Momma. He also found Mrs. Chapman to be soft-spoken and polite, yet too reluctant to answer direct questions such as those Mother posed to her about her home, its location, her late husband.

Chapman, apparently, was a common name in the Virginia colony. It might not even be this woman's name. She might have taken it from her master, were she a runaway servant, or from a name she knew would not be easy to trace to its original family without going to the colony itself.

For one thing Micah believed about Sarah Chapman without a hint of a doubt was that she was running and hiding. She refused to go into the inn itself and rarely emerged into the yard unless needing to chase after Eliza, who in turn chased after one of the stable cats each time an opportunity presented itself. She worked in the kitchen without having to be asked, washing dishes, scrubbing pots, rolling out crust for a meat or onion pie. But when Mother asked her to carry a platter of chicken into a group of guests, Mrs. Chapman refused.

"I will turn the ham on the spit." And she turned her back on Mother and began to do just that.

"I am sorry I brought her to you if she is always this defiant," Micah said. "Perhaps she should earn her keep in the bakehouse instead."

Mother hefted the platter of roasted fowl. "And hide in your storeroom?"

"If she likes."

The stiffening of Mrs. Chapman's shoulders told Micah she heard every word they said.

"Bring her tomorrow," he said.

"I would rather stay here," Mrs. Chapman responded.

"But Mrs. Drake has been asking about those cakes you said you can make," Micah reminded her.

Mrs. Chapman gave the spit another turn. "I can bake them from here."

"I don't have a good oven as Micajah has," Mother pointed out then vanished into the inn.

"Tomorrow," Micah repeated.

He and the widow stood alone in the kitchen, the first time they had been alone since they met. Though ten feet separated them, he experienced a discomfort that few females gave him. Likely from the fact she never looked directly into his eyes. Until that moment, when she turned her head and held his gaze for no more than a breath, a heartbeat, both of which seemed to snag in his throat.

"I have to look after Eliza."

"And how long have you been doing that?" he asked.

"Not as long as a mother should." She gave him a view of her slim, straight back. "I was too occupied with frivolities. That's why I can bake fine cakes and nothing else."

"We shall see." He attempted to maintain his chilly demeanor toward her, but something in her honesty about herself softened his heart just a bit.

So much, though, that he procured a copy of the *London*

Connecticut Gazette the next morning to have a second look at the notices of runaways—servants, slaves, and even wives. Nothing appeared that matched Mrs. Chapman's description, which proved nothing one way or the other. News traveled slowly from the southern colonies to the northern ones then up the Connecticut River to Glassenbury. Yet she said she had been on her way north for five weeks.

On her way north to what? He really needed to ask her. When she came to the bakehouse. If she came to the bakehouse.

Which she did not do anytime that day. His leg aching from an onset of cold, wet weather, he didn't take dinner at the inn, but ate leftover bread and cheese in his quarters above the bakehouse. Later in the evening, he presented himself at the kitchen door in time to find Mrs. Chapman scrubbing a stain from the pine kitchen table.

"I will pay you a fair wage to work in the bakehouse if you can indeed produce cakes," he said without greeting.

She didn't pause in her work. "I will not leave my daughter without someone to care for her."

"My mother or Clara will look after Eliza," Micah said. "I cannot have you slipping out the storeroom door with her when I am otherwise occupied."

Her scrubbing grew powerful enough to reduce the surface of the work space to splinters in a few more minutes. "And of course you have no reason to take my word that I will not."

"Will you give it if I say I will?"

"I need the money," she admitted, still without looking at him. "I will be there."

Accompanied by his mother, she arrived early the next morning before many folk in the town had awakened. Cap frills fluttering, she marched up to the serving counter, bringing the clean, sweet fragrance of lavender and rosewater with her, mingling with the aroma of baking bread. "I have arrived, and if anything happens to my daughter because I am here, it will be on your head."

"You promised to bake cakes for me to earn your way." He spoke more harshly than he intended, but something seemed to be wrong with his breathing. "Can you keep that much of your word?"

"The Lord will provide for you for doing your Christian duty in helping her," Mother said.

"That remains to be seen." Micah glanced at the *Gazette*. "There's still nothing in the newspaper, but I would rather have you close at hand, whether you are telling the truth or not. If you are, you are safer here than at the inn."

The instant he said the words, he realized they were foolish. He could never defend her if a villainous man were indeed chasing her. No doubt Micajah Ingersoll would get in the way of her renewed flight rather than fend off an assault.

Another reason why no female in town wanted him— defending their honor or possessions with a loaf of bread sounded like something from a pantomime or farce.

"I will agree to stay as long as my daughter and I are safe." Mrs. Chapman gave him a steady gaze. "Where do you want me to start?"

He smiled at her. "Where you started here before—in the storage room. Find the ingredients you need for your cakes."

"Do you have any spices? Nutmeg or cinnamon or ginger?"

"I do. I keep them locked away. Tell me when you need them."

"Eggs?"

"In the storeroom."

"All right." She rounded the counter and headed back to the storage room. Though he rarely needed them, he had purchased a basket of eggs just that morning, counting on her appearance.

"I'm willing to give her a chance," he said to his mother.

"Good. I believe her."

"How can you? We do not even know her true name."

"I do." Mother rested her hands, fine hands with long fingers, but a little red and rough from work, unlike Sarah's hands, smooth and white now that they were clean. "Her name is Sarah Chapman."

"Or so she says."

"Aye, and I believe her. She, as you know, was widowed last September. A month ago, her husband's factor abducted her and her daughter, trying to force a marriage."

"I have never heard of anything like that, not even up in the New York wilderness."

"It happens in the southern colonies where they do not have many preachers. People do not. . .er. . .get married with the blessing of the Lord or the Crown outside the cities unless they have a great deal of money."

"And she said she is an heiress."

"She is, but this Woods is not a rich man. He only wants to be."

"As I said," Micah scoffed, "a drama right off the London stage. London back in England, that is. Sounds preposterous to me."

"It does." Mother nodded. "But so preposterous, I believe it is true."

"But I will keep looking for runaway servants in the paper. This one is a week old." Micah folded the sheets of print and set them on a shelf below the serving counter. They worked well for wrapping up loaves of bread.

And he had loaves of bread ready to come from the oven. Though he had acquired a clock with the bakehouse, he had gotten so he could know if the bread was ready by the way it smelled.

These loaves he pulled from the oven built into the side of the hearth were a perfect golden brown. He used a long, wide blade to lift them onto a wooden rack so they could cool. While he worked, Mother waited quietly on the other side of the counter. From the storeroom, Sarah's voice rose and fell in quiet recitation, as though she repeated a recipe again and again. Then her footfalls sounded on the wooden floorboards and she came into the shop.

He glanced down at her shoes for the first time. Foolish of him. Shoes told stories of a man's—or woman's—life.

Though the leather of Mrs. Chapman's shoes was scuffed and scratched, it had once been fine, expensive material, though her shoes were nothing anyone should walk in for long. They appeared more like the hour-glass-shaped heels ladies wore when dressed in their finest. The buckles were real silver, as any lesser metal would have tarnished. She could have sold the buckles for passage or food, but she might not know she could fasten shoes with twine. Or maybe she wasn't willing to sink that low.

A servant given her mistress's cast-off shoes would use string or perhaps ribbon to fasten them.

Gripping the doorframe, Mrs. Chapman raised one foot with the sole toward him so he could see the trodden-down edge of the heel and the thinness of the leather bottom. "The heels are worn down, too. Ridiculous shoes to run away in. I told your mother I was a pampered wife. I had nothing more sensible."

Another note in her favor.

Micah couldn't help himself. He laughed. The short guffaw sounded rusty to his own ears, and he couldn't recall the last time he had so much as snorted in mirth. He didn't trust this female to be telling him the truth, and yet her indomitable spirit, her courage, even if she were a runaway servant, impressed and, yes, amused him.

And amused his mother. She grinned broadly and turned toward the door. "I will leave the two of you to bake without my supervision. I need to oversee the inn. We have several guests heading into the mountains for the autumn hunting at present."

"You work too hard, Mother." Micah tried to hurry forward to open the door for her. He led with his right leg, a lifetime of habit, and his knee buckled. His right hand shot out to catch a solid surface for balance.

His fingers closed on a feminine arm instead, small-boned, yet smooth. No sleeve covered the delicate forearm. She had tucked up the sleeve ruffles to protect them. Only a light dusting of flour graced her fine skin.

"Will you forever be covered in flour?" He intended to sound exasperated but sounded amused instead. He barely suppressed a groan. Mother probably thought this banter was a sign he had decided Mrs. Sarah Chapman might be exactly what she said and, more, that he had decided to get to know her better.

He wished his mother weren't right.

Chapter 6

As Mrs. Ingersoll closed the door behind her, a peal of laughter drifted back into the shop.

Sarah snatched her arm away from the warmth of Micah's strong fingers curved around it. "I—I am sorry. The bread. You were about to grab the bread."

"Considering how many customers I owe loaves, that would have been a disaster." He stared at the crusty bread rather than her. Beneath his shining dark hair, his ears burned red.

"How did it happen?" Sarah asked.

Mr. Ingersoll stared at her. "I beg your pardon?"

"How did you injure your leg?"

A bold question for her to pose to him, yet the limb obviously gave him trouble, so she may as well also have that honesty between them.

Still not looking at her, he gave an offhand shrug. "I ran off and joined the Sixth Connecticut Militia and fought in this nonsensical war with the French. A French musket ball found me."

"I am so sorry. Is that why you became a baker? I mean—" Her cheeks heated as though she were too near the fire. "I mean, I thought bakers were old and fat, not young and hand—" She started to clap a flour-dusted hand over her mouth.

He caught her wrist before her fingers touched her face. "You cannot continue to waste my flour on your face. Your skin is pale enough."

He reached out his other hand toward her cheek, as though about to smooth a fingertip over her skin. "How a runaway could keep her skin so fine, I cannot imagine."

Fingers tingling where he gripped them, Sarah stared at the scuffed toes of her once-expensive shoes, imported from Italy. "I had a hat until the day before I arrived here. I traded it for a penny loaf."

"Is that all?" Mr. Ingersoll's gaze flew to her hair, where one of his mother's frilly caps perched. "It must have been in poor condition."

"It was not, but I was hungry and Eliza was crying from the pain in her stomach." Speech delivered, she spun on her heel with a flurry of cap ruffles and wide skirt and hastened back to the storeroom. She tried to lose herself in blending eggs and butter, flour and sugar, while her ears pricked to the sound of Micajah Ingersoll moving about the bakery—the slight drag of his right leg over the boards, the *slap, slap, slap* of those broad hands with their long, strong fingers working the dough. Her mind's eye saw him reaching toward her face, a strange light in his eyes, a glow that made her feel too warm, made her want him to caress her cheek.

"Don't like him," she warned herself. "At any moment, you will have to run again."

She wished she didn't have to. The days at the inn had been a welcome respite of warmth and good food, clean clothes, and Eliza crying less than she had since that dark night when Sarah snatched the child from her bed and fled from the plantation before Benjamin Woods could carry out his plan to force her into a marriage without the sanction of the church or Crown.

The family was kind. Even Micah had softened toward her. If her cakes turned out well and sold, he might soften more, might help her get to safety in Boston.

She needed the precious spices to make the batter complete but waited until a band of customers left the shop. Just because the entire town knew her name didn't mean they had to know where to find her. In the warmth of the storage room, surrounded by barrels of flour and loaves of sugar, tins of salt and bowls of yeast, and, most of all, with Micajah Ingersoll between her and the only unlocked door, she felt safer than she had since her husband's death. If only Eliza were there, close at her side, ready to flee if necessary.

A man with a bad leg couldn't chase them—another reason to feel safe in Mr. Ingersoll's company. Only Woods, not tall but strong and whole in all his limbs, could catch up with them. If only he had gone to Boston, followed the false trail she had tried to lay.

The shop door closed behind the last customer, and Sarah rushed from her thoughts of Woods's handsome but florid face to request the key to the spice chest.

"I won't waste any, I promise." She didn't look at him. She couldn't. She had been unable to do so often, for every time their gazes met, a jolt like the sensation of an imminent lightning strike raced through her. "I only need a pinch of cinnamon and nutmeg. And—and tomorrow I'll make macaroons—if you have any almonds, of course."

"I do not, but my mother may. We shall see how the cakes

sell first." Mr. Ingersoll gave her the key to the spice chest. He, too, only looked at her from the corner of his eye.

Because he felt the same jolt?

Hoping the cakes would not sell and she could return to the inn kitchen, warm and friendly and close to Eliza—even if it were not as safe as the bakehouse and its sad proprietor—Sarah slipped into the bakeshop with a bowl filled with fragrant batter and a request to use the ovens. "And a pan to bake these upon."

"There are irons aplenty beside the hearth." Mr. Ingersoll stood at a table kneading more bread, his hands never ceasing their rolling, pushing, lifting motion, the fingers flexible, the wrists beneath the folded-back cuffs of his shirt, supple.

Who cared if a man had one bad leg when he possessed hands and arms like that? Hands strong enough to turn a mound of dough to the texture of satin, gentle enough to sooth a fractious child.

Sarah's insides felt as soft as the butter she smeared onto the iron sheet before she scooped the thick cake mixture into mounds upon the pan and carried it to the oven.

"I became a baker," Micah said abruptly, "because I loved cakes and thought I could have them all the time if I baked."

"But you don't make anything other than some sweet biscuits." Sarah concentrated on not tilting the sheet of cakes. "What do you call those cinnamon sweets?"

"Snickerdoodles. They are Dutch. I learned how to make them when I was in Albany on the way to the fighting. They are a stiff dough that stays put."

"Ah, I understand." Sympathy tightened her chest.

He did not make cakes because his gait was too uneven

and he might tilt the pan, causing the batter to run all over the sheet.

"You could make wafers," she suggested. "The iron keeps the batter inside."

"The occasional sweet biscuit is all anyone wants," he snapped out. "I expect you will use my ingredients for naught."

"Perhaps, and I told you that cakes and macaroons are all I know how to bake."

"Of course, you are an heiress." He didn't keep the hint of sarcasm from his tone.

"I was not always. I should have learned more practical baking." She closed the oven door with a gentle clang of metal against metal but did not turn to face him. "But my father wouldn't allow it. He had plans for me to marry Ralph Chapman nearly since I was born."

"I expect you were not opposed to the notion of becoming wife to a rich plantation owner."

She shrugged. "I was not opposed to marrying Ralph. He was gentle and kind, and we had been friends all my life, it seemed. My father was his tutor, you see. We grew up together on the plantation, like you must have with girls here in—" Sarah stopped and darted into the storeroom as though she had forgotten something vital, which, of course, she had—the way the females in Glassenbury treated Micajah Ingersoll now that he had come home a wounded militiaman.

"I despair of him ever finding a wife," his mother had bemoaned. "The older females are married and the younger ones think a man with a lame leg cannot be a good provider."

Silly females. Money did not make a happy marriage.

Sarah had not been unhappy, and she and Ralph remained friends, but she never felt the tingling warmth, the melting joy her friends described or she read about in the poets' works.

Inside the bakeshop, Mr. Ingersoll kneaded the bread again, though the force of the pounding of the dough sounded more like he tried to tan a hide than blend the ingredients to the perfect texture for bread. It was an angry sound, or the sound of a man in pain trying to focus that anguish on something else.

Sarah cringed in the storeroom, waiting for the baking time for the cakes to pass. She cleared away her mess from mixing the batter. She inspected Mr. Ingersoll's stores to see what else she might bake. She tried not to hear him beating the bread dough beyond submission.

She succeeded at the first three tasks. She failed at the last one. Her ears strained toward the sound of his uneven footfalls, the way he swept the floor with smooth, even strokes, the rumble of his deep voice when he spoke to customers.

That voice made her feel as though he sang ballads to her. If any female were wise enough to listen to him talk, she wouldn't care for a moment that he might not be able to hunt or carry anything abnormally heavy or dance at a festival. Yet the females who came into the bakery treated him with a cool politeness that suggested he was nothing more than a mere acquaintance.

She began to tidy up the shelves of the storeroom, rearranging jars and small casks, dusting the shelves. On one shelf a pile of old newspapers lay. Micah used them for wrapping up bread and rolls and those cinnamon sweet biscuits he made sometimes. She began to straighten the stack so every corner was even.

They were at least a week old and some appeared a bit too handled around the edges. She removed those sheets from the stack. She could make fire spills out of those and keep the clean ones for wrapping.

She saw the notice in the third paper down. No wonder Mr. Ingersoll hadn't seen a notice of her being a runaway in any recent paper. It was in an older paper, an advertisement requesting the return of a runaway wife and child, "For she may not be in her right mind."

The description fit Sarah perfectly.

How Benjamin Woods had gotten the information into a Connecticut newspaper so quickly took Sarah a few minutes to work out. Of course he had come north ahead of her, had likely ridden, so he moved faster than she with a child who hadn't obeyed well until recently. He had expected Sarah to go north to Ralph's grandmother. He had simply lain in wait and no doubt peppered the papers with notices to have her returned to him.

"But you're not my husband, whatever you claim," she growled to herself. "We never shared so much as a house, however much you lie."

Yet who would believe her?

Quickly she began to tear the newspaper into curled twists of paper for starting fires. But this belonged to Micajah Ingersoll. She couldn't destroy it. Newspapers were expensive, were they not? Paper certainly was, and this appeared to be several sheets' worth. She could simply hide it, tuck it at the bottom of the stack. By the time he got that low, she would be long gone with Eliza or have convinced him she was telling the truth.

She must start out by proving she told the truth about being able to bake delicacies. Sarah wanted to avoid any of the customers seeing her now she knew a notice had been posted, but she needed to remove the cakes from the oven. Head down, Sarah scurried out to the hearth and wrapped a linen cloth around her hand so she didn't burn herself opening the oven door. The instant the iron grate separated from the box, the aroma of spices swept into the bakehouse.

"What is that?" Mrs. Drake cried. "Not apple pie. I don't smell apples."

"Currant cakes," Mr. Ingersoll said. "My new assistant is trying to prove her worth."

"I want one immediately," Mrs. Drake insisted.

"I need to test them first." His footfalls approached Sarah. "Must ensure they are fit for consumption."

Despite the potential unkindness of the words, his tone suggested a hint of teasing instead, as though he believed her cakes would be fine.

They looked well, a perfect honey gold bursting with the dark, dried berries. Still, Sarah bit her lip, and her hands shook a little as she set the pan on the table. If they weren't delicious, she would have no way to earn her keep. His mother didn't need Sarah's services at the inn. She would have to take Eliza away, head north without any money, before the winter snows arrived. "Well?" Mr. Ingersoll prompted.

"We are all eager to have cakes we can buy," Mrs. Drake said. "I know we can all make them ourselves, but it is so much better to buy them from someone who has mastered the art."

"They should be cool enough," Sarah murmured. She lifted one from the pan, thanking the Lord that it didn't stick.

Mr. Ingersoll took it from her hand. For a moment their fingers entwined. Sarah fought the impulse to hold on, beg him to give her another chance if this one failed. "I—I have not baked since my husband died," she whispered.

"They smell very well," Mrs. Drake said. "Micajah, do hurry and give us your opinion."

Mr. Ingersoll lifted the cake to his lips, leaving Sarah's entire body cold despite the heat inside the bakehouse. He took a small bite with strong, white teeth, and chewed slowly. His expression remained bland.

"Well, how are they?" Mrs. Drake demanded.

"Passable." Mr. Ingersoll's blue-gray eyes twinkled at Sarah and he laughed. "Better than passable. You have a light hand, Mrs. Chapman."

"Then I will take half a dozen," Mrs. Drake said.

In minutes, she departed with several cakes wrapped in paper and her coin shining on the counter.

"I do believe," Mr. Ingersoll said in his melodious voice from close behind Sarah, "your cakes are a success and you will be worth keeping on at least as long as the ladies of Glassenbury think them worth the cost."

Or he found the paper she should have destroyed rather than hidden.

Chapter 7

You have changed your mind about her, have you not?" Mother waylaid Micah the instant he entered the kitchen door of the inn.

Quickly he glanced around in search of Sarah Chapman, assuring himself she couldn't hear his mother's declaration nor his response. "I have changed my mind about her not telling the truth about being able to bake and no lady in Glassenbury willing to pay for the sweets."

Indeed, in the week since Mrs. Chapman had begun to bake her currant cakes, Shrewsbury biscuits, and almond macaroons, every female in Glassenbury had slipped through his door, even several who baked their own bread. Despite the cost of the sugar and other expensive ingredients, he had made more money in the past six days of work than he had made in the previous six weeks.

"I will pay her a fair wage for her time," he said, "and expect she will run away from us."

"But not for any ill reasons." Mother drew Micah into the yard despite the cold, late October day. "I do not believe for a minute that she is a runaway servant or wife and think you do not either."

Micah shrugged.

"Stop making that rude gesture in front of me, young

man." She tapped his arm and gave him an exaggerated frown. "You are one of my sons, which means you are not weak-minded. You know what you think."

"I do, and I continue to read the *Gazette* for notices."

"Stop it. She is a lovely young woman, and Eliza is a sweet child."

"She is naughty."

"She is spoiled. Servants were given care of her and never made her do anything she did not want to."

"Which does not speak highly of Mrs. Chapman—if she is Mrs. Chapman."

Mother sighed. "Micajah Ingersoll, will you give no one an opportunity to make mistakes and learn? You know God gives us a second chance in life after we have been sinners and come to Him."

"And does that mean we do not pay for those mistakes?" He cast his gaze down at his right leg.

"Sometimes we do," Mother admitted, her face softening. "I believe Sarah is paying for her mistakes with Eliza in that you and others do not believe she is her daughter."

"I beg your pardon?" Micah gave Mother his full attention. "What are you saying?"

"You may ask her. Indeed, I think you should take her for a walk this evening. The moon is full."

Micah glanced into the sky, clear and bright with stars. In the east, a moon hung as heavy as a filled grain sack, nearly as yellow as the sun. "A good reason not to take her for a walk. But I will go on one myself if you will excuse me." He turned on his heel and strode away with as much speed and dignity as he could muster.

If he didn't leave, he knew what the next words from his mother would be: "She is perfect for you."

She wasn't. Just because she had increased his profits and had proven a tremendous help, not to mention good companionship, in the bakehouse didn't mean she was someone he would want to marry. He couldn't, by law, marry a servant who had run away and certainly couldn't even consider a courtship with a woman who might still be married. Or married again. How Mother could think he should baffled him, or proved how desperate she was to see him wed. Just because the ladies of Glassenbury pitied him rather than fawned on him as they had before he went off to war didn't mean he needed to grab the first female who came along and take her to wife.

He should have reminded Mother how she always told them that God would provide a wife when the time came. Odd she would forget her own words of wisdom and try to foist Mrs. Sarah Chapman onto him. Perhaps she, like God, had given up on him, on trusting that God would oversee his future.

He would oversee his future, however lonely that might be, in his rooms above the bakeshop, suppers with his mother and married brother, visits from his nieces and nephews as they grew older.

Walking past the businesses and homes of the town, seeing families enjoying the company of one another, Micah's future felt as bleak as a January night—cold and dark. He should go home and sleep, but the idea of his empty rooms, cold from the fire being out all day, prompted him to take advantage of the clear night and bright moon for a walk.

Walking strengthened his leg and felt good after mostly standing all day.

He turned toward the river, and footfalls clattered behind him. He paused, glanced back. Pale gold hair shining nearly as bright as her white cap in the moonlight, Sarah Chapman dashed toward him.

"Mrs. Ingersoll sent me." She caught up to him, panting. "Mrs. Jonathan Ingersoll, that is. I was to be sure to tell you your mother did not send me."

"And why did Clara?" Reflexively, he offered her his arm.

She took it and laughed. "The same reason, I expect."

"I am sorry. So you know they want to matchmake?"

"I know. It it foolishness, of course."

His perverse heart clenched inside his chest at her words. Even a desperate female didn't want him.

"You do not believe my story," she continued, "and no one can have even a friendship based on distrust like that."

"I am not sure what I believe anymore."

Not when he liked the feel of her hand on his arm, the whisper of her skirt swinging against his leg as they walked, the light, slow speech of her voice.

"Then I would like to be on my way to Boston as soon as I have earned enough money." Her fingers clenched on his arm for a moment. "That is, if you will let me go."

"You are not a prisoner. I cannot stop you."

"But you should if I am a runaway."

"For your own safety."

She said nothing until they reached the river. A few boats bobbed at anchor in the water, but no lights bloomed on their decks. The only brightness shone from the moon reflected in the rippling dark surface. It was the sort of autumn night about which poets wrote, the sort that made a man think about a female at his side throughout the coming frosts and then snows of winter and beyond. The sort of thoughts he would not allow himself to have. He should pull away now before he decided he trusted her.

"Why did you run away and join the militia?" she asked abruptly.

He started, glanced down at her upturned face. "I was bored. That's the best explanation. Perhaps I was rebellious. I didn't like the baker all that much. He would not let me do more than sweep up and stoke the fires, when I wanted my hands in the dough or wanted to create recipes." He let out a harsh bark of mirth. "I like to cook. My brothers used to tease me about it, and yet I find something satisfying about creating food that fills a man's—or woman's—belly with satisfaction."

"So you just left the baker without assistance?" she asked.

Micah hesitated, remembering that last night, that last straw. "I did, but it was not mere selfishness."

"No?" she prompted.

He started to shrug, remembered Mother telling him that was rude, and turned his face away upriver to where he thought he'd find freedom and adventure. "I never told anyone. It would have made my brothers angry and my mother—well, she likely would have ruined the man from ever working in the colonies, and I couldn't let that happen. So I just left, encountered a friend who was joining up, and went with him."

Again she gave him that gentle pressure on his arm.

"What did the baker do?"

Micah hesitated a moment then decided anyone knowing, now that the man was in his grave, wouldn't matter. "The baker had spilled oil on the floor and expected me to clean it up, but I did not know about it. When I carried in a load of wood, I slipped and dropped it. Some shavings got into a batch of dough and ruined it."

"I expect he was furious."

"Quite." Micah shifted his shoulders in memory of the rage, the result. "He grabbed the nearest object to hand and started striking me with it."

"Which was?"

"A poker."

"Mic—Mr. Ingersoll, that is terrible! He could have killed you."

"I am not sure he did not want to. I lit out and did not come home until last year, when I was nearly dead from my wound."

"And he was gone."

"He had been for years. Had an apoplexy not long after I left, so the bakehouse stood empty. People used the ovens for baking their bread, as most people do not have their own, or not big enough for more than a meat pie. I started helping with the baking, as I could not do much else, and eventually took over the entire shop again."

"For which the women of Glassenbury have been most grateful, I am certain."

"Yes, I believe they are."

"I always appreciated having a servant to bake and one to cook and one to do everything else for me, I thought. But now. . ." She paused and ground a scuffed toe into the soft earth near the river. "I believe I like having a reason to get up in the morning. The way these hardworking women look so happy when they bite into one of my macaroons or York cakes or puddings. . . It's more satisfying than reading poetry and writing letters when there was little about which to write that wasn't gossip. Though I do miss visiting the poor." She gazed down at her ruined shoes and laughed. "I guess I am the poor now."

"What happened to your inheritance?"

Surely what she answered would reveal some of the truth of her past.

"It is still there along the James River. Prospering, no doubt. Mr. Woods will be seeing to that, as he wants it, but I cannot go back." Her fingers dug into his and she added, "I cannot risk being at his mercy again. Please."

She was shaking hard enough for him to feel it, and he covered her fingers with his free hand. "Unless you are a runaway, I do not have to send you back. If you are, Mrs. Sarah Chapman, I do not have any choice."

"I am not a runaway." Despite her declaration, she bit her lip and looked away.

Shame? An admission of guilt? Definitely an evasion.

Heart heavy, Micah turned toward the road home. "I need to be getting to my rest. Tomorrow is a workday."

Despite the silent and tense ending to what had begun as a pleasant stroll, Micah wanted to repeat it as long as the weather remained cold but mostly dry. Walking with the calm and understanding presence of Mrs. Sarah Chapman at his side felt far more pleasant and natural than walking alone.

Too pleasant and natural. So much so, he avoided any more than necessary contact with her for several days. Yet for every minute of every day, he felt her presence, smelled her lavender and rosewater fragrance from Mother's handmade soap, heard the rustle of her petticoats, caught a flash of gold hair beneath the white cap. She remained out of sight from customers most of the time, preferring to keep herself occupied in the storeroom, cleaning or mixing or reading through the newspapers he kept in there for wrapping bread if the customer didn't bring his or her own sack. She read every paper he purchased, and he purchased the few that came up the river, enjoying the news from the other colonies and his own, curious, in spite of his experience, in the progress of the war with the French and their Indian allies.

The latter didn't seem to be progressing at all. The other news remained much the same. Life in America meant hard work and was generally a pleasant way to live. Some fretted at England's control and lack of understanding that life in the colonies was different than life in England.

He also looked at the notices. Still nothing appeared. And with each listing of runaway servants, children, and spouses he encountered, a nugget of hope began to expand, rise like yeast.

But she spoke of nothing but going to Boston and the home of her late husband's grandmother. "I would like to get there before you all get the snows for the winter," she said at the family supper that evening. "When will I have earned enough money?"

"I expect within a week or so," Micah admitted.

The reluctance with which he spoke came through, and

Mother and Clara glanced at him with wide smiles.

He shook his head. "Now, ladies, with all due respect—" he rose abruptly—"I do not think I banked the fire properly; we were so late closing up the bakeshop this evening."

With this half-truth drifting behind him, he strode from the room and into the drizzle of the night.

"Meow," one of the stable cats greeted him.

He bent and stroked the damp fur. "You should go inside. The weather outside is no place for a cat to be, and you will not find any mice." He continued across the yard, leaving the yowling cat behind him.

The bakeshop would be warm, dry, empty. It was always empty these days, no longer the haven of solitude he had needed after military life. Just solitary. Seeing Jonathan and Nathaniel so happy emphasized his own silence. Alden didn't mind his bachelorhood. He was still young and knew what he wanted to do—become a physician first and then find a bride.

"All right, Mother," he said to the solid walls of the bake-house, "I admit it. I want a wife and family now."

Mother had always told them to pray for mates. Micah had as a young man. No more. He had gone to war against everyone's advice, broken his promise to the baker, and now God showed him with every disinterested female that he had sacrificed his future as a husband and father. Still he prayed but didn't trust God to listen to him now.

Weary of the silence, he set out a stack of clean papers and bread starter for the next day, noting the former was growing low, then banked the fire properly and headed for the steps leading to his rooms above the shop.

A knock sounded on the door then it opened. "Mr. Ingersoll?" Mrs. Chapman's voice rang to him soft and clear. "Mr. Ingersoll, are you here?"

"Yes." He pivoted on his left leg, grabbed the handrail, and made his slow progress down the steps. "What are you doing here so late?"

"I am sorry." She wrung her hands at her waist. "We—we cannot find Eliza." She started to cry. "I am such a terrible mother. I never should have left her."

"Where did you leave her?" Stumbling a little over the bottom step, Micah rushed to her side and rested a hand on her shoulder.

As fragile as a bird's wing, it shook with her silent sobs. "In—in her bed. She was asleep in our room off the kitchen. I thought she was safe."

Though he had considered her to be a terrible mother when she abandoned her child in the barrel, regardless of her reasoning, he now found soothing, reassuring words spilling from his lips. "You are not a terrible mother. You thought she was sleeping."

"But I was not near. I was not watching over her. Oh, Mr. Ingersoll." She clutched his arm and gazed up at him with wide, bright eyes. "What if he—if Benjamin Woods took her?"

Either her fear was real or she was indeed an actress of the finest order. For whatever reason this Benjamin Woods was chasing her, the man did exist, Micah believed wholly now.

He covered her hand with his, finding it ice cold. "Let us go back to the inn and begin the search."

"Everyone is out looking for her now. I cannot believe she would go far. She never does. She plays in the innyard with the cats or sometimes with other children, but she has never gone away." She snatched her hands free and covered her face. "I should never have left her alone. God is punishing me for being such a terrible mother all her life. I left her to servants because I was so—so selfish."

"I do not think God punishes us for sins we have repented of." Micah found himself using his mother's words. "That was what Jesus' death on the cross was for."

"I know, but I've only thought of myself." She turned toward the door. "Perhaps she would have been better off if I had stayed on the plantation with all the servants who love her and care for her."

Though she began to walk swiftly, Micah caught up with her and pulled open the door then clasped her hand and headed back toward the inn with her. "Why were you so against marrying this man?"

Or being married to him?

He shoved the thought aside. "Was he cruel to you?"

"Not physically. But he said things that frightened me. He's a fine factor. At least, the plantation prospered under him. But even if I didn't so dislike him, I don't. . .love him."

"And you want to love your husband?"

"Yes, foolish female that I am." She wiped her eyes on the edge of her shawl. "If I did not think I should be able to marry a man I love, rather than another *mariage de convenable*, now that Ralph left me the plantation entire, Eliza would be safe."

"We do not know that she is not." Micah squeezed her fingers and released her hand as they entered the innyard.

Two cats began to wind themselves around his ankles,

nearly tripping him. He stopped to gently shoo them out of the way and let out a sigh. "Looks like we will be getting more kittens soon. Now tell me where everyone has begun to look?"

"All the different streets and down—down to the river. There could have been a boat. Ooo." She pressed her hands to her middle.

"Where is Mother?"

"In the kitchen."

"Good. Go join her. I—oh, that silly cat." It planted itself in front of him, meowing. "Go into the barn where it is dry."

The cat didn't move.

"I want to look, not stay here."

"But if it is this man who has taken her, he could grab you, too."

And Micah didn't want that to happen. He didn't want her to be a runaway servant, property of another man at least for the length of an indenture.

"You may stay with me," he decided.

"Thank you." She clung to his arm. "But where to start?"

"Micah, you cannot be out in the wet," Mother called from the kitchen doorway. "You are barely well again, and if you slip. . ."

Micah cringed with embarrassment.

"I am with him, ma'am," Mrs. Chapman said. "We'll be near at hand in the event the others find. . .something." She wiped a mixture of tears and drizzle off her face. "If only we knew where to start instead of everyone scattering about."

"Ye-es." Micah stared down at the obviously expectant cat. The second one had disappeared, presumably into the stable. But the soon-to-be mother cat prowled around the door, no doubt begging for scraps of food.

"Eliza likes the cats, does she not?" he asked.

"She adores them, and they are so gentle with her. But they never go far—oh." Her eyes widened. "Could we be that silly?" Hope brightened her face in the dim glow of a lantern over the kitchen door.

"Perhaps."

As one, they headed for the stable.

"She has always liked animals." Mrs. Chapman spoke more quickly than her usual drawl. "She had several cats and made pets out of my husband's hunting hounds on the plantation."

The stable was dry, warm, and fragrant of horses and hay. A single lantern hung above the outside door, casting a dim, shadowy light inside. The horses of guests munched or shifted in their sleep with a rustle of straw. One roan fellow poked his head over the door of his box and poked Mrs. Chapman's shoulder as they passed.

She reached up and patted his nose with an affection that said she liked animals as her daughter did. "Have you seen a little girl, you beauty?" she asked the horse.

He blew through his nose.

"Eliza?" Micah called.

Hay rustled and a cat meowed from a nearby empty stall.

"Eliza," Mrs. Chapman called, "are you with the kittens?"

They peeked into the stall. Two cats lay in a bed of clean straw, but no little girl joined them there or anywhere else.

"Eliza?" Mrs. Chapman called again, an edge to her voice now. "Are you here?"

Another rustle brought wisps of hay drifting from above. Micah glanced up, caught a pale blur and a whimper.

"Are you up there?" he asked calmly.

"Ye-es." Now he heard the sniffles.

"Eliza." Mrs. Chapman headed for the ladder to the hayloft. "Eliza, how did you get up there?"

The ladder was steep and narrow, and the rungs surely too far apart for a small child to climb. Yet she must have.

"I heard babies up here," Eliza called down. "But now I'm scared."

"You should have thought of that when you went up." Mrs. Chapman stared at the ladder.

He could guess what she was thinking—climbing it in a gown and petticoats would be difficult at best. Climbing it with his lame leg might be more difficult, coming down with the child worse. Yet he had to do it. He had to do something for her after how he had doubted her.

He took a step toward the ladder. "Mr. Ingersoll?" Eliza's face peered over the edge for a moment then shrank back. "Momma, come get me."

"Do not watch," Mrs. Chapman said. "I will have to tuck up my skirt."

"No, I will retrieve her." Micah grasped one side of the ladder then waited, expecting her to say he couldn't do it.

She gave him a brilliant and grateful smile. "Thank you."

"Please," Eliza whimpered.

"I will be there in a trice." Or two.

Micah began to climb. One rung then two. His left foot up then his right. Left, right. Weight on the left, not the right. If he remembered that going down. . .

He reached the top and held his arms out to the child. She ran to him and clung. "You saved me again. I couldn't climb down."

"You should not have gone up at all," Mrs. Chapman said from the stable floor.

"But I had to see the kittens. Babies." Eliza clung to his neck.

She was a sturdy thing, hard enough to carry on a flat street, harder down a ladder. If he dropped her, she would surely break something. If he fell, he could injure his leg again. Sarah Chapman would look at him with disgust or pity, certainly not admiration.

He wanted her admiration. He fully admitted it. But his breathing grew rough, his heart rate faster.

"Hang on tightly," he murmured.

Left foot first. Leave his weight on the left. The right wouldn't fully bear his weight, let alone his and the child's. But Mrs. Chapman never doubted for a moment that he could do this.

Slowly, one step at a time, concentrating, he descended the ladder. He didn't realize he held his breath until both feet stood on the solid floor and Eliza wriggled for him to let her down.

"Kittens, Momma." She ran to her mother. "Babies with closed eyes."

"You should never have gone up there." Mrs. Chapman's tone was gentle but firm.

"But you should see them."

"The only thing I want to see is you in your bed where you're supposed to be."

"Why? I didn't hurt myself." The lower lip protruded.

Her mother pursed her own mouth, and Micah realized how full and pink her lips were. Soft looking, too, giving him notions.

He turned his face away. "Do you wish me to carry her?"

"No, she can walk." Sarah took Eliza's hand. "If you will excuse us, I need to talk to my daughter about her disobedience."

Eliza began to cry.

Mrs. Chapman's lips quivered, too, but her footsteps were firm as she stalked from the stable towing the dragging child.

Micah followed and waited in the kitchen while Sarah entered the bedchamber off the kitchen usually reserved for a maid who lived in. Though faint behind the thick door, voices rose and fell, one pleading, the other lecturing. The child cried. The mother waited until silence fell. The others returned, and Micah told them where Eliza had been.

"You climbed up?" Nathaniel looked surprised.

Mother just smiled. Micah guessed what she was thinking—"I told you so." Nonetheless, he waited for Mrs. Chapman to emerge into the passageway outside the kitchen.

"I told her to never leave the inn without someone with her. Perhaps she will listen to me now." She held out her hands to him. "Thank you for fetching her down."

He took her hands in his. "I was happy I could do so."

"Why could you not? Oh." She flicked a glance to his leg. "It did not stop you from going up."

"And you are learning how to be a good mother, judging from the scolding you gave her."

"I love her. I have always wanted nothing but to keep her safe."

And he loved Eliza's mother, Mrs. Chapman. Sarah. He wanted to keep her safe. He knew in that moment, holding her hands, the aromas of baked meats and lavender drifting around them, her hair a shining cloud about her cheeks, her face turned up to his with her pretty lips parted.

He bent his head and kissed her. She drew in her breath, and for a heartbeat he feared she would pull away, but then she relaxed against him, into the arms he circled around her. She slid her fingers into his hair, pulling it from its queue to make a curtain about their faces.

The click of footfalls on the kitchen floor sent them staggering apart, but if his expression was anything like Sarah's—dazed and dreamy—whoever exited the kitchen would know in an instant what he'd done. What they'd done.

"Do I apologize?" he asked.

Sarah shook her head.

"Good, because I'm not going to."

Mother walked out of the kitchen, glanced from one to the other, and laughed. "Very good. Tomorrow after the shop closes, we'll discuss my son giving you a proper proposal."

"Oh, no, he needn't. I shouldn't have." Hands to her crimson cheeks, Sarah fled back to the room she shared with Eliza.

"Of course I will." Heart singing, Micah strode to the door without a bit of hesitation in his walk. "And you can say I told you so all my life, Mother."

He barely felt the rain pouring down outside, the cold wind off the river, the pavement beneath his feet. Of course

Mother was right. He had been attracted to Sarah from the beginning—to her audacity, her courage, her gentleness. He would indeed propose to her the next day, and in the morning not the afternoon.

But in the morning, while he wrapped the first loaves of bread in paper, he found an old newspaper with a notice about a runaway wife. It fit Sarah's and Eliza's descriptions to perfection.

Chapter 8

The instant she arrived at the inn, Sarah knew something was wrong. Micah didn't greet her when she walked through the door shortly after sunrise. He simply pointed to a chair then returned to his kneading. She opened her mouth to ask what was wrong then saw the paper lying on the counter and closed her lips, folded her hands on her apron, prayed.

God had brought her this far, had given her shelter through the Ingersolls, had given her a man she wanted to love within days of meeting him. He would not let her down now unless she was wrong and she was not to remain with Micah.

But Micah had kissed her. He had held her and kissed her.

Her heart pounded so hard her stomach hurt. And still Micah didn't speak until he divided the dough into loaves and washed his hands free of flour. Then he faced her, his arms over his chest. "You lied to me. I have fallen in love with—I have kissed another man's wife. You knew it and you kissed me back."

"Will you believe me if I tell you the notice is a lie?" Sarah ventured in a small voice.

"Then why did you hide the paper?"

"I could not destroy it. Paper is expensive. I thought you would not notice."

"But you hid it. Oh, Sarah, Missus—whatever your name is. . ." He swallowed. He speared his fingers through his hair, pulling it loose from his queue as she had the night before. He turned his back on her. "Come along."

Sarah didn't move. "Whe–where are you taking me?"

"Where I should have taken you the first night—to the sheriff."

"And you cannot believe me?" She sprang from her chair and rushed across the room to face him, blocking his path to the door. "You say you love me, and yet you do not trust me to be telling the truth? And here I trusted you to fetch my child from that ladder when I know no one else believes you can do as much as any man. I believed you loved me when you kissed me. I believed you were a fair man worth loving."

"No woman believes I am worth loving." He started to step around her.

Sarah grabbed his arm. "No, Micajah Ingersoll, it is you who thinks you are not, who believes you are being punished because you ran away. And now you think everyone who runs away from a terrible situation should be punished. But you are wrong."

"You are the one who is wrong. I only think you should be returned. If I had been younger, if someone had returned me—" He stopped, gazed past her shoulder. "You need to face your life, Sarah, not run from it."

"Then don't run away from me." She stepped close to him. "From us."

"We cannot be, you and me. You belong to another man."

"You only believe that to justify going in the opposite direction from loving me. But you have to trust I am telling the truth and trust that God knows you are sorry about the past and forgives you." She touched his cheek, his skin smooth from the morning's shave. "But you are right. I must return to the plantation and risk encountering Benjamin Woods so I can prove to you I am telling the truth." Running, she left the bakehouse and headed for the inn.

Where she found an uproar because Eliza had vanished again.

Micah trotted after Sarah as fast as he could. Not until that moment, when he couldn't run after her, did his leg injury bother him so much. Not the pity from females who had once cast eyes at him, not the way others tried to do things for him he knew he could do for himself, not since he returned to Glassenbury humiliated did he care so much that he was lame. By the time he reached the inn, neither Eliza nor Sarah could be found.

"The child was in the yard with the cats," Mother said, "and then she wasn't. Then Sarah came running in here like a mad hound was after her, and the minute she heard Eliza was gone, she vanished out the door."

"We have to find her." Micah gave no explanation for his actions, simply climbed the steps to his mother's private quarters, took his father's old pistols from the high cabinet in which she kept them, ensured they were primed and loaded, and returned downstairs. "She's in danger," he said as he exited the inn.

"Wait." Mother rushed after him, cap flying from her head. "Micajah, you cannot go after her. Let me fetch your brothers."

"She is my lady. I will find her."

If he hadn't been too much of a fool for her to still love once he did. If he didn't stumble at a crucial moment. If—

"If you want us to have a future together, Lord, You will guide my steps." For the first time in the year since he'd been wounded, Micah placed his complete trust in the Lord.

Then he began to ask everyone he passed if they had seen Eliza or Sarah.

"Saw a big man carrying a little girl 'bout an hour ago," a river trader said. "Noticed 'cause she was screaming."

And so it went. Some had seen the child, some Sarah. They had gone toward the river. The river meant a boat and—where? Down toward the sea or north toward the hills?

Downriver. Benjamin Wood would take Sarah and Eliza back to that southern colony that paid little heed to the recent English marriage laws requiring licenses and preachers giving the blessing over the union. He needed a boat. He could row perhaps faster than someone could sail. Nathaniel would have one.

He didn't ask for his brother's permission. He simply took the boat from its mooring.

"Micah, wait." Nathaniel sprinted from his workshop. "You cannot go rowing."

"I can." Micah bent his back to the oars. It was strong. His arms were strong. His need to catch up with Sarah stronger.

The current helped, carrying him downstream. It would help Woods, too. He didn't know what the man looked like. He should have asked Sarah. He should have asked her a great deal.

Upriver, Nathaniel gestured and talked, haggling with

some men for the use of their boat. Behind him, smoke from cooking fires spiraled into the sky, reminding Micah he'd left the bakehouse fire blazing on the hearth. He prayed for no fire to damage the town. If the bakehouse burned, he wouldn't care. He and Sarah could rebuild together if she would have him.

He rowed harder, faster. He scanned every craft he drew near, every one that passed whether propelled by sail, oar, or paddle. Nothing. No one. No golden-haired lady or raven-haired child. Many strangers. He called to several, asking if they had seen the woman and child. None had.

Micah's arms began to ache, his back throb. The pistols lay heavy against his thighs, close at hand, ready for him to use. He could shoot. He would shoot straight.

"Micah." Nathaniel's voice rang across the sunlit water. "Farm."

Nathaniel, in a boat with a friend of his, gestured toward shore.

Micah glanced around. A farm sprawled down to the water's edge with its own landing. Two boats bobbed there. One lay empty. The other lay too low in the water to not hold a passenger, but Micah could see no one above the gunwale.

A man stood on the narrow jetty, short, broad, muscular. A well-enough looking fellow, save for a thin tightness to his mouth that suggested cruelty. "Keep moving," he barked. "My property here."

"No, it's not." Micah drew alongside and threw the painter over a mooring post.

The man reached to toss it back.

Micah cocked one of the pistols. "Do not touch it, fellow."

"I don't want you here." Despite the defiant words, the man froze.

Micah smiled. "I will move along as soon as you give me the lady and child."

"I don't know what you're talking about." But the man glanced toward the boat.

Micah could still not see inside. No help for it, he had to step out of the boat. Too easily, this man could shove him off-balance and into the river. If Micah had to fire the gun, the recoil might throw him off balance and into the river. Between the cold and the current, he was unlikely to survive.

For Sarah's sake, he must take the risk.

He led with his left leg, one hand on the mooring post, the other gripping the pistol. "Do not try to push me off, or I will fire."

"She is my wife," the man insisted.

"She says she is not."

"She is mad. She stole our child and—" The man lunged toward Micah.

With one leg on the jetty and his weak leg still on the thwart of the boat, Micah fired. The man reeled back, clutching his arm. Micah teetered then flung himself forward and hauled himself onto the jetty. He landed with one knee in the middle of the man's belly.

"Are you Woods?" he demanded.

"I need an apothecary." The man's arm bled freely.

"You may have one. What is your name?"

"All right. I am Woods and she is my—*ooph*."

Micah's knee drove the air from the man's lungs.

Now he saw into the other boat. Sarah and Eliza lay there

tied together and gagged. Eliza wept, but Sarah's eyes were wide and as clear a green as new spring grass.

Leaving Woods for Nathaniel to take in hand, Micah knelt and leaned forward to cut their bindings. "And while I am on my knees," he said with a smile and duck of his head while he worked, "may I beg your forgiveness and ask you to be my wife?"

Free from her gag and bindings, Sarah laughed and hugged a sobbing Eliza then rose on her knees and grasped Micah's hands. "You came even when you were not certain I was telling the truth."

"You were telling the truth. I was just a fool who thought I am of no use as a husband, so let myself believe lies."

"But you trust me now." It was a statement, not a question.

He leaned forward and kissed her then gathered Eliza into his arms to lift her from the boat.

"I want a snicker biscuit," she said.

"I do not have any," Micah said.

"But we can bake some," Sarah added.

Micah stared at her for a moment, suddenly ill. "Since you were telling the truth about everything, I just realized that you are an heiress. You will not want to work in a bakeshop when you have servants to do that for you."

"Money and servants kept me from my child. I will not let them keep me from you, and if that means baking cakes the rest of our lives, I will bake cakes the rest of our lives."

"You are certain? I could go to the plantation, but I know nothing about farming. And my family is here."

"I am certain."

"But it is hard work."

"Micajah Ingersoll," Sarah scolded, "are you trying to run away from me?"

"No, I will run to wherever you are."

"And that means back to Glassenbury and family and work baking cakes." She perched on one of the thwarts so she could kiss him. "I can think of nothing sweeter."

MACAROONS

The following recipe is taken from *A New and Easy Method of Cookery* by Elizabeth Cleland, 1755.

To make Macaroons, Blanch and beat a Pound of Almonds very fine, keeping them wetting with Orange-flower Water: Take an equal Quantity of fine Sugar, pounded and sifted, then beat up the Whites of eight Eggs, and mix them all together; place them handsomely on Wafers, then on Tin Plates or Papers. Bake them in a slow Oven.

Author's Note: After some digging into eighteenth-century dictionaries and cookery books, I deduced that a "wafer" was a special iron implement designed to produce thin, flat biscuits or, what we now know as cookies. Think the crispy part of an Oreo.

If you wish to try this recipe, you can use an ungreased cookie sheet in a low oven, probably around 300 degrees, though I have seen modern macaroon recipes calling for an oven as low as 250 degrees.

You can substitute vanilla extract for the orange flower water, or, if you like, use a few drops of orange extract.

By the way, the word *cookie* comes from a Dutch word meaning "little cake."

Award-winning author **Laurie Alice Eakes** has always loved books. When she ran out of available stories to entertain and encourage her, she began creating her own tales of love and adventure. In 2006 she celebrated the publication of her first hardcover novel. Much to her astonishment and delight, it won the National Readers Choice Award. Besides writing, she teaches classes to other writers, mainly on research, something she enjoys nearly as much as creating characters and their exploits. A graduate of Asbury College and Seton Hill University, she lives in Texas with her husband and sundry animals.

IMPRESSED BY LOVE

by Lisa Karon Richardson

Dedication

To Joel, Ethan, and Olivia,
you make me want to be a better me.

Chapter 1

HMS Aries, *off the coast of New England*
October 1762

Phoebe flinched as another round of cannon fire slammed into *Aries*'s hull. The crew answered the blow valiantly, their great guns spewing round shot and fire. A muted cheer went up from one of the gun crews. Their ball must have found its mark. But it wouldn't be enough to save them. The French ship of the line had twice as many cannons.

Lips moving in silent prayer, Phoebe paced the confines of the gun room to which she had been relegated. There must be some way she could help without getting in anyone's way. She was an Englishwoman after all. Should she stand by and raise not a finger to defend the ship?

She heaved open the door and stepped into the companionway just as another barrage from the French punched holes in the ship's stout timbers. Her foot caught and she tumbled forward, striking the bulkhead as a cloud of splinters filled the air. She flung up an arm to cover her face. For a long moment she crouched on the deck, making herself as small as possible. Blood pounded so loudly in her ears she could hear nothing else.

It took her awhile to realize that the men were cheering.

Had they beaten the French back? Phoebe dared to peek then straightened to her feet. Beneath her the frigate seemed to dig into the water like a thoroughbred gaining purchase for a final sprint.

Thinking to return to the gun room, Phoebe turned, but a gaping hole marked the place where the door had been. A jagged crevice in the deck opened to the bread room below. Her mouth went so dry she couldn't swallow. The choice had been made for her. She couldn't go back, so she would go forward.

She made her way up and out into the waist of the ship. Something warm dripped onto her arm, and she raised her hand to her forehead. Blood. She must have been scratched by a shard of flying wood. She reached into her sleeve for her handkerchief, but it wasn't there. Instead she dabbed at the cut with the back of her hand. How was she going to be any good to anyone if she didn't even have sense enough to carry a handkerchief?

She stayed where she was, out of the way of the toiling gun crews, until at last she caught sight of Uncle John on the quarterdeck. He stood tall and proud, the gold lace on his captain's uniform gleaming in the afternoon sun, his sword slung at his side. Deep in discussion with his first lieutenant, Mr. Loring, Uncle John motioned toward the shoreline looming closer and closer.

For an instant, Phoebe thought he meant to run the frigate aground in order to keep her out of French hands, but then she realized they were aimed toward the mouth of a river. Wily Uncle John. He must hope to escape by navigating waters too shallow for the larger vessel. She grimaced. God grant that the waters weren't also too shallow for *Aries*.

Behind them, the French ship's chasers barked and spat. The cannon fire tore through the rigging, showering the quarterdeck with tackle and wicked splinters. Phoebe plastered herself even closer to the bulkhead.

When she looked again, Uncle John had collapsed to the deck. Heedless of the danger, she raced forward and hurled herself up the ladder.

Uncle John was conscious and trying to regain his feet.

His lieutenant held him down. "You musn't, sir. I've sent Midshipman Hollis for the surgeon."

Phoebe sank to her knees next to her uncle. Her gaze shied away from the stain spreading across his coat. "I am here, Uncle. We will take care of you."

He didn't seem to hear her. He grasped Mr. Loring's arm. "Take us. . .Glassenbury. They've—" His words broke off in a grimace. His breathing grew reedy as he struggled to master the pain. "Shipyards."

Gasping and pale, the midshipman appeared. "The surgeon is dead, sir."

Phoebe's gaze locked with the lieutenant's. Tight as her throat was, she managed to squeeze out a plea. "We have to get him to a physician."

Mr. Loring nodded. He stood and gave orders to the helmsman.

One thought pulsed through her. *Please, God, do not take someone else I love.*

❧

He musn't forget the laudanum. Alden turned on his heel and paced back the way he'd come. He unlocked the medicine cabinet and selected a dark bottle. Carefully he stowed the tincture in his bag.

The front door burst open, but he didn't glance up. "I am coming, Connor. Your father will be fine."

"Are you the doctor?"

Alden snapped his head up at the unfamiliar voice. "Who are you?"

A tall bruiser in white duck breeches and a blue jacket stepped inside. "We need the physician." Behind him three other fellows crowded into the doorway, each as seedy looking as the first.

"I am afraid I am on my way to another call." Alden hefted his bag. "If the matter is urgent, you had best call upon the surgeon. If it can wait, I will attend you once I have treated my neighbor." He moved to usher them out, but not a one budged.

The tall fellow yanked off his hat. "Listen, mate, our captain's hurt bad."

Alden removed his spectacles and put them in a breast pocket. "Your captain?" He rubbed the bridge of his nose.

"Had a nasty scrape with a French ship of the line, we did. Had to come up the Connecticut to get away from them frogs."

A fellow wearing a disreputable straw hat stuck his head around his taller companion. "Our surgeon was kilt."

The men were obviously deeply concerned for their captain. Alden modified his tone. "My neighbor has fallen from his roof. When I have tended him, I will come straightaway."

The tall fellow looked at his mates, unspoken communication crackling between them like heat lightning. "That's not good enough, sir."

"It will have to do, lads."

"No sir." The big fellow took a step forward. "You're coming with us."

Alden planted his feet, refusing to back up. "I think you better go now."

The other intruders stepped forward as well, making a wall.

"No sir. I hate to have to do this, sir. It'd be a lot easier if you'd just come with us nice and easy like."

Surely they weren't so deluded as to think he'd allow anyone to dictate which patients he'd see. "I think not."

The fellow sighed. "Then I got no choice. See, we're Royal Navy."

Alden tasted something bitter at the back of his throat. "I have asked you politely. Now get out of here before I raise a hue and cry."

The fellow said sadly, "Afraid I can't do that. You're being pressed, boy'o."

Impossible. For a moment, Alden's mind went blank as a fresh-washed slate.

He shook his head. But the men closed in on either side, despite his attempt to deny reality. His fingers clenched around his bag, ready to thump someone.

The shortest of the lot, a stout fellow with impressive side-whiskers and a red neckerchief, moved in to grab Alden's arm. Alden swung the bag and caught the lout under the chin, snapping his head back. Alden spun and jabbed his elbow into the biggest bruiser's solar plexus.

But there were too many of them. He was overwhelmed

in a matter of minutes. One of the brutes pulled his arms behind him and clamped manacles around his wrists.

The bewhiskered fellow picked up Alden's medical bag then led the way out of the office. Alden considered his options, but with two men on either side, there was little chance of escape.

Connor Martin moved to intercept them. "Dr. Ingersoll, Papa needs you!"

"Run for the surgeon. I will come when I can."

Tears shone in the child's eyes. "But he's hurt real bad. He could die."

That tears it. Alden grunted and yanked the chains free of his captor's grasp. He darted past the boy. "Run, lad!"

He made it less than a hundred feet before a blow caught him above the ear and the world became a wash of swirling color and pattern. He pitched forward into the mud of the street.

The sun flickered like a candle in a draft and winked out.

❧

"You shouldn't have hit him so hard. Now what good is he?" The voice was feminine—lilting but with an edge of tension.

The sound of a man's response was engulfed in throbbing pain that radiated from the side of Alden's skull. He swallowed against nausea and squeezed his eyes shut. A groan escaped his lips and at the sound the woman spoke again.

"Oh! I think he must be rousing." The voice came closer. "Dr. Ingersoll?"

As appealing as the voice was, Alden wished it would go away.

"Dr. Ingersoll? Are you feeling better?" The whisper brushed his cheek.

It startled him and his eyes popped open. He immediately regretted the rashness of that act and closed them again but not before his brain had been imprinted with an image of the loveliest creature he'd ever seen.

Mahogany curls, pert nose, and coffee-dark eyes looking at him expectantly.

He wasn't in the street anymore. Where was he? And who was this woman?

An altogether rougher voice shattered the quiet. "I wouldn't have hit him at all if he'd come quiet-like. He'll come round any minute and won't be worse for wear."

Recollection snapped his eyes open again. The view was far less enchanting this time. The big Royal Navy fellow loomed above him.

It wasn't just an effect of the blow to his aching head; he really was swaying. He was on board a ship.

"I protest." It didn't come out as strongly as he wanted. More a kitten's mew than the lion's roar he intended. He tried again. "I protest!"

❧

Phoebe looked pointedly at the bosun who suddenly seemed to find the stitching on his hat fascinating. She turned to the physician. "Dr. Ingersoll, I must apologize for the manner in which you have been handled. Mr. Harcourt here did as he thought best. I hope you will forgive him."

The doctor made to rise, and instinctively she moved to assist him. The feel of warm muscle bunching beneath the linen of his shirt brought with it the burning revelation that she'd never touched a man in such an intimate fashion.

Humiliation stung her cheeks, and she knew she was turning as crimson as a marine's uniform. As soon as he was upright, she pulled her hand free and clasped it tightly in her other hand to make certain she didn't make some other impulsive and inappropriate move.

"I don't think you understand, Miss—"

"Carlisle," she supplied.

"Miss Carlisle. I was on my way to tend a patient."

"I am afraid that is not possible. My uncle has been gravely injured in a battle with the French. He needs your help."

"There is a prior claim on my attention."

Harcourt cleared his throat. "Badgering the lady won't help you a jot. Not now. You've been pressed nice and legal."

The doctor stared at Harcourt as if he were speaking a foreign tongue.

"I am afraid it is true, Dr. Ingersoll," Phoebe said. Her heart hammered in her throat and she wiped damp palms against her skirt. There was no way to soften the blow. "You serve at the pleasure of His Majesty's Navy."

An angry wash of red swept up past his loosened cravat and bled across his cheekbones. "And if I refuse to treat your captain?"

The bosun grabbed for the doctor. "Then I'll keelhaul you myself, and that's after I take the lash—"

Phoebe forestalled Harcourt's threats with an upraised hand. "Please, Dr. Ingersoll, as a physician, you must be a man of compassion. My uncle is dying." The tears she'd tried to keep at bay overran her defenses. Blinking rapidly to keep from humiliating herself, she covered his hand with hers where it rested on his chest. "Surely even righteous anger is worth little in comparison to a man's life."

He glared at her for an interminable moment. Just when she thought he would demand to be keelhauled instead, he sighed. "Take me to him."

Sweet relief rushed through her along with the realization that she was holding his hand. She pulled away. "Thank you."

His stern expression melted a bit. "There may be little I can do for him."

Phoebe had to look away from the grave truth mirrored in his eyes. "I understand." But she didn't want to understand. No, she had to believe that God had provided the physician they needed for a reason.

Chapter 2

The world spun around Alden as he tried to stand. He clutched at the side of the berth to keep from falling. After that clout on the head, he had more business being a patient than treating one. Still, the sooner he took care of the captain the sooner he could leave. Surely they wouldn't keep a man of standing in the local community. They just meant to force his cooperation. He put his feet experimentally to the deck.

He swallowed hard as the ship rolled beneath him. Prickles of sweat beaded his forehead. He would not be ill in front of these people. Especially not Miss Carlisle. Lips clamped tight, he took a step forward and reached for the door.

"Would you care for tea?" Miss Carlisle stood at his side, brow furrowed as if she'd bought a faulty clockworks doll and was trying to think how to return it to the shop.

"No." It came out harsher than he'd intended, and Harcourt stiffened. Alden fumbled for his glasses. Let the brute try something. One-on-one, Alden could give as good as he got. He hadn't grown up with three older brothers without learning a trick or two.

"Then my uncle is in the orlop deck with the other wounded men." She swept around him into the companionway, leaving him to stumble along in her wake.

The deeper into the bowels of the ship they went, the fouler the air grew, until it seemed a physical presence as real and wicked as a pair of hands wrapped around his throat. Just when it seemed he could bear it no more, they descended into the orlop deck and the stench doubled. No, trebled.

He covered his mouth with his hand. He might as well have tried to turn back fog with a lady's fan. There was no masking the reek. Alden staggered and grabbed for the bulkhead. Miss Carlisle plucked a handkerchief from her sleeve and shrouded her nose and mouth.

This is where they keep their injured and ill? It was a wonder any of them survived. "Where is he?" He managed to grate out the question.

Miss Carlisle pointed at a table against the far wall.

At least they didn't have the fellow in one of the hammocks strung throughout the low-ceilinged compartment. Alden set his jaw and picked his way through the crowded aisle to the captain's side.

The man's complexion held the gray pallor of dirty linen. A befouled bandage encircled his head. Alden put his ear to the captain's chest. His breathing was shallow and erratic. In the light of the swaying lamps, Alden could tell little of the wounds. But if the state of the bandages was an indication, they were grave.

"He must be moved out of this squalor."

Miss Carlisle motioned for Harcourt. "Could you see that he is moved back to his cabin immediately?"

"Where will you sleep, miss?"

"Perhaps the carpenter could replace the bulkheads and partition the cabin so I may stay near him."

"Righto." Harcourt motioned for a young man wearing what looked like a butcher's apron to help him. Together they shifted the captain. The man moaned and a grimace twisted his features.

Alden glanced back at the wounded men still lying in the foul recesses of the ship. Who would see to the poor wretches?

Miss Carlisle soon outstripped her uncle's bearers, darting up the ladder and out into the light and air. Alden followed more slowly. The others weren't his responsibility. If he tried to treat them all, he'd never get off this ship. He'd take a look at the captain, prescribe a treatment, and then they'd surely let him leave. He'd pray for these fellows. And if the ship was still in port after he'd seen his patients, perhaps he'd come back.

He hurried up the hatchway after his newest patient. The poor fellow looked as if the coffin fitter ought to be called.

How would this crew take it if their captain didn't recover? The near silence of the ship took on a sinister air. Officers and sailors alike followed his progress with their eyes. Alden glanced up into the rigging. Even the men in the tops had their attention focused on him rather than their duty.

Right. Well, he'd just have to do everything in his power to see that their captain recovered. He adjusted his spectacles and stepped into the captain's cabin.

❧

Phoebe opened the door and held it wide as Harcourt and the loblolly boy carried in Uncle John. She took in the cabin with a more critical eye than she had employed in months. The guns had been cleared away, but the carpenter's crew had not yet replaced the bulkheads, and the compartment was one long chamber. Still, windows banked the far wall, letting in light and air. The decking had been swabbed clean, and the sea cot rehung. Surely this would satisfy even the fastidious Dr. Ingersoll?

That gentleman bent slightly to clear the doorframe. He surveyed the chamber. "I suppose it will do."

Feeling like a hostess whose offerings have been snubbed, Phoebe let the door bang shut with the motion of the ship. The doctor moved out of the way just in time. The look he cast her showed he had no idea why she might be piqued.

Was he really the best physician in the town? This fellow was handsome, but that was no indication of professional skill. And he seemed closer to her own age than a learned physician ought.

Dr. Ingersoll leaned over Uncle John and gently began to unwind the bandage wrapped haphazardly around his wound. A grunt revealed his dissatisfaction with what he found.

Imperiously he held out a hand. "Where are my instruments?"

"Your. . .instruments?" Phoebe looked around, at a loss for why he might think she had his instruments.

Harcourt tromped toward the door. "I'll get 'em."

Dr. Ingersoll turned his attention back to Uncle John. Phoebe stifled a gasp as he removed a dressing and revealed a half dozen angry red wounds.

"Your presence is not required, Miss Carlisle. If you are uncomfortable around the injured, do not distress yourself by staying." The doctor did not look up as he spoke. "I do not need another patient to tend."

Phoebe blushed. "I am not some ninny likely to faint away at the sight of a little blood."

"As you wish." The doctor continued his inspection.

Phoebe planted a fist on her hip. A bad habit. She jerked it away. "Can I be of assistance?"

At last the infuriating man deigned to look at her. "I believe the bosun went for my bag."

"I am capable of more than fetching and carrying."

He sighed. "The loblolly boy is here to assist me. And in truth, I do not know what I am going to do yet."

"What?" Phoebe couldn't keep the sharpness from her tone.

Dr. Ingersoll straightened with wintery hauteur. "Your uncle is suffering from several different injuries. To begin, he has a broken clavicle. Not an uncommon injury but painful to the patient. There are half a dozen serious cuts and gashes that will require stitching, the worst of which is a laceration to the brachial artery in his left arm. The tourniquet was properly applied, which may have saved his life, but he will certainly lose the arm. And then there is this head wound. I do not know that he will ever wake up. He has undergone a terrible shock. I cannot promise he will recover."

Phoebe could feel the blood drain from her face. Her eyes grew hot and prickly. She squeezed them shut. When she was sure she would not cry, she opened them again. "Just tell me what to do."

His expression softened. "This is no job for a lady."

"The loblolly boy has his hands full with the other injured. Would you rather leave them unattended?"

"Surely there is someone else on this blighted ship who can assist me."

"They all have tasks, and as you can see, I am idle. He is my uncle. I want to help him."

"Say a prayer for him."

"I will, but I would like to do something practical as well."

"I cannot imagine what would be more practical than prayer." He held up a hand. "I will need a man of some strength to help keep him still. Besides which, I doubt your uncle would appreciate you being exposed to such sights."

The comment cut off her protests. He was right. Uncle John wouldn't want her to see him in the agony that was to come. He deserved to retain his dignity.

Lips pressed hard together, Phoebe left the captain's quarters as Harcourt returned. She paced the deck outside the door, her hands kneading one another, her lips moving in silent prayer. Surely God would heed her. He must.

Jimmy, the loblolly boy, came and went a half-dozen times.

The sun set with its usual burst of brilliance.

Lieutenant Loring joined her. "The captain has a remarkable constitution. He'll be shipshape in a fortnight."

Phoebe couldn't quite force her lips into the expected smile. "The physician said he would need to remove Uncle John's arm."

"We're lucky he did not balk at performing a surgeon's task. Don't worry, miss. Many a naval man has done without an arm. It will not signify to the admiralty."

"What am I to do if he dies, Mr. Loring?" The question spilled out.

"Don't fret." He patted her arm awkwardly. "I shall take you to your family in Halifax as your uncle intended. They will welcome you with open arms."

Phoebe brushed away hair the wind had blown into her eyes. At least there were still people around to map out her future. She would never be expected to make a truly important decision. Though she'd sought the reassurance, it irritated her. "I wanted to stay and assist, but Dr. Ingersoll would not allow it."

"I'm sure he was wise. Let the physician go about his business without interference."

The cabin door opened and Phoebe swung toward it, her pulse hammering in her throat like a maddened woodpecker.

Dr. Ingersoll stepped out. His apron was covered with blood, but he must have rinsed his hands. He removed his spectacles and rubbed the bridge of his nose.

❧

Alden already regretted his harshness toward Miss Carlisle. He could not prolong that look of wide-eyed terror, though he feared it might soon return and would not be so easily banished. "You may go in now, Miss Carlisle. I have dosed him with laudanum, so do not try to rouse him."

She snatched up her skirts and darted past him.

The officer who'd been standing with her put his hands behind his back. "Good work, Doctor. I trust everything possible has been done."

"Everything my skill can devise."

The man nodded and made to move away. Alden reached out to detain him. The lieutenant glanced at the hand on his arm and then back up at Alden with a look of reproof so strong Alden immediately let his hand drop to his side. It couldn't stop him from speaking, however. "I've treated your captain, and I will agree to come and check on his progress. May I go now?"

The lieutenant stiffened. "I'm afraid that's not possible."

Alden replaced his spectacles. "I have patients on shore who require my care."

"Dr. Ingersoll, you have been impressed into the British navy. You have no patients outside the confines of this vessel. You have no home outside this vessel. You serve at His Majesty's pleasure."

"You are not going to let me off this tub?"

The man scowled at the denigration of his ship. "While the captain yet lives, it is not a decision I can make. But we are in desperate need of a good medico, and you were highly recommended."

"You cannot do this. My whole life is in Glassenbury. Everything I have worked for, everything I care about."

The officer met his gaze, though the line of his jaw relaxed a fraction. He softened his voice. "It's already done, I'm afraid. I cannot release you without being party to desertion." He clasped Alden's shoulder. "It isn't such a terrible life." He raised his voice again. "Mr. Harcourt."

The odious bosun emerged from the captain's cabin. "Sir?"

"Keep an eye on the good doctor here."

"Yes sir."

With nowhere else to go, Alden all but dove back into the captain's cabin. How was he going to fix this?

Chapter 3

Alden did not immediately see Miss Carlisle. When his eyes adjusted to the relative gloom, he realized she was kneeling next to her uncle's berth. He plopped wearily onto a stool and let his head fall into his hands.

How was he going to get out of this mess? Did his family yet realize what had happened? He had promised to dine with Mother at the inn this very evening, but if he didn't arrive she would assume he had been called away to tend an emergency.

Perhaps she could rally the mayor to demand his release. There must be something that could be done. These people couldn't simply spirit away whomever they liked on a whim.

But of course they could.

The war still limped along, and as long as it did, these sailors could enslave any man they pleased.

"God, I'm going to need your help."

The words were a bare murmur, but Miss Carlisle turned toward him.

"I'm sorry?"

He raised a hand. "I was just. . .joining you in prayer."

"Thank you. I fear he needs it."

Alden rose and joined her side. He had done an elegant job, if he did say so himself. The head wound had been neatly stitched and bandaged. As had the arm stump. He had even managed to realign the clavicle with the help of a bolster under the captain's back and a push on his shoulders.

Still, Captain Carlisle looked even paler than he had before. Alden checked his pulse again. The captain was cold to the touch, despite the warmth of the day, and his pulse sped like a fury.

"Is there anything else you can do?" The girl's question was tentative, as if she didn't really wish to know.

"I. . ." Alden ran a hand through his hair. "He has lost a great deal of blood."

"But is that not a good thing? You will not have to bleed him."

"In this case, I fear it has gone too far. The humors are unbalanced, to the opposite extreme."

"Is there any sort of treatment?"

He continued to stare at his patient's pale visage. "I have been reading of some experimental treatments developed in London and Paris nearly a century ago. They involve transfusing blood from animals into the injured."

"That can be done?"

"It was not always successful, which is why the treatment fell by the wayside. I have theorized that it would be more effective to transfuse blood from a family member rather than an animal. They do say that 'blood will tell.'"

"I am a family member. Could you do it for Uncle John?"

Alden wheeled to look at her. "You must be joking!"

"If he needs blood he can have mine." She spread her hands. "I am sure I am due for a blood letting after all the excitement aboard ship. Why ought it go to the leeches if there is the slightest chance it might help him?"

"I have never attempted such a thing."

"How does it work?"

"A small incision is made in the veins of both patients and a tube is connected. I do not recall all the details. I never expected to actually employ the technique. I will not do it."

"Please, Dr. Ingersoll. I beg you to reconsider. There can be no real danger. Do not let him die for lack of something I could freely give."

Alden scrubbed his face with his hands. *Could this day get any worse?* What had he been thinking to mention transfusion at all? He'd wanted to sound erudite and well-studied in front of a beautiful young woman. He was daft. That was all there was to it. But he'd never have expected her to jump at the notion so eagerly.

Although. . .she had a point.

The captain's need was grave.

With a sinking sensation, he knew he was about to give in. He gave a final gasp of protest. "I would need several medical texts from my office, and the first lieutenant has made it abundantly clear that I cannot leave the ship."

"I will gladly fetch anything you require."

He smiled. "I thought you disliked fetching things."

In spite of herself, Phoebe smiled back. "I merely said I am capable of more."

❧

Phoebe clutched the list of books in her hand as if it were a ten-pound note. The pair of ten-year-old midshipmen who had been sent along as escorts were having trouble keeping up with the pace she set, but she didn't care if she left them behind entirely. Time was of the essence.

The town had appeared charming from the ship, but now with night firmly in control of the horizon, she could see nothing beyond her thin circle of lamplight. Appreciation of Glassenbury's attractions would have to wait. She had a task to fulfill.

The door to Dr. Ingersoll's office hung slightly ajar. He had indeed been taken in haste.

Despite the open door, the interior of the office was tidy as a monastery. Inhaling the pungent scent of herbs and books, she walked through the front room to an examining room where she found the glass-fronted bookcases Dr. Ingersoll had described. He had a surprisingly large library for a colonial physician—at least a hundred volumes. She perused the spines. And not all medical texts, either. Dr. Ingersoll had a wide range of interests. She handed the requested volumes to Midshipman Hollis.

Her gaze lingered on the remaining books. What sort of man owned these disparate works? She found everything from a slim volume of Gray's poetry to the works of the famous historian, Herodotus, to a *Robinson Crusoe* that her fingers itched to open and delve into. She spun on her heel and marched toward the door. It wasn't any of her business what kind of reading material the good doctor enjoyed.

She stopped short, making the midshipman do an awkward hop to the side so as not to collide with her. The stairs to the private quarters were right in front of her, and Dr. Ingersoll had been snatched from his home without any sort of notice.

She made a decision. "Hollis, take those books back to

the ship. I will follow along shortly." It would be kind to bring Dr. Ingersoll some clothes and personal effects. He wouldn't be ready to do the transfusion until he'd gone over his references anyway.

Taking up her skirts, she mounted the stairs. She pushed away all doubts of the propriety of her actions. Surely the law of kindness was more important, and it wasn't as if she were visiting a man's chambers when he was in residence.

The rooms were well proportioned and comfortably furnished. A broad mantel crowned a brick fireplace. It held several small, carved images. She approached and found the artistry impressive. A handful of human faces looked as if they might speak at any moment. But there were others as well: a miniature dolphin and an eagle, wings spread as if he were diving after his prey.

Perhaps the doctor passed long winter nights by whittling. Her fingers brushed the glossy wood. These were finished though. The work of a craftsman. Even if it was not his own work, he obviously appreciated beauty. The doctor certainly was turning into something of an enigma.

She was dallying. Reluctantly she turned from the intriguing bits of statuary.

In the bedchamber she found a wide bed, its hangings pulled back to reveal a plump pillow and skillfully embroidered counterpane. A table beside the bed held yet more books and what must be a spare set of spectacles.

Phoebe took up the spectacles and the first volume of *Tristram Shandy*. The doctor's clothes hung from a neat row of pegs along the far wall. Folding the garments tidily on the bed, she focused on the task at hand rather than considering the advisability of her actions. Though her cheeks burned, her hands were steady as she added clean linens and stockings to the pile. Now, what to carry it all in?

In the kitchen she found a marketing basket. She sighed. It was no sea chest, but it would have to do. She carried it back up to the bedchamber and placed the garments inside before adding the book and glasses. Hands on her hips, she made a final survey of the room. There must be something personal he would want to remind him of home.

Then she spotted it. No carvings adorned the mantel here. Just a single miniature. Phoebe took up the painting and held it to the light. Small enough to fit in her hand, it nevertheless captured an inordinate amount of detail. It depicted a young lady with eyes the color of the Atlantic after a storm, lustrous skin, and dark, luxurious hair. She held a posy of violets and appeared delighted with the world.

Dr. Ingersoll must have a sweetheart. Or a wife.

For some reason the thought had never occurred to her. But of course, such a man must be attached. Phoebe sighed and sat on the edge of the bed. The girl was lovely. Phoebe hesitated. Perhaps it would cause more pain to be reminded of this girl when he could not be with her? Phoebe would never be able to compete with such a prize.

Catching the drift of her own thoughts, she sprang to her feet. She tucked the miniature into the basket and snatched up the burden. She was being ridiculous. She had no intention of competing with the young lady in the picture.

☙

Alden closed the last treatise and rubbed his eyes. Why had he allowed himself to be persuaded into this scheme?

The procedure seemed fairly straightforward, but what if he managed to botch things and killed both the captain and Miss Carlisle? Harcourt would devise something far worse than keelhauling.

Bowing his head, Alden said a prayer for wisdom. While he was at it, he mentioned the captain and his niece, too. His further plea that God would help him figure a way out of the British navy was interrupted by Miss Carlisle's return.

She hauled a basket with her that looked—familiar. She thrust her burden at him. "Here. I thought a few things from home might make the situation easier."

"You went through my things?" He spoke slowly, trying to decide whether to be angry at the intrusion or grateful that he once more owned something other than the clothes he stood in.

Her cheeks blossomed pink. "I did not mean to pry. Only to make you more comfortable in your new circumstances."

Alden accepted the basket and peeked inside. Mother's miniature lay on top and he pulled it out. Had she yet heard what had happened? Would she be able to rein in his brothers when they heard?

He said another quick prayer that they didn't attempt anything foolhardy.

"I thought you might wish to have that with you. She is very lovely."

He nodded. "Always was the belle of the ball."

"I am sorry you will not be able to see her for a while."

"I do not know what she will do when she hears what has happened."

"But surely she loves you?"

Again he nodded, his eyes fixed to the tiny portrait. "Of course."

"Then I am sure she will wait for you."

He glanced up. "Wait for me to do what?"

The becoming pink in Miss Carlisle's cheeks spread. "Come back and marry her."

He laughed and turned the portrait so she could see it as well. "This is my mother."

"Your mother?" She clapped a hand to her mouth. "I am so sorry. I convinced myself I was not prying, and look at what I have done."

Alden suddenly made up his mind not to be offended. "I am pleased you brought the portrait. It will remind me of home."

"Are you ready to try the transfusion?"

The question jolted Alden, returning him with a profound thump to the deck. "Are you certain you want to go through with this?"

She looked at her uncle. "If I do not, he will die."

"Not necessarily." Alden grabbed for the text he'd been reading. "We could try it with a lamb."

"Doctor."

He stopped flipping pages, compelled by her quiet steadiness to meet her eye.

She continued, "Please let me do this. I am not frightened, and I must do something to help him."

He sighed. "All right. We will do the procedure here rather than transfer him back to the orlop deck. The jostling would not be good for his wounds."

Miss Carlisle nodded.

Alden licked his lips. "He still might die, you know."

"At least I will know we tried everything."

Chapter 4

While Dr. Ingersoll made arrangements, Phoebe changed into her nightdress and wrapped herself in her dressing gown. With quick, neat movements honed by years of practice, she took down her hair and plaited it. At last, prepared and with nothing else to do to stave off unease, she knelt by Uncle John's sea cot. Her prayer was simple but heartfelt.

A knock at the cabin door proved prelude to Dr. Ingersoll's return. The loblolly boy held the other end of a high, narrow table, and they maneuvered it through the door awkwardly.

They placed the table next to Uncle John and Phoebe stared at it.

"I need you to lie on top."

"I. . .see."

She rested a hand on the table considering how she was meant to get up there.

"Let me help you." He encircled her waist with one arm and scooped her up with his other hand behind her knees.

Phoebe stiffened and threw her arms around his neck. Then she laughed. "You took me by surprise."

Dr. Ingersoll's cheeks reddened but he laughed with her. "Apologies. I should have warned you." He settled her atop the table and withdrew.

"No apology is necessary." Trying not to feel like a suckling pig, Phoebe lay with her hands clasped across her abdomen. He spread a coverlet over her and placed a small bolster under her head, his touch gentle but with the swift assurance of a practiced physician.

He pushed his spectacles up on his nose. "I would dose you with laudanum to deaden the sensation, but it would slow your pulse."

Phoebe licked her lips. "I understand."

The door smacked open. Lieutenant Loring stalked in. "What is this I hear? You're performing experiments on the captain and Miss Carlisle now? I'll not hear of it."

Phoebe pulled the coverlet higher about her neck. "Mr. Loring, I have reque—"

The lieutenant bowled through her words as if they were skittles. "Don't think that you could ever get away with harming an officer of this vessel because you dislike having been pressed. I'll have you brought up on charges—"

"Mr. Loring!" Phoebe sat up.

He paused and glanced at her. His cheeks turned scarlet at her dishabille.

Phoebe snatched for the blanket and moderated her tone. "I appreciate your concern, Lieutenant. However, I have *asked* Dr. Ingersoll to proceed with this treatment. It is none of your affair."

"Miss Carlisle, during your uncle's incapacity, I feel as if I must act as your guardian."

Phoebe lifted her chin a notch. "You overstep, Lieutenant. I owe you no obedience other than that of a passenger on your vessel. I owe my uncle a great deal more."

Loring looked to Dr. Ingersoll as if he might now expect aid from that quarter. "You must know this is a ridiculous risk."

The doctor straightened to his full height, a good four inches taller than the lieutenant. "The captain is failing. You can see for yourself."

For a moment the lieutenant's eyes shifted to take in Uncle John, who lay still as death and twice as pale.

Dr. Ingersoll continued, "The transfusion may indeed be the best option to help him."

The lieutenant threw up his hands. "Don't say I didn't warn you." He turned on his heel, but his sword caught between the table legs and he had to do an awkward sidestep to pull free.

Phoebe met the doctor's gaze as the door banged shut. She smiled, and an instant later they were laughing together. "Forgive me. I must not make you mock a superior officer."

"I have yet to find my sea legs in that regard. I—I still cannot imagine that I will not be going home when your uncle's treatment is concluded."

The raw disbelief Phoebe heard in his voice grated across her conscience. Her amusement faded and she lay down again.

Doctor Ingersoll turned his gaze to the instruments the loblolly boy had laid out. "It will not take long, Miss Carlisle."

Phoebe trained her gaze on the planks directly above her. She didn't want to see what was happening.

❧

Alden took up a lancet. He'd placed Miss Carlisle on the table so she would be slightly higher than her uncle, and gravity would help rather than hinder them. She flinched as he made the incision but made no sound. It took only a moment, and then he placed the stripped quill that would act as funnel and bound it in place.

Now for the captain. Another incision and he inserted the other end of the quill.

In essence it was a simple procedure. There wasn't much more to do but sit back and wait. Alden looked from one patient to the other. If it worked, perhaps he could use the circumstance to his advantage and persuade the captain to release him.

His gaze settled on the view through the windows. The green of the woods beyond the town offered a refuge. If he could escape the ship he could take to the woods. There were families outside town who would take him in until the British were gone and it was safe to return to his life.

Loring had made it more difficult by ordering Harcourt to watch him. Alden wasn't the only impressed man on board, and the lieutenant had suspended shore leave due to the risk of runaways. No one would be willing to turn a blind eye, since he'd resent someone else gaining their freedom.

Maybe he ought to wait until dark. He could simply jump over the side and swim like mad for shore. But guards were posted at night. At the splash the sailors would be on his trail in a trice. There'd be no chance to find a safe haven. Alden sighed.

"Is everything all right?"

Miss Carlisle's soft inquiry startled him from his reverie. He jumped and jostled the quill. She winced.

"I am sorry, Miss Carlisle. I was woolgathering. Does it hurt much?"

"No more than a normal bleeding."

Alden nodded, then cast about for something more to say. "What brought you aboard a Royal Navy vessel?"

She closed her eyes. "My grandmother died. I lived with her in Kent since my parents and younger brother died from the smallpox in 1750. Because I have no closer relations, I am on my way to live with Uncle John's family in Halifax."

"A long trip."

"Excessively." She closed her eyes, opened them again, and a sad smile twisted her lips.

"I have never been more than a hundred miles from home," he said.

"Did you grow up in Glassenbury?"

"Yes. My mother operates the Red Griffin Inn."

"Do you have any brothers or sisters?" she asked in a dreamy voice. "I always wanted a sister."

"Three older brothers. I am the youngest of the family, and they teased me incessantly." She smiled again, so he continued. He'd long ago learned how to chatter so as to take patients' minds off their discomfort.

Her eyes drifted shut again. "Doctor." She interrupted the flow of his words. Her own words were slurred. "I feel a bit. . ."

When she didn't continue he checked her eyes. They'd rolled back. She'd fainted. He all but ripped out the quill and had her arm bandaged well before he thought to breathe again. He waved the smelling salts under her nose. She didn't so much as twitch.

❧

Phoebe blinked. The world spun like the time that dreadful neighbor boy had twisted her swing until she'd gotten sick. As sick as she was about to be. She rolled to her side. A bucket appeared in front of her, and she emptied the contents of her stomach.

Someone rescued her braid from danger of being fouled. The same hand rubbed her back in gentle encouragement. With a groan she at last lay back. Her eyes met Dr. Ingersoll's, and she realized that it had been he ministering to her at such a moment.

She squeezed her eyes shut. If she tried hard enough perhaps she could disappear. Why, oh why, did it have to be him?

He was a doctor; he'd probably seen worse things.

But not from her.

She groaned.

"Are you feeling better, Miss Carlisle?"

"Hm? After that you may as well call me Phoebe. My physician back home always did. I tend to get ill after being bled. I ought to have told you."

"The reaction is not uncommon. I was ready." He nudged the bucket with his foot.

"You are very kind, Dr. Ingersoll."

"Just Alden will be fine. If I am to use your given name, you ought to have the liberty of mine."

"My previous physicians would disagree."

He bent a little closer. "Your previous physicians are not here."

"You are right. They would never have let me proceed with the transfusion."

"Then they might have lost your uncle."

"Is he well?"

"Not well, but I believe he may mend. The rhythm of his heart has slowed, and his color is a touch improved. We will see how he fares when he wakes from the laudanum."

Warmth spread through Phoebe. Perhaps, at long last, she had done something really worthwhile. "Is there anything more I can do to help?"

"You have helped enough. For the rest of the night you are a patient."

That wasn't so terrible. Movement still made her head spin. "May I stay near Uncle John?"

"For the time being. If I need to operate again, I'll have to have you moved."

"Thank you." The knife of guilt flayed her conscience. He had been so kind to her, and not at all condescending as most physicians. He had even acted as a surgeon to save Uncle John's life. How would he feel if he knew it was her fault he was here?

Chapter 5

Alden awoke in the tiny surgeon's berth with a crick in his neck from the hammock and no notion of the time. How did men survive years of this life? At least he wasn't bedding down with the sailors. Those poor wretches were packed in like stacked firewood.

A knock sounded at his door and one of the midshipmen, he couldn't tell them apart, poked his head through the door. "Lieutenant Loring's compliments, sir. And he would like to see you."

"I am coming." Alden groaned and hoisted himself out of the hammock. He dressed. *God bless Miss Carlisle for fetching clean garments.* Scraping a hand through his hair, he decided his appearance would have to do then presented himself to the quarterdeck, where the lieutenant was holding court.

"Ah, Doctor. How fares the captain?"

"Better, I believe. He regained consciousness in the wee hours and we spoke briefly. He was lucid, with no lingering hallucinations from the medication. Barring infection or fever, he will mend well enough."

"That is good news. And Miss Carlisle is well after her ordeal?"

"I believe she suffered no lasting ill effects."

"I'm glad to hear it. And what of your other patients?"

"My other patients?"

"The sailors injured in the fighting."

"I have not seen any other patients."

Lieutenant Loring clucked his tongue. "Doctor, I know you weren't pleased to be brought on board, but I hadn't expected you to be remiss in your duty."

Alden stiffened, his jaw settling into a hard line. "I was kidnapped from my home to tend your captain. I have done that."

"No sir. You were impressed into the Royal Navy to replace our surgeon. I suggest you get about the task."

Alden whirled and stomped away without another word. He didn't trust himself to speak. If he once let loose with what he thought of that officious...smug...son of a sea hag, he'd be hauled up and flogged. He ground his teeth at the unfairness.

He slammed into the captain's quarters to check on his patient.

Miss Carlisle—Phoebe—was sitting next to her uncle's cot with a book open in her lap. The sun gilded her form until she seemed to glow like a Renaissance madonna. She was easily the most beautiful thing he'd ever seen, and his breath hitched in his throat.

The sight of her cooled his fury slightly. Her smile as she looked up heated his blood in a different way. The lieutenant didn't matter a whit. Just a few days more tending the captain for Phoebe's sake, and if need be the crew, and then he'd escape into the woods.

She motioned to a bowl on the table beside the captain's sea cot. "I fed him some broth, but he fell back asleep after a few minutes."

"The body requires a great deal of rest while it heals." Alden checked the bandage. Noted with pleasure the sight of laudable pus and wrapped a fresh cloth around the wound. Many physicians didn't bother changing the bandages, but it seemed to help the smell.

"I would like to help tend him today, if I may."

"That may be a good idea. I have been informed by Lieutenant Loring that I have neglected my duties." Alden nearly spat the words, his temper rising. "As if he has a right to assign me any task. I am a free man. A landowner. He has no right."

Phoebe paled, and he wanted to kick himself. Of course, Loring had the right by virtue of his position. By virtue of laws written a world away and the sovereignty of a king Alden had never seen. His outburst put Phoebe in an awkward position. Her loyalty must lie with the navy, of which her uncle was a part.

He ran a hand through his hair. "I am sorry, Miss—Phoebe. I should not have spoken to you thus."

"Oh, Doc—Alden." Tears shimmered on the edges of her lashes. "Please, I should be the one to apologize. I—I did not realize at the time. It was all happening so fast. And I was so worried. But it is all my fault."

❧

Phoebe could hardly breathe with the weight of guilt pressing against her heart. The doctor's handsome brow furrowed. He'd likely never smile at her again. Those eyes of his would never light up with wit and friendship, at least not for her. But she couldn't go back now. He deserved to know the truth. If he kept blaming Harcourt or Lieutenant

Loring, it would only lead to trouble.

"When our ship put in, I made inquiries for the best doctor in town."

He drew back.

Phoebe sucked in a breath. "I learned your name and where your office was located. But then I feared that you might not come with me. So I asked the lieutenant to send a few men." She swallowed. "I even suggested that if you were not amenable, they could press you, though such a thing is not usual with surgeons."

He looked at her as if she'd struck him. "*You* did this to me?"

Mouth as dry as ship's biscuit, she nodded. "I never considered. I never thought of the consequences to you. I was just so worried—"

"You will excuse me, Miss Carlisle. I have patients to tend."

She might have been Medusa, the way his face had frozen in hard planes. Back rigid, he turned and stalked away. She wished he had slammed the door behind him. It would hurt less if she could be angry rather than ashamed. Once again she searched in vain for a handkerchief. She'd have to do without. Just as she'd have to do without the doctor's approbation.

Her tears spilled over, and she covered her face with her hands. Why hadn't she just asked him to come herself? He surely would have obliged. Then he wouldn't be trapped here. But instead she'd wanted her own way above everything. She certainly hadn't prayed and gotten God's approval on her machinations. Father had always told her that just because she could get her way didn't mean she should. This was what he must have meant.

"What can have my girl so upset?"

Phoebe jerked upright at the sound of her uncle's voice. Thin and scratchy as the day's growth of stubble on his chin, it nevertheless sounded marvelous.

"Oh, Uncle John. You are going to be all right, are you not?" It came out as more of a question than the affirmation she intended.

He groaned. "I do not think you will be rid of me quite yet."

Phoebe grasped his remaining hand and brought it to her lips. "I am so glad. So glad."

Her tears rained on him and he sputtered. "It would be a pity to drown now after escaping the French."

Phoebe instantly pulled back and smiled. "I am sorry."

"What has you weeping?"

"Everything. The doctor, and my own wretched hubris, and you, and grandmother."

"What has the local doctor to do with your troubles?"

"That's just it. He is not just the local doctor. He has been pressed into the navy, and it is all my fault."

Uncle John's eyes drifted closed. "You rousted him with a billy club no doubt."

"Go ahead and laugh, but it is the truth. Please, can you discharge him? Once you are better, of course."

He reached to squeeze her hand. "I told you when you came on board not to question the running of the ship."

"This is different." Phoebe poured out the tale. Uncle John would have words of wisdom to share. He could set things right. If she could just find the right words, she might even win back the doctor's regard by securing his release.

She glanced over to Uncle John. His eyes were closed, his breathing deep. He'd fallen back asleep.

Phoebe closed her own eyes. There'd be no help from that quarter.

❧

Alden took refuge in his cabin. He paced the confines for a good five minutes. How dare she meddle? Did she think she was some sort of deity that could toy with people's lives? He'd thought her possessed of Christian feeling, but that couldn't be. Not with that level of disregard for her fellow man. She had been the one bright spot in this whole farrago. The sense of betrayal stung nearly as much as the offense.

He slammed his fist into the wall of his cabin. A howl of pain and rage escaped him. It had been stupid. He stared at knuckles split open from the force of the blow. "Physician, heal thyself," he muttered.

He retrieved a roll of bandages from his case and awkwardly bound the wound.

The change of watch sounded. Alden rubbed his forehead. It was time to see about his other patients, before Loring took it in his head to inspect the sick bay. With the orlop deck stench fresh in his memory, he tied his handkerchief around his mouth and nose. He breathed in deep and said a prayer. God was going to have to figure out this mess.

With the gunports open to catch the breeze, the air in the sick bay wasn't as fetid as the orlop deck. He lowered the handkerchief and made the rounds with Jimmy, the loblolly boy, at his side. His patients were a miserable lot, with a range of illnesses and injuries that would make a heartier constitution than his quiver. It seemed the treatment had mainly consisted of grog and gruel, with the lad making a special effort to remove the worst of the splinters if they were easily reached.

It was going to be a long day. Alden put on one of the surgeon's leather aprons.

When the worst of the injuries had been handled, his mind began to wander. Surely it couldn't be so very difficult to get off the ship without anyone noticing. The eyes of the lookouts couldn't be everywhere at once.

After he ministered to these poor men he could escape this ghastly tub with a clear conscience. He'd forget about Phoebe Carlisle as soon as he was free. His cheeks heated with a renewed sense of betrayal every time he thought of her. The sooner he could get away, the better.

The bit of him that always subverted his best attempts at self-pity spoke up. He muzzled it. But whenever he turned his attention elsewhere, the little voice piped up again. *She was trying to save her uncle's life. She didn't know what she was doing to you. She's naive. What would you do if Mother needed help? Would you be any less ruthless?*

The voice kept at him, an incessant pricking. He might just go mad before he had a chance to escape.

She didn't deserve forgiveness, he assured himself. And he'd find a way off this ship. An idea occurred to him. His eyebrows rose, lips pursed. It just might work. He could use Miss Carlisle's regret to his advantage. She would help him escape without ever knowing she had.

Chapter 6

Phoebe looked up from her prayer at the sound of the door opening. She hoped it would be Dr. Ingersoll, but it was her uncle's steward with another bowl of broth. The fellow placed the tray reverently on the table by the head of his cot, and when Phoebe insisted she would feed the patient, he nodded gravely and departed with the assurance that he would bring her meal directly.

Phoebe touched her uncle's shoulder. "Uncle John, you need to take some nourishment."

He groaned in response and made to turn away from her. But the movement seemed to cause him pain. His face contorted in a grimace of agony.

"Uncle John!"

His eyes popped open, the whites showing his alarm. "Phoebe?"

"Uncle John, are you all right?"

"No, I am not all right. An arm I no longer have itches, and the stump feels none too pleasant. My head aches as if Cerberus is gnawing on it, and this infernal collarbone hurts like blue blazes."

Perversely, Phoebe smiled. Uncle John had ever been known as the worst possible patient. He was generally so robust that any infirmity put him in a foul mood. He wanted nothing of drams and doses. He wanted to get back to commanding his ship. Enforced idleness wore on him like no amount of work could.

In other words, he was becoming his old self. "Pipe down, Captain Carlisle. You will be able to hound your crew only when you are better. So you might as well take some broth and stop your grumbling."

She stood and piled bolsters behind him to prop him up. He harrumphed and would likely have crossed his arms if one had not been missing. But he opened his mouth and allowed her to spoon in some soup.

"You are too slow." He took the bowl from her and slurped the contents without resorting to niceties such as a spoon. "There," he said, handing it back. "That's efficient."

Phoebe leaned forward and kissed his cheek. "I am so glad you are on the mend. You had me worried."

He patted her shoulder. "Truth be told, my girl, I was a mite concerned myself."

The door opened again and Phoebe turned, anticipating her lunch. Instead Dr. Ingersoll stooped to enter. He said not a word to her but examined his patient with every appearance of concern and skill.

Phoebe sat by silently, listening as he instructed Uncle John on the importance of his diet, bed rest, and fresh air. It was a good thing she was here, or Uncle John would promptly disregard everything the doctor said.

"You are making good progress, Captain, but you will be weak for several days, possibly weeks. The headache should gradually wane as the swelling within your skull reduces, and the stitching without heals. The transfusion was a remarkable success. I—"

Uncle John's eyes, which had been drooping, popped open. "What?"

"I employed a treatment known as transfusion. In fact, your niece helped."

"What has Phoebe to do with any of this, other than playing nursemaid?"

Dr. Ingersoll colored as if he knew the answer would not be well received. "It is a process by which blood is funneled from a healthy person into an injured person. I assure you there is precedent for the treatment."

"You asked my niece to do what?" Uncle John struggled to sit up.

Phoebe intervened, placing a mostly gentle hand on his chest and helping him to lie back. "I insisted, Uncle John. It was no different than being bled for some ailment."

"But you were not sick. You might have thrown your humors out of balance and made yourself ill."

"Nonsense. Every doctor I ever met seems to think we are all in need of a good bleeding. Now, if you do not get better, we may have to do it again."

"Not under any circumstances." He shook a finger at the doctor. "I do not know what kind of quack you are, but do not let her do it again, or I will send her to the masthead and you to the brig."

Phoebe planted herself between them. "You would do better to thank us both kindly for saving your life."

Uncle John snorted and glowered, but within a few moments had fallen asleep again.

The doctor turned to leave.

Oh, no. He wasn't going to get away that easily. Phoebe reached out and touched his arm. "Dr. Ingersoll, please. You have every right to be angry with me, and I do not intend to try to talk you out of it, but please, is there any way I can make amends?"

❧

Alden hesitated. That had been too simple. He had been braced to manipulate her into making such an offer. But it appeared God was smoothing his way. It had to be a sign that this trial was nearly over. He'd be free and home in a day or so. He could be patient for that long. But he was getting ahead of himself. "Do you think you might see your way to performing a small service?"

"Anything."

"I wrote a letter to my mother explaining where I am." He drew it from his waistcoat pocket. "And bidding her farewell." *And instructing her whom to contact about finding me a hiding place once I gain shore.*

"I would be delighted to deliver your letter. If Jimmy can sit with Uncle John, I will go now."

"I will sit with him." Alden gave her directions on how to find the Red Griffin and handed over the letter, ignoring the pinch of conscience. He wouldn't have been forced to such an action if she hadn't had him practically kidnapped. At least he could be sincere in his gratitude for her cooperation. "Thank you."

Miss Carlisle ran her fingers over the makeshift seal he'd managed to produce from candle wax and his thumbprint. When she looked up, there was no mistaking the reproach in her eyes at his lack of trust. "Is there any other message or token you would like me to take to her?"

Alden bit off an apology. "No, but if you could wait for a reply?"

"Certainly." She stood and moved around him with a circumspect swish of skirts, as if afraid of brushing too closely.

The captain stirred and she looked back anxiously.

"We will take excellent care of him while you are gone."

She nodded. "I will just fetch my cloak. Is there anything further I can bring you from your home?"

The thought enabled him to harden his heart. He shouldn't need to pack up the detritus of his life. He should have the freedom to return to his things and his life. And if he didn't go soft in the head and blurt out his plan, he would be going home. The pause was stretching too long. He forced a grim smile. "You have already brought me everything I require."

She nodded and departed so quickly it was obvious she was glad to escape his presence.

Alden sighed and dropped into the chair she'd vacated. As much as he hated to admit it, even to himself, he wanted her to smile at him again. But there was little chance of that now. Especially after she found out he had duped her.

Phoebe took only a moment to tie on her cloak before requesting the use of the jolly boat for the afternoon. Lieutenant Loring was exceptionally accommodating, and she had to decline his escort rather more forcefully than she might have wished. She had an idea there might be naval prohibitions against an impressed man communicating with his family while in his home harbor. Well if there were, she preferred to remain in ignorance.

She kept the letter tucked safely out of sight and carried with her a large, empty basket that implied her desire to visit the shops. Feeling like a traitorous spy, she sat staring at her clasped hands as the oarsmen pulled steadily toward the dock. When at last she was handed ashore, she turned her gaze to the town.

It was a handsome, prosperous-looking place. Its tall clapboard buildings looked as if they were pleased with themselves but not smug, merely content. Late flowers still bloomed here and there despite the nip in the wind.

Unlike in London, numerous trees lined the walkways. A few of these grand old dames were already changing their fashions for the reds, oranges, and golds of autumn. With Dr. Ingersoll's precise directions, it didn't take long for her to find the inn his mother owned.

It was perhaps the most charming establishment she'd ever seen. Vibrant orange chrysanthemums, russet helenium and snowy-white asters filled window planters and mounded along the walk. The building itself was painted a cheery red, brighter than brick, but in no way showy. Spotless windows were flung open to welcome the sun's rays. All in all, an air of cheerful bustle promised excellent housekeeping and a staff that knew what they were about.

Phoebe hesitated on the stoop. Alden had asked her to wait for a reply. What if they expected her to make conversation? There would be no way to avoid the questions that would come her way.

The decision was made for her when a neatly starched young maid flung open the front door. The girl yelped and hopped back. "Oh, glory, miss. You gave me a fright."

Phoebe apologized and asked for the mistress of the establishment.

"I'm afraid I can tell you we're full up this evening."

"I am not in need of lodging. It is a personal matter."

"Oh, well we've got all the staff—"

"And I am not in search of employment. I have brought her a message."

Curiosity blazed in the girl's eyes. "I'll fetch her down."

"Thank you." Phoebe stepped into the front hall. Her fingers kneaded the wicker handle of her basket.

The Red Griffin was as pleasant as she had expected. Well-scrubbed floors were dotted with bright rugs. The furnishings weren't new but appeared to be good quality and well cared for. The aroma of roasting chicken and something else delectable hung in the air. The scent alone would entice every weary traveler in the district to lodge at this establishment.

The maid returned and opened the door to a small sitting room. "Mistress invites you to have a seat in here. She'll be down directly."

Phoebe went through and perched on the edge of a settee. This chamber didn't look like a public room. A secretary desk bursting with papers occupied one wall. Sketches and paintings hung in joyous abandon, some straight, others less so. The mantel held carvings similar to the ones she'd found in Dr. Ingersoll's home.

In spite of herself, Phoebe crossed the room to examine them. She was almost certain these came from the same talented hand, perhaps a member of the doctor's family.

Above the fireplace a series of four charcoal sketches caught her eye. The artist had limned the faces of four young men. A younger version of Alden was captured in the drawing on the right. The others must be the brothers he mentioned. Phoebe stared at the sketch of Alden until it seemed it might speak. He looked more at ease than she had ever seen him. His smile warm and open, not tinged with bitterness as it was aboard ship. Had circumstances changed his smile before he came to the ship? Was this the way he looked at home? Or was the loss of that ebullient grin her fault?

A sound behind her made her spin.

The lady who had materialized in the doorway wasn't so different from her miniature. Plumper, perhaps, and wearing a mobcap over dark hair that was now streaked with silver. But the penetrating power and good humor of those blue-gray eyes were as self-evident in person as they were in the painting.

"I always did like those drawings of my boys. The artist did an excellent job of capturing their personalities."

Phoebe murmured agreement.

"Now, what might I do for you, young lady? Marianne said you have a message for me?" Mrs. Ingersoll's glance swept Phoebe's person, obviously taking in the quality of her garments and marking her down as a most unlikely messenger.

"Yes ma'am." Unsure whether or not she should explain herself, Phoebe pulled Alden's letter from its hiding place and handed it over.

Lips pursed, his mother slipped open the seal, removed the letter, and began to read. The color drained from her face. "Alden!"

Blindly she groped for a seat. Phoebe stepped forward, but the woman collapsed onto the settee before Phoebe could offer assistance.

Mrs. Ingersoll couldn't seem to tear her eyes from the letter. She held it in trembling hands. Eyes wide with more emotions than Phoebe could name or even guess at turned suddenly toward her.

"What do you know about my son?"

Chapter 7

Phoebe cast about for words, an explanation, anything to turn those baleful eyes away. Though in truth, she deserved the reproach radiating from the woman. "I…I believe he explained in the letter." What had he written?

Mrs. Ingersoll turned her attention back to the letter. Her eyes seemed to devour the lines of neat script, darting across the page and back again.

Phoebe willed her feet to remain planted. They wanted so badly to flee the cozy inn that they ached. She hadn't considered how difficult this interview would be. Just another headlong tumble into trouble. Why couldn't she ever look before she leaped?

She had to stick it out. She'd promised Alden she would wait for a reply.

A bit of color seeped back into Mrs. Ingersoll's cheeks, though they were nowhere near the comfortable rosy shade she'd exhibited when she entered the room. Abruptly she stood and pointed a finger at Phoebe. "Wait here." Then she turned on her heel and marched from the room.

Phoebe heard a tiny crack as the handle of her basket gave way beneath the pressure of her fingers. She loosened her grip instantly. Her cheeks burned. Her throat was tight enough that she might never swallow again, and her vision seemed to shudder. She couldn't focus. Every bit of her wanted out of this room and safely back on *Aries*.

Safely? Why had she thought that? Did she really think Mrs. Ingersoll meant her harm? What if the woman decided to hold her as a hostage in exchange for the doctor? It would be illegal of course, but that would be little consideration to a mother in danger of losing a beloved son. England was at war, after all. Phoebe hadn't just signed the doctor up for a pleasant cruise down the river. *Aries*'s battered condition was proof enough of that.

No. She was being ridiculous. No one meant to kidnap her.

In the hall she could hear the scurry of rushing feet. Lowered voices murmured just below what she might have overheard. Somewhere a door slammed.

After an eternity that the mantel clock insisted on calling a mere quarter of an hour, the door opened again. Phoebe swallowed convulsively, though it did no good. Her mouth and throat were parched. Mrs. Ingersoll entered first, followed by two men, their faces flushed, their postures intimating tightly leashed anger. Both of them wore aprons over working clothes. But whereas one was dusted with flour, the other was flecked by sawdust. The befloured man walked with a limp and had maple-colored hair. The other looked more like Mrs. Ingersoll, with darker hair and sea-washed eyes. Phoebe glanced at the drawings to confirm her guess. Yes. These were two of Alden's elder brothers.

Mrs. Ingersoll spoke first. "I haven't questioned her yet. I wanted you boys with me."

The sawdusted one eyed Phoebe like she was a louse, though his remarks were addressed to his mother. "How long do you think it will take for Jonathan to get here?"

"I do not know. I sent Marianne to fetch him, but it will depend on whether he is out on the river or not."

"Perhaps we ought to start without him. I am sure that Miss. . ." The other brother looked at Phoebe.

"Carlisle," she said.

"Miss Carlisle must be wishing to return to her uncle."

Phoebe nodded eagerly. "I should very much like to get back to the ship."

Mrs. Ingersoll was less conciliatory. "I have a few questions first. Tell me exactly what has happened to my son."

Whalebone from her stays prodded Phoebe in the ribs. Or was it guilt? She ought to tell the full truth and simply accept the consequences. She had wronged these people nearly as much as she had the good doctor.

She licked her lips, trying to find a way to make them understand that she had been frantic. She couldn't say that she hadn't meant to do what she'd done. She'd planned it out. But she was sorry. She had failed to take into account the physician whose life would be upended.

"I ought—"

The door to the sitting room flew open and another young man marched in. Three handsome young women entered hard on his heels. Mrs. Ingersoll was engulfed in hugs. Noise and movement and energy filled the room. Everyone was talking at once, either demanding to know what had happened or busy trying to explain. Several small children joined the chaos, and with them an energetic little puppy.

Phoebe tightened her grip on the arms of her chair and

stayed very still as the storm raged. Was this how normal families acted? She could hardly recall. Her own upbringing had been one of straight spines, stiff upper lips, and cold dinners alone with a nurse in the nursery. Grandmother had not believed in noise.

For all the clamor, there was a good-naturedness about the madness. They obviously cared for one another.

One of the younger tykes began to cry when she heard that Uncle Alden had been taken from them. Tears came to Phoebe's eyes as well. God forgive her for what she'd done. Was her uncle more important than this child's? Why hadn't she thought things through?

At length, Mrs. Ingersoll raised her hand, and the room quieted by degrees. The children were sent outside and the adults took seats, ranging around the sitting room in a comfortable sprawl of familiarity.

"Now," said Mrs. Ingersoll, "we were just about to listen to what Miss Carlisle can tell us of Alden."

Phoebe's hands were becoming sore with the constant kneading. "Dr. Ingersoll was impressed aboard *Aries*. I"—her voice quavered—"I'm afraid it was my idea. My uncle is the captain and he was terribly injured. Dr. Ingersoll saved his life. But I am so sorry that I never considered what impressment would mean to him or to his family. I want to make amends."

The family members looked one to another. Phoebe tried to decipher their emotions. Doubt, suspicion, worry, fear, anger, a host of others, but none pleasant.

Where was the relief that confession was meant to bring? No one would look at her. It was almost worse than when they'd all been looking at her. Phoebe jumped to her feet. "Perhaps you would like to discuss matters? I will wait outside for your answer."

"I think that would be best, my dear," Mrs. Ingersoll said, her voice quiet.

Phoebe hastened outside. She could not stop trembling. On the stoop she realized she'd forgotten her basket, but it would have taken an army to make her go back for it.

Staring at the flagstones that Alden must have traversed a thousand, nay, a hundred thousand times, she made a decision. It might mean betraying her uncle and *Aries*, even the laws of England, but she was going to help Alden escape. She had to make matters right.

Alden rubbed his temples. Would the carpenter and his crew never finish with their infernal hammering? His head now pounded as much as they did.

He'd made his rounds after lunch, checking on each of the sailors and allowing three to return to their duties. Then he returned to the captain's cabin and dismissed Jimmy.

A hand to his patient's wrist established that he had a steady pulse. A touch rapid. But not nearly the frenzied race it had been on the night before. His color was better, too. Still wan but without the waxy quality of a man begging entry at heaven's gates.

Gently he unwound the bandage around the captain's arm. When the wound had been exposed, he examined it. Pleased with the look of it, he took a breath and opened a jar of ointment he had made. Compounded of wool wax and comfrey, it had a unique stench that made his eyes water and his nose hair sizzle. He ought to have opened the windows before he started this.

His patient groaned.

Alden hesitated.

"What is that?"

Alden held up the jar so the captain could see it. "An ointment. I know it reeks, but I assure you, I have used it before with great success."

The captain grimaced in a way that Alden thought might have been meant as a smile. "Lad, a sailor thinks the more unpleasant a medical treatment, the more effective. Smear away."

Alden did so, eager to be able to close the jar. "I think your arm will do. You show no signs of infection."

The captain grunted.

As soon as he closed the jar, Alden applied a fresh bandage. If nothing else it would muffle the stench of the ointment. "You will still be weak for at least a fortnight. It would be best if you remained abed for at least that long."

"I have a ship to command."

Alden squinted at his patient then realized why the man was so fuzzy and put his spectacles back on. British captains were supposed to be nearly godlike in their powers over the lives of their men, but Alden was well used to recalcitrant patients. "Lieutenant Loring is doing a fine job of seeing to the repairs, and you are at safe harbor. Your vessel will not fall apart if you take time to recover your health."

The man snorted. "Discipline might."

"What good would it do your crew for you to kill yourself by early exertion? The choice is yours, of course. You need only listen to me insofar as you wish to get better and stay better. Although I will say that I hate to have my good work ruined by ungrateful patients."

"Me, ungrateful? You allow my niece to participate in quack medical experiments, and I am considered ungrateful?"

Despite his own misgivings on that score, Alden sensed that if he gave so much as a particle of ground, the captain would insist on his own way. "She saved your life with her gift. Yes, I would say your attitude is ungrateful."

Clearly, Captain Carlisle was unused to disagreement. He harrumphed and shifted in his berth. "I am grateful to Phoebe, of course. You are the one that ought to have put a stop to that ridiculous procedure."

"If I had, your niece and crew would be attending your funeral today. Now, take this." Alden handed him a dose of laudanum.

The captain accepted the cup but did not raise it to his lips. "Where is my Phoebe?"

"She has been here almost constantly." Alden was not about to admit to the favor he had asked of her.

Captain Carlisle nodded. "She needs to rest."

"And so do you. Drink the medicine."

The captain grimaced but obeyed. "You are an impertinent young man."

"I have not yet become accustomed to naval life."

"Well, in spite of everything, I appreciate that you came aboard to treat me."

"I was press-ganged, sir. I had little choice." Alden regretted the words immediately.

The captain's eyes widened. "My men impressed you?"

At your niece's bidding. Alden restrained himself and said neutrally, "They were greatly concerned for you."

Subdued, the captain lay back and swallowed his dose of medicine. "I believe I recall Phoebe mentioning it. But then this must mean our surgeon has passed? I had hoped she merely insisted on a physician."

Alden nodded.

"And the men? God forgive me, I have been remiss in considering any pain but my own." Captain Carlisle rubbed his head. "Was the butcher's bill very high?"

By the time Alden finished giving his report of the wounded, the captain's head was nodding. His eyelids closed once more, and before long a gentle snoring filled the cabin.

Alden sighed and crossed to open the windows. Then he took the seat Phoebe had vacated. He'd taken no pleasure in giving the captain bad news. It was apparent the man cared for his crew as much as they cared for him.

They had all been right that their captain would die without assistance, and when he had refused to come with them, they must have felt their options limited indeed. Some of the resentment smoldering in his gut fizzled.

"Lord, help me to know what to do. I do not know why You brought me here, and I want to go home. But please, help me not to overlook Your guidance due to my anger." He lifted his face to enjoy the breeze off the water. His eyes drooped closed. His head bobbed and he shook it, trying to clear it of cobwebs. He was just so tired. He'd had at most two hours of sleep in the past thirty-six hours. His eyes were so heavy. If he rested them for a moment, he could go back to figuring out what God wanted with him. His eyes shut.

"Doctor?" A sweet voice plucked at him. A small hand squeezed his shoulder. "Are you well? Should I call the boy?"

Alden fought to free himself from the tentacles of sleep. With an effort he managed to pry his eyelids apart. "No. I am all right. A little sleepy."

"You ought to be." Phoebe settled beside him. "You have been run off your feet since coming aboard."

Alden shrugged. "Were you able to see my mother?"

"I was. You have a lovely family."

"You met them all?"

She nodded. "Most of them, I think. How many are there?"

He snorted. "At times it seems like too many."

A dreamy look crossed her face. "I think I would enjoy having a large, close-knit family. It was just Grandmother and I for so long that the silence became oppressive."

He met her gaze and felt the heat of shame burn his cheeks. He was trying to get back to them all. How could he pretend they were anything but a blessing in his life? "Did they give you a reply?"

She pulled a letter from her basket, along with a paper-wrapped parcel. "You mother sent this along as well. She said likely you were not eating right and wanted you to have something from home."

Alden accepted the package and opened it to find an apple, a slice of ham, an entire loaf of bread, and three crullers. He shook his head and sighed. Mothers. At least she hadn't sent along clean drawers.

Cheeks warm, he glanced up to find Phoebe smiling at him. He shrugged. "She worries."

"Of course she worries. You are her son."

"I am also a grown man."

"I am not sure that matters."

His raised his eyes from the package and was surprised anew at how beautiful she was. The urge to stroke that petal-soft cheek overwhelmed him.

"Dr. Ingersoll, I. . ." She moistened her lips with the tip of a pink tongue. "I have to apologize. I am so, so sorry, for what I have done to you. I—no excuse is good enough. But I will try to make it up to you." Tears glittered in her eyes.

Unthinking, Alden stepped closer. He reached forward and cupped her cheek in his hand. She leaned into his palm.

"It is all right, Phoebe. Of course you wanted to save your uncle. It is all right. I forgive you." His fingers moved to stroke her hair. He might be starting to see why God brought him here.

She lifted her face and met his gaze. And the urge was too much. Still gently cradling her head, Alden lowered his lips toward hers.

❧

The breath caught in Phoebe's throat. Her lips tingled in anticipation. And then his lips were on hers. Somehow both firm and soft at the same time. He moaned a little in the back of his throat and pulled her closer. Willingly she yielded and wrapped her arms around his neck.

She'd never been so swamped by sensation. Eyes closed, she raised herself on tiptoe to better welcome his mouth on hers. Nothing existed outside the contact of her body with his.

Uncle John snorted and mumbled something, and almost at the same time the cabin door opened to reveal the chaplain.

Phoebe sprang away from Alden.

Breathing hard, she brushed her lips with the back of her hand.

Eyebrows raised, Reverend Malcolm nodded a polite greeting. "Good day, Miss Carlisle. I hoped to be able to offer some small service to the Captain, if only to sit with him. I do hope he is feeling better."

Lips still feeling the force of Alden's kiss, Phoebe nodded. "I am certain he will appreciate the company. He was just stirring."

Alden had turned to inspect the instruments and bottles that had accumulated on the table. She wished she could see his face. What was he thinking?

Did he regret kissing her?

She didn't regret it, except. . .it was going to be even harder to help him escape when she really wanted to keep him near always.

Looking at the rigid line of his back, she knew she had to try at least. He deserved to be happy. And she was the one who had to make certain he could go home where he belonged. Hand pressed to her chest as if to calm her racing heart, Phoebe hurried into her cabin and shut the door.

It was time to begin planning.

Really, it oughtn't to be so hard. They were, after all, within hailing distance of the shore. If she could just get him to town, he would be able to find shelter among his friends and family. He was well loved.

Phoebe nearly smacked her head on a beam. The new cabin that the carpenter's mates had knocked together for her was a good deal smaller than her former lodgings. She turned on her heel and resumed pacing.

Could Alden swim? She sighed. There were so many unanswered questions. Well, she wasn't going to let that stop her. She retrieved a book of foolscap and began to write out her ideas. There had to be a way.

Chapter 8

Over the next week and a half, Alden found himself falling into step with the routine of the ship. The life wasn't so unpleasant. If he had been starting out, he might almost have enjoyed the demands of shipboard life. There was something to be said for routine and discipline. But every time he went on deck or glanced out the gun hatch toward Glassenbury, longing for his home and his family seared him.

On the other hand, every time he caught a glimpse of Miss Carlisle, he ached to hold her again. To have her near. To touch her hair and hear her say his name.

One thing was clear. He couldn't have them both. If he was going to escape, he didn't have long to figure out why God had put him aboard *Aries*. The repairs were almost complete, and the frost was coming thicker and thicker every night. Captain Carlisle and Lieutenant Loring were worried about the early ice on the Connecticut River. They could not afford to wait too long and end up trapped. Alden could sympathize.

Not only that, but it seemed the townsfolk had heard of his impressment and most had refused to do business with *Aries*'s crew. The officers had a hard time refitting and replenishing their stores. And the men had been discouraged from going ashore by the hostile reception they received.

His attention was caught by the scrape and bump of a boat coming alongside. The bumboats had largely disappeared from *Aries*'s vicinity. The occupants were either angry about the press or fearful of being pressed themselves. He craned his neck to see what was going on through the gun hatch.

Phoebe sat in the bosun's chair. He'd never seen a back so stiff, and she clutched the ropes with fingers that looked to be made of white marble. Without stopping to put on his greatcoat, he bounded out of his cabin and up on to the deck. She freed herself from the apparatus and stood with a manner so regal that he could only imagine some insult to her dignity. Her eyes were suspiciously bright and her color high. Had she acquired a fever? Pain pierced him at the thought of her falling ill.

But no, the midshipmen swarming aboard via the nets looked like they had been in some sort of tussle. Clothes disarranged and torn, they looked like they'd wallowed in a pigsty.

As he drew closer he realized that her cloak had been decorated with splotches of some sort of noxious substances. There was no fever. This was in a way worse, because it was personal. Someone had targeted her. The fearful pang of worry that had squeezed his heart twisted into searing heat. He'd never so desperately wanted to be ashore.

Dear God, if he could just get his hands on the ruffians who had done this he would teach them a lesson, and he wouldn't even care if it took splitting his knuckles open again. He tried to catch Phoebe's eye, but she hurried down to her cabin immediately.

Alden turned to where the captain had been taking the sun on the quarterdeck. The man struggled to his feet and might have fallen if his lieutenant hadn't been there to catch him. Knowing that his place was with his patient, Alden allowed only his gaze to follow Phoebe's retreating form.

The captain refused Alden's steadying arm at first but relented enough to allow himself to be assisted down the ladder.

"Shall I see you to your cabin, sir?" Alden asked.

"No. I want to speak to Phoebe."

"I am sure she would be happy to wait on you."

Captain Carlisle snorted. "Then you do not know Phoebe as well as you think you do. She does not want to wait on anyone at the moment."

Alden tilted his head and looked sidewise at the man. "Then perhaps she ought to be allowed a bit of privacy."

The captain stopped short. Glared at Alden. Sighed. "Oh, all right. Take me to my room and then send in my steward."

Alden nodded understanding. "Shall I tell him you want tea?"

"No, but you can tell him to have cook make some of those sweetmeats Phoebe likes."

"Yes sir."

Alden opened the door and helped him negotiate the stoop. The captain shook off his hand then and moved to take his favorite seat. Alden turned to go.

"You know what happened to her is your fault, don't you?"

The caustic tone halted Alden in his tracks. He turned. "I feared so."

"Your presence has complicated what should have been

an easy stay in a pleasant port."

"My mother would tell you that I have the tendency to complicate a good many simple things. It is one of my greatest flaws."

"You are impertinent, too."

"Another of my flaws. I beg you to excuse me."

The captain grunted and waved Alden to a seat. "The worst of it is that my Phoebe is taking the brunt of this. She has taken it into her head that she is responsible for seeing you pressed. I tried to tell her that my men do not take orders from female passengers. In the absence of orders from a superior officer they rely on their own judgment and experience, but she will not hear a word of it."

Alden was all too aware of Phoebe's determination to retain her guilt, but he didn't know what to say.

Captain Carlisle continued, "She blames herself for everything from the ill feeling in the town toward our crew, to depriving you of the home and practice you have built. She would blame herself for the French attack if she could figure out just what she did to put them on our track."

Alden looked up from studying the worn leather of his shoes. "Sir, I did try to convince her that I do not hold her accountable. That I have forgiven her. I think the Lord may have put me here to some purpose, I just do not know what it is." *Or how long I'll have to stay.*

The captain regarded him for a long, appraising moment.

"If there is anything further I can do or say to try to convince Miss Carlisle that I bear no grudge, please—"

The captain moved his stump in a gesture of dismissal. "I believe you. You have given every indication of. . .kind feeling toward her." Something unsaid in the captain's demeanor made Alden blush. "Guilt is a vicious master, however. Even though she understands your protestations with her head, she has not forgiven herself enough to let them into her heart."

"What would you have me do?"

It was the captain's turn to sigh. "I wish I knew, lad. I wish I knew." He sounded more fatigued than he had in days, and Alden rose to check his pulse. The captain flapped at him. "I am all right. Just go fetch my steward. And do not stir the pot. For Phoebe's sake."

Alden nodded and all but ran from the room. His errand took only a moment, as he met the steward in the companionway and passed on the message. Then he sought out Reverend Malcolm. He found the clergyman in the gun room and begged an audience. The good reverend immediately set aside the volume he had been perusing. "Certainly, Dr. Ingersoll. I am in need of a distraction. It is a pity to find the folk of the town so poorly disposed to us."

"Yes, well. That is a bit of what I wanted to talk about, I suppose."

The reverend patted his arm. "I am afraid the gun room is not conducive to private conversation. Follow me." He led the way out and up onto the main deck and then began to climb the rigging as if he were one of the hands.

Alden raised an eyebrow, but he knew his way around a ship and grasped hold of the ropes. The farther he climbed from the ship, the freer he felt. Perched on the platform, he gazed down on both the ship and the town.

Reverend Malcolm smiled. "Now, what is it you wanted to talk about?"

With a few hitches and starts, Alden poured out the conflict tearing at him. "I would feel better about it if I knew what God wanted me to do here. As it is, I cannot seem to find any peace."

The reverend nodded sagely. "It sounds like the problem may be that you are looking in the wrong place."

"In what way?"

"Simply put, any peace you have based on circumstances will be fleeting. True peace arises not from the pleasantness of our situation but from our relationship with the Creator."

"But I do believe in Him. I try to follow His guidance."

"Ah, but you tell me that you cannot tell what He wants from you."

Alden shook his head. "I know what I want. I don't know what He wants."

"But you believe He placed you here."

"He must have. I'm here."

"Then why are you so anxious to leave the place He's brought you to?"

Alden swallowed. "I. . .if I don't get off this boat before they sail on the tide, the chance of escape almost disappears. I'll be stuck for years, and who's to say I won't get turned loose just to be taken to serve another captain?"

"You know, when we sign up to follow the Lord, we give up many of the rights we hold so dearly. All of them, in fact. Except the right to follow the Lord and do His will. You have the right to be angry for the way in which you were brought aboard this ship, but you can choose to set that aside and consider why God has allowed it. You never know what might happen if you abandon your rights and your will.

He has a way of working things around that never ceases to amaze me."

"But what if He does not?"

"Then you will still have been obedient."

"But what if He wants me to take a stand—to escape?"

The reverend pantomimed looking around. "Obedience is the key, no matter the call."

Alden sighed. "I thought for a bit that I might know why He brought me here. But the more I think on it, the more ridiculous it seems. I do not stand a chance, and even if I did, it would mean leaving everything I have ever known."

Reverend Malcolm winked and stretched. "Nothing is impossible with God." He lowered himself through the lubber's hole, leaving Alden to ponder.

Alden stared at the scarred platform, scored by the blades of innumerable bored midshipmen. If God had brought him here, did he have any right to demand to leave before God opened the door? The more he thought on it, the more he realized his turmoil came not in the decision to leave the ship, but in leaving Phoebe.

He had to admit it to himself. Somehow in the few days he'd known her, he'd fallen in love. She was everything he could desire in a wife, and much more.

Alden swung himself out to the ropes and climbed down. He headed to the orlop deck, where he took out his frustration on dried herbs, grinding them to powder in the mortar. It didn't work. He slid to the floor, letting his head fall back against the bulkhead. He covered his eyes with his hands. He would stay. He would wait on the Lord, and he would enjoy what time he could with Phoebe. She would leave the ship in Halifax, and he'd likely never see her again. But either way, he'd trust the Lord to direct his steps.

"God, I hope You can work through all this. I just don't see any hope for us to be together."

❧

Phoebe paced her cabin. Her hands had stopped shaking an hour ago, but she couldn't seem to sit still. She had never been treated so dreadfully in her life. And though a part of her felt she deserved to be reviled, most of her ached to slap those schoolboys. They didn't know anything about her.

And besides, she was working to make things right.

She kneaded her hands as she considered her plan once again. It ought to work. Her only difficulty might lie in distracting the midshipman on watch. With good weather and a friendly harbor, there wouldn't be many men on duty. It should all be as easy as flicking open a fan.

How she would miss him. It seemed impossible that he should occupy so much of her thoughts and heart when they hardly knew one another, but he did. His departure would leave a hole in her life. But considering only her own desires was what had brought her here. For once it was time to consider someone before herself. If she loved him as she suspected, then she should seek his happiness. She would have to trust God to fill the gap in her heart that Alden would leave behind.

Phoebe sucked in a breath of fresh air through the gun hatch and stared out at handsome little Glassenbury.

Evening seemed to take an inordinately long time to arrive. When she finally did, it was as a fashionable lady, late to the ball but trailing a gorgeous gown of stars. Her escort, the moon, was only a sliver, high above and far away.

Good. Phoebe didn't want too much light. They would need every advantage they could possibly gain. Though it hadn't been officially announced, everyone knew this would likely be *Aries's* last night in Glassenbury.

The watch would be on their guard for an escape attempt. But they wouldn't suspect her. She prepared for supper with exquisite care. She wanted to look her most fetching. Ostensibly to appeal to any guards she met, but also, truth be told, because she wanted Alden to remember her looking her best.

At her suggestion, he was to dine with them. She'd also invited the chaplain and Lieutenant Loring, to mask her intent.

The dining table had been spread with Uncle's second best. But it gleamed and glowed enough to assure the guests of their welcome. The men stood at her arrival, and Phoebe self-consciously took the seat Lieutenant Loring pulled out for her.

She glanced over at Uncle John and he winked. He was looking almost his old self. If nothing else good came from all this, at least God had used Alden to save her uncle's life. She really couldn't ask for more.

Covertly she looked to where Alden sat, wearing his best coat, with his dark hair pulled back in a queue. His spectacles perched on his nose, and his linen glowed snowy white in the candlelight.

He looked like. . .he looked like a thoughtful Adonis. That was it.

But when he met her gaze, he affected her more like Zeus

slinging a lightning bolt that stole her breath and pinned her to her chair. His smile, at once tender and determined, also held something more ineffable.

"Is something wrong, Miss Carlisle?" Lieutenant Loring's voice brought Phoebe back from the ether in which she had been floating.

"No, of course not." She realized her hand had been poised over her fork for several long seconds without picking it up. Snatching up the utensil, she launched into trivial conversation. The first course was presented and consumed without any blunders. Then came the next course and finally the pudding. Phoebe's heart beat faster as the time for action drew closer. But her bright smile never slipped.

At last it was time to drink the loyal toast. The men stood and raised their glasses.

Phoebe did likewise. Then with a little moan she sat heavily back in her chair. The men clustered around her. She raised a hand and spoke faintly. "Dr. Ingersoll, suddenly I do not feel well. Would you see me to my cabin and perhaps prepare a draught for me?"

"Certainly, Miss Carlisle. Do you feel well enough to stand?"

"I. . .I think so." She fluttered her eyelashes and sagged against him.

He put a hand under her elbow.

The look of concern in Uncle John's eyes made her cringe, but she couldn't turn back now.

Alden nodded to the officers. "Please excuse me, gentlemen."

In the companionway, Phoebe straightened. "Come with

me. I have a plan to get you out of here," she whispered.

"What?"

"Do not worry. It will work." She grasped his hand, tugging him forward. They couldn't afford to dally.

The cold on deck slapped her cheeks and seared her lungs.

"Miss Carlisle—"

Phoebe shushed Alden. "We do not have time for you to argue."

"Now stand over here." She pushed him into a shadowy corner and moved to intercept the bosun. "Mr. Harcourt, I believe the captain wishes to speak with you."

The bosun's eyebrows rose a bit in surprise that a ship's boy hadn't been sent with the message, but he nodded and headed toward the hatch. Good. That just left the midshipman. Phoebe whirled to fetch Alden, but he was already at her back.

"You were supposed to stay hidden," she hissed.

"Miss Carlisle. I have decided—"

A light from below allowed an eerie glow to edge along the deck. They were wasting time. She grabbed his hand and tugged him toward the waist of the ship.

Up near the bow, a chorus of a drunken song erupted. Feet thundered on the deck toward the disturbance. Alden straightened, his head cocked toward the tumult. Phoebe made sure the midshipman had abandoned the quarterdeck and dragged Alden up the ladder.

A hiss sounded from the dark and she peered over the rail to find Jonathan Ingersoll in a small skiff. Beside her, Alden peered down into the darkness, too, and his jaw dropped. "Did my brothers put you up to this?"

Phoebe began uncoiling a rope over the side of the ship. She forced a tremulous smile. "I put them up to it. Now all you have to do is climb down."

Alden took her hand. "I do not want to go. Not if it means leaving you." He drew her closer.

Below, Jonathan hissed again and motioned for him to hurry.

Alden ignored him. "I believe God brought us together for a reason. I love my family, but I cannot leave you."

All the feeling in her hands seemed to have drained away. The rope fell from her fingers. The deck felt suddenly unsteady. "You would stay for my sake?"

He nodded.

"You do not resent me?" Her eyes prickled with the heat of imminent tears.

"How could I? You only acted to save your uncle."

"But what of your practice?"

"People get ill everywhere. When I am discharged from the navy, we can settle wherever you like."

She shook her head. "I cannot let you do this."

"I am afraid you have no choice. Unless you intend to reject my suit."

She stared at him, almost wishing she could find the strength to deny him, for his own good. And then she threw her arms around him. "I want to, but I cannot."

Their lips met in a sweet, soaring kiss.

Alden's lips moved along the line of her cheekbone until they nuzzled her ear. "I love you, Phoebe. I will go anywhere for you."

A light flared over his shoulder, blinding her. She jerked

away from him and her foot tangled in the coil of rope. Before she could so much as gasp, she hurtled overboard. Arms flailing, she hit the water on her back. It forced the air from her lungs. Almost as quickly, the frigid water snatched at her skirts and dragged her down.

Chapter 9

For an instant, Alden's heart seemed to stop. Behind him came the sound of shouts and curses. He kicked off his shoes and vaulted over the side of the ship. Fingers plucked at him. Caught his shirt, tried to hold him back. But he was free. His body knifed through the air after Phoebe.

The water closed over his head in a rush of cold that sent a jolting shudder through him. He kicked, driving himself deeper into the river. Trying to find Phoebe by touch alone. *God, grant me light! Help me find her.*

A warm glow of lantern light filtered to him from above. Below him and to his right, Alden caught a glimpse of something pale. It was Phoebe. Hands clawing at the water, she was yet dragged toward the bottom. Air bubbles streamed from her mouth. Her eyes were open, silently begging for help.

His lungs burned, threatening to burst, but he pushed forward until he could catch the cloth of her skirts in his grip. With every bit of energy he could muster, he hauled her up toward the light.

His head broke the water, and he sucked in a lungful of air. Men's voices battered him, but he couldn't heed the angry tumult. He found Phoebe's face in the mass of fabric from her dress and held it above the water. All the while prayer pulsed through his veins. *Don't take her, God. Please let her be all right.*

Rough hands snatched at him and pulled him from the water by his collar. Other hands pried Phoebe from his grasp. The wind made him realize how cold he was, and his body convulsed in shivers. Somehow he landed in a pile on the deck. He scrambled to his feet looking around wildly for Phoebe.

She lay huddled on the deck, looking tiny and fragile. He lunged forward, but arms prevented him from moving. He scrabbled at them, trying to free himself. Men clustered around Phoebe until he couldn't see her anymore. Everyone seemed to be shouting.

A bellow cut through the chaos. "What is the meaning of this?"

Harcourt shoved Alden forward. "He tried to take a runner, sir. And knocked Miss Carlisle in when she got in his way."

Still shuddering and gasping for air, Alden could only say, "No!"

The blood leeched from the captain's face until he looked as ill as he had when Alden first saw him. His eyes burned like live coals when he stared at Alden. "Throw him in the brig," he roared.

"No. That's not what happened."

Hands clamped on Alden's arms and he was dragged away.

Reverend Malcolm joined the captain. "Sir, you might want to have the doctor tend her before you lock him up."

"Turn her on her stomach. Loosen her stays," Alden

shouted over his shoulder. "Get her warm." A fist struck the side of his head and set his ears ringing.

Still he struggled.

Lieutenant Loring appeared at his side. "We've got your brothers, Ingersoll. Looks like we'll have three more fine new hands."

Alden shook his head. It couldn't be happening. *God, where are you?*

There was a gasping, choking noise and someone retched. It was the sweetest sound Alden had ever heard. The men cheered.

"Phoebe, are you all right?" Desperately he yanked free of his captors. He didn't make it far.

A whispery imitation of her voice scratched at the air. "Alden? Alden!"

The men holding him slowed, looking at one another questioningly. Alden stilled as well. "I am here, Phoebe."

The men parted and he saw her. She still lay on the ground, but swathed in blankets, her uncle kneeling by her side. She turned her head to Alden.

He ached to run to her. Instead, he met the captain's gaze. "Sir, I did not knock her into the sea, and I was not trying to escape."

"What? No!" said Phoebe. Her voice still achingly weak. A grimace twisted her features as she tried to sit up.

Uncle John pressed her back down. "Calm yourself, my girl."

"It is my fault," she rasped. "I fell." Her hand fluttered out from under the blankets and extended toward Alden.

He took a step toward her, and this time no one restrained

him. He kept moving until he, too, knelt by her side. He looked up at the captain, who appeared confused. "We need to get her out of this wind and into dry clothes."

"In my cabin." The captain stood with difficulty.

Alden gathered Phoebe into his arms and followed.

❧

Phoebe leaned her head against the hollow of Alden's shoulder. So this was what it felt like to be cherished.

If only she could enjoy it.

But someone was attacking her head with an ice pick, and her throat and chest ached. In the great cabin he lowered her into a seat. Uncle John's steward appeared at her arm with a clean, dry dress. The gentlemen departed so she could change.

The warm cloth stilled the worst of her shivers, but she retained one of the blankets. When she opened the door she found Alden also wearing dry clothing.

"Phoebe." Uncle John's voice sounded as it had when she was eight and he had caught her in some infraction. "I think it is time for you to explain."

He settled behind his desk and gestured for her and Alden to sit. The pent-up story tumbled out in a swirling eddy of words.

Uncle John's face remained stony until she came to the part where she fell over the side. "That would seem to clear up the matter of Mr. Harcourt's allegations. Doctor, please accept my apologies for the accusation."

Alden bent his head in grave acknowledgment.

At some point during the interview, she had reached for Alden's hand. They now sat linked together as they awaited the captain's judgment.

Uncle John sat back in his seat and rubbed his face. "My darling, do you love him?"

Feeling as if she were tumbling through space again, Phoebe turned to meet Alden's gaze. "I do."

"And you love my niece?"

"With all my heart." Alden squeezed her hand.

"You would be willing to stay as our surgeon?"

"I will do anything to stay near her."

The captain nodded. "That is what I wanted to know." He pushed away from his desk and stood. He stuck his head out the door and ordered the steward to fetch Reverend Malcolm and Lieutenant Loring.

The lieutenant arrived first.

"Mr. Loring, please prepare the ship for sail. We will go with the tide on the morrow."

The lieutenant's curiosity radiated from him like a skunk's stench, but he saluted and left to attend his duty.

The reverend arrived. "You asked for me, Captain?"

"Yes, Reverend. I have need of your services. Do you have your prayer book?"

Reverend Malcolm patted his pocket. "Always."

"In that case, we are in need of a marriage ceremony."

Phoebe jumped to her feet. "Uncle John, do you mean it?"

He raised an eyebrow.

She looked to Alden. "Is this what you want?"

"More than anything."

She flung her arms around his neck. "As do I. But not like this. Reverend, you may put your prayer book away just for a bit."

Alden cocked his head at her, eyebrow raised.

"You must have your family here."

In short order, Alden's brothers were procured from the brig. They filed in, each holding his hat before him like a penitent schoolboy. Uncle John announced that he wasn't going to hold them, and some of the tension eased from their shoulders. Then Alden announced his impending marriage, putting his arm around Phoebe's waist and pulling her to his side.

Silence as the brothers gaped, and then there were cries of congratulations and a round of backslapping. Phoebe's hand was shaken, and she sensed each one covertly inspecting her.

As dawn lit the sky, Alden's mother and sisters-in-law and what seemed at least a dozen nieces and nephews were helped aboard.

Mrs. Ingersoll embraced her son fiercely, driving the air from his lungs in a whoosh. Phoebe clapped a hand over her mouth to stifle a laugh at her suitor and then decided that, upon occasion, impulsiveness might not be so terrible. And she allowed her joy to well up into a full-fledged laugh.

Mrs. Ingersoll stretched a hand toward Phoebe. "I knew in my bones I would be seeing more of you when I first spied you in my sitting room."

"Then the thought of this wedding is not too distasteful to you, Mrs. Ingersoll?"

"Bless you child, I raised my boys to listen to the Lord's voice. I am just glad Alden finally found someone. He is the pickiest one of the bunch."

The comment sparked laughter from the surrounding family.

From the basket hanging over her arm, Mrs. Ingersoll

produced a bunch of helenium and asters from the Red Griffin garden. "These are for you. Every bride ought to have flowers."

Phoebe accepted them, tears brimming in her eyes.

"And call me 'mother,' if it suits you, dear."

"Oh, thank you." Phoebe embraced the older woman.

Chattering and laughing, her new sisters took her hands. "You must get ready!"

They accompanied Phoebe into her makeshift cabin and helped her dress her hair. Then she donned her best gown.

When at last she was deemed properly enchanting, she was led on deck. Alden's smile when he met her eyes was even broader and more engaging than in his mother's sketch.

It wasn't the wedding Phoebe had ever imagined, but it was perfect.

A wedding breakfast was prepared, and Phoebe reveled in her new family's noisy, joyous festivities, so different from her grandmother's mausoleum of an existence.

When at last the breakfast drew to a close, Alden gave his mother a hug. "I will be back to visit when I can."

Uncle John approached and put a hand on Phoebe's shoulder and one on Alden's. "I have not given you your wedding gift yet. You are hereby discharged from His Majesty's service."

Alden looked to Phoebe, his eyes shining. "What do you want to do?"

Phoebe's heart was so full it felt as if it might burst. "We have to stay here. Your life is here, and my life is with you."

She flung her arms around Uncle John. "I will miss you."

His one-armed hug was still tight enough to catch her

breath. "I will miss you, too. But I thought you might say that." He gestured over the side at his cutter, which had been lowered into the water. It already contained her trunks.

Tears misted her eyes. "I love you, Uncle John. Thank you."

He nodded and turned to hide his reddened eyes. "Now I am about to miss my tide. Be off with you."

Within minutes the entire Ingersoll tribe stood on shore. Phoebe waved and waved as *Aries* grew smaller and finally disappeared.

At last she turned to find her husband gazing at her with a complicated mixture of pride and worry and love. He kissed her temple. "Are you ready to go home?"

She smiled. "I cannot wait."

Apple Fritters à la Bavarre

The following recipe is taken from *A Complete System of Cookery in Which is set forth a Variety of genuine Receipts collected from several Years' Experience under the celebrated Mr. deSt.Clouet, sometime since cook to his Grace Duke of Newcastle.* By William Verral, Master of the White-Hart Inn in Lewes. Suffex, 1759.

Pare and quarter some large pippins, lay them to soak in orange juice, fine sugar, cinnamon and lemon-peel, and toss them often. Your dinner being almost ready, dry them in a cloth, tumble about well in fine flour, and fry them all very tender in hogs lard; dish them up, and sift plenty of fine sugar over them, color nicely with a salamander, and send them up.

Author's Note: Nowadays a salamander is a super broiler mostly used in restaurants, but traditionally it was a long utensil with a flat metal head, which was heated very hot. Sort of like a branding iron used to caramelize sugar.

Influenced by books like The Secret Garden and The Little Princess, **Lisa Karon Richardson's** earliest writing attempts were heavy on boarding schools and creepy houses. Now that she's (mostly) all grown-up she still loves a healthy dash of adventure and excitement in any story she creates, even her real-life story. She's been a missionary to the Seychelles and Gabon and now that she and her husband are back in America, they are tackling new adventures—starting a daughter-work church and raising two precocious kids.

College of the Ouachitas Library